Kneeling in the Silver Light

Stories from the Great War

READ ORDER

37 (6)	25	43	67	231
15	93	177 (14)	115 (16)	251
57	191 (12)		131	
83			149	
105			213	
167				
203 (10)				

Published by The Alchemy Press

Astrologica: Stories of the Zodiac

Beneath the Ground

Doors to Elsewhere

In the Broken Birdcage of Kathleen Fair (ebook)

Invent-10n

Kneeling in the Silver Light

Merry-Go-Round and Other Words

Nick Nightmare Investigates

Rumours of the Marvellous

Sailor of the Skies (ebook)

Sex, Lies and Family Ties

Shadows of Light and Dark

Swords against the Millennium

The Alchemy Press Book of Ancient Wonders

The Alchemy Press Book of Pulp Heroes

The Alchemy Press Book of Pulp Heroes 2

The Alchemy Press Book of Pulp Heroes 3

The Alchemy Press Book of Urban Mythic

The Alchemy Press Book of Urban Mythic 2

The Komarovs (ebook)

The Paladin Mandates

Touchstones

Where the Bodies are Buried

www.alchemypress.co.uk

Kneeling in the Silver Light

Stories from the Great War

Edited by
Dean M. Drinkel

The Alchemy Press

Kneeling in the Silver Light
Copyright © Dean M. Drinkel 2014

Cover painting copyright © Chris Rawlins

This publication copyright © The Alchemy Press 2014

Typesetting and design by Peter Coleborn

Published by arrangement with the authors

First edition

ISBN 978-0-9929809-1-7

Published by The Alchemy Press
Cheadle, Staffordshire, UK

www.alchemypress.co.uk

Contents

Copyright Details

Acknowledgements

I would like to personally thank the following:

Scott; Vincent; Christophe; Stephan; Kristin; Martin; Justin B.; Clive Barker; Chris Alexander and the staff of *Fangoria*; Chris and the staff of The Tavern, Cannes; Rob & Sheri Moon Zombie; Brandon Crouse; Chris Hall; Jim Mcleod; Simon & Lizzie; Joe Mynhardt; Peter & Jan Coleborn; John Gilbert; Tom Pergola; Ed Ward; Suzanne Kendall; James Powell; Barbie Wilde; Chris B.; Gary; Chris T.; Niven, Janine, Emily & Sarah; Ronan Farrow.

Mario Götze; Antoine Griezmann; Steffen Iversen; Jonathan Blondel Bradley Will Simpson Robbie Robertson

Harri & Charley; Sinead, Zac & Alex

Love to you all
Dean M Drinkel
Paris, France, June 2014

This book is dedicated to:

My brothers – heroes both;

My mother

And in memory of:

Maurice Francis Drinkel
&
Louis George Drinkel

"Show me a family of readers, and I will show you the
people who move the world."
Napoleon Bonaparte

Introduction

Okay, Gentle Reader, I'll try and keep this short. If you know me then you'll appreciate that won't be easy – you see, I want the anthology to speak for itself rather than pages and pages of text from me...

So, let's begin here: if memory serves, I first met Peter Coleborn in late 2012 or early 2013 through his partner (and excellent writer/editor) Jan Edwards, whom I had worked with on a number of other anthologies. It was either at Fantasycon (in Brighton) or one of the British Fantasy Society Open Nights (in London) that we first spoke and of course, I was in complete awe because of what he had been doing with The Alchemy Press.

From that first meeting, several "face to face" chats and a few emails in between, I pitched the idea of compiling/editing an anthology of stories with the Great War as a backdrop. Luckily for me, Peter really dug (see what I did there?) the idea and rapidly *Kneeling In The Silver Light* was born.

The cover was put together first (isn't it amazing?) and we put an open submissions call on The Alchemy Press website, as well as my own blog and Facebook pages. I have to say, I was absolutely inundated with contributions – the majority of which were simply brilliant, and the rest – well, they were very good as well. I know it sounds a cliché but, Gentle Reader, it was a very hard decision to make on which tales were going to make the final cut or not. I do know that if I was ever to do a sequel then it too would be full of outstanding tales!

Peter and I were clear with the tone of the anthology and the types of stories we wanted to include – I hope I have kept to that brief and that you enjoy what follows.

When choosing both the writers and their stories, I very much wanted a "world view" of the Great War, rather than a clutch of stories by British writers – and boy, do we have that:

Australian, American, Canadian, Danish, French, English, Welsh … just to mention a few. I was also lucky with having a heady mix of both male and female writers. I truly believe the anthology is so much stronger with these varied voices from around the world.

*

As I sit here on my balcony in Northern Paris, putting these few words together, sipping a well earned espresso, something very strange has just happened which I feel I need to record here as I'm a firm believer in co-incidences (as an aside, I hope that you'll see there are lots of connections between the stories – by that, I just don't mean because the Great War is the theme. For instance, there is a clear lineage from Bryn Fortey to Paul Woodward's tales – even if Paul's is set in an alternative reality. Another? Okay, check out Rima's and Emile-Louis' … then to open with the bloody brilliant Christopher Fowler and Allen Ashley's cracking read to end … I have been truly blessed this time around).

Originally, there were going to three subjects covered in the introduction: my own brother's experiences in Iraq; a friend who was having problems finding a job; and thirdly the erection of a statue of Gavrilo Princip in Sarajevo.

However, as I attempted to weave those three strands into one single narrative, I happened to Google my great-grandfather's name as I wanted to check something. He wasn't a Drinkel so don't bother wasting your time looking – anyway, he was quite "big" locally and held several political offices throughout his life. During the Great War, he was decorated a number of times as well as being mentioned in Dispatches. Quite the hero.

As I continued my search, I noticed there were thousands and thousands of "hits" – this blew me away; I knew he was a "personality" but this was getting beyond a joke. However, on closer inspection, I saw that there were so many hits because his medals had been put up for sale by auction.

The sellers, though doing nothing illegal, I fathomed (as he apparently had been given them), perhaps needed to look within themselves at the morality of what they were now doing

– particularly when making claims that there was no-one else alive in the family to the pass the medals onto: um … hello … over here!

My father was very close to his grandfather and as he is not here anymore, either, I felt that it was my duty to try and find out what had happened at the auction (as it was in late 2013), who had bought them, and make a decision on what to do next with all the facts to hand...

...after several weeks of investigation, I was informed by the auctioneers that they couldn't give me all the details (Data Protection and all that) but they did assure me that someone else from within the family had caught wind of the story and had purchased them in the nick of time. Great, I could rest easily.

So, a short story with a happy ending.

As history more often than not tells us, there are not many who come out of a war with a happy ending. Whether it is a family member or friend that is sadly killed in battle, there are those that return physically or mentally wounded.

And that's just the "front-line" troops – not to mention girlfriends, wives, boyfriends, husbands, brothers, sisters, fathers, mothers … the list can be endless...

In closing, a personal thanks for taking the time to read this and (hopefully) purchasing this anthology – a lot of effort went into producing it for you.

I thank Peter for allowing me to follow the project through.

I thank the authors for their contributions – let them know via their blogs/websites what great stories they've written Gentle Reader.

Support small presses – they really are important and the bedrock of the genre community.

Okay, espresso finished, I'm taking a trip out today. An exhibition has opened at the Musée de le Grande Guerre in Meaux. If you didn't know, in late September 1914, in Marne, the British joined with the French armies and stopped a German march into Paris.

If the Germans had managed to get into in the capital so quickly after the outbreak of the war, the French would have

capitulated and the Great War might have had a very different ending indeed ... I feel a story coming on ... auf wiedersehen.
Peace and love.

Dean M. Drinkel
Paris, France
June 2014

The Dead

Rupert Brooke

Blow out, you bugles, over the rich Dead!
    There's none of these so lonely and poor of old,
    But, dying, has made us rarer gifts than gold.
These laid the world away; poured out the red
Sweet wine of youth; gave up the years to be
    Of work and joy, and that unhoped serene,
    That men call age; and those who would have been,
Their sons, they gave, their immortality.

Blow, bugles, blow! They brought us, for our dearth,
    Holiness, lacked so long, and Love, and Pain.
Honour has come back, as a king, to earth,
    And paid his subjects with a royal wage;
And Nobleness walks in our ways again;
    And we have come into our heritage.

The Scent of Roses

Christopher Fowler

"It is a story I have dared not tell anyone," said the man seated opposite. "But now the weight of it is destroying me. I will speak and you may listen. At the end, you will decide what must be done. Will you take coffee?"

He talked in riddles, and yet it seemed to make a kind of sense. Lulled by the warmth of the summer day, the dappling of light beneath the trees, Fritz Urban had been dozing in his chair when I approached and seated myself at his table. The day was still hot, but now the café benefitted from the breeze lifting up from Lake Geneva. The waiter set cups before us as Urban regarded me for a moment, then began.

"I was not always a salesman. I was born in 1885, and grew up poor in the outskirts of Dusseldorf, but I had no desire to become a farmer, and escaped my violent father at the first opportunity. I had always loved cars, but had never ridden in one. Then one day, at a trade fair that was held in Vienna, I saw something that changed my life, a Benz Motorwagon of gleaming lacquered metal, and at that moment I knew the world was about to be transformed. I could see that there would be no more need for horses and carts. The piston engine, transplanted into a personal carriage, could become a mode of transport for the entire world to use. In America, I heard, the Oldsmobile factory was beginning mass production of such vehicles, so that people of all classes could afford to ride them.

"Of course, I could not afford an engine or even have access to such a marvel, so I did the next best thing; I requested an apprenticeship at an automobile engineering firm. Soon I became a driver for the new Motorwagon, a profession few had been able to master. I quickly saw in it a way to make money. I

drove the first Daimler-Mercedes. I was one of the few men in
Austria who had mastered this skill, and soon my services were
greatly in demand. I was asked to go to America and train
further there. But—"

" —there was a woman," I suggested.

"Yes sir. There was a woman named Hannah, with whom I
had fallen in love. And, I felt sure; my love was to be
reciprocated."

"To be reciprocated?" I was puzzled. "It was not initially?"

"No. We were separated by our stations in life. Hannah was
a Lady-In-Waiting to the Duchess of Hohenberg. High-born
and highly strung. She had no interest in a man such as I. And
yet, with each meeting, her attention grew stronger."

"How did she come to meet you?"

"I was delivering cars to the palace. The royal interest in the
new automobile was strong. At this time I had the great good
fortune to become a chauffeur in the service of Count Harrach,
a nobleman of the Austro-Hungarian Empire who was also a
close friend to the heir of its throne. A most important
personage whom I was to have the great privilege of serving."

"Not bad for a boy who had been expected to become a
farmer," I said, lighting my cigar. "Did this levelling of the
classes endear you more to Hannah?"

"I like to believe that she warmed to me for who I was, and
not because of my new position in life," said Fritz coolly. "Over
the next few months, we saw more of each other, and I was
invited to walk with her – chaperoned, of course – on several
occasions."

"And you proposed."

"At the first available opportunity. It was difficult to get
Hannah to myself, to find the privacy for such a conversation.
As you can imagine, she was usually surrounded by members
of the household staff. But one afternoon in the gardens, I was
able to separate her from the others and spoke of my
intentions."

"She accepted, I take it?"

"She asked for a period in which to consider my proposal.
For the next few nights I was unable to sleep—"

"It's very romantic," I said, impatiently waving smoke from the table. Without looking at my watch, I knew my train would soon be arriving. "Let us assume she accepted and you were married."

"Indeed, sir, that was the situation. I was wed with the blessing of her family, although some members stayed away from the nuptials, feeling that my parents were below hers in station. We began living as man and wife, and all was well for a while."

"But something happened?"

"Something happened." Fritz gave a bitter laugh. "I fear to tell it, for you really will think I am quite insane."

"I am used to insanity," I replied, taking a sip of my bitter coffee. "I'm afraid I must hurry you. I will have to leave very shortly."

"Then I shall tell you of my dreadful shame," said Fritz. "Tell me, do you believe in fate?"

"Most certainly," I said. "Our paths through life are set as rigidly as roads, but we alone control the vehicle of our destiny."

"I did not believe in fate before these events, but I do so now. And if, as you say, we control our lives, then the fateful day came when I changed not just my fate, but the fate of the entire world."

Fritz sat back as he remembered, his head illuminated by the late summer sun. "My hours were long," he said, "and I was sometimes required to drive great distances for the Count, which took me away from Hannah. Often my trips were for the most trivial of reasons – the collection of a vase, the delivery of a letter, but the job was well paid and I became an expert Mercedes driver. Meanwhile, life in the royal Bohemian household required Hannah to be at the beck and call of her mistress at any time of the day or night, although as the now married Countess Sophie Chotek had herself been a Lady-In-Waiting, she proved a kind and understanding employer.

"Still, in the first few months of 1914 Hannah and I seemed to spend less time than ever in each other's company, a situation that made us both fractious and argumentative. I realise that now; I had been spoiled by my new position. I had been ushered into a world that no-one in my family had ever seen, and still I could not be entirely happy. I can see that the downfall of men hinges on tiny things – in my case a stray glance, a new shoe, a perfume bottle, a pair of scissors. These were enough to bring about the disaster for which I must now hold myself accountable. The thought if it makes me ashamed that I am still alive."

"You do look a trifle pale," I said, wondering if I could delay for a few minutes and catch a later train, for I sensed that I could be of use. I attracted the waiter and ordered Napoleon brandies for us both. "Let us drink together. I usually find the effect most beneficial."

Moments later a pair of gold-rimmed glasses arrived and we touched them together. "To your health."

"It began with a girl of some seventeen summers," said Fritz sadly.

"There is always a girl," I sighed.

"This one was radiantly beautiful; the niece of the Count, and when Elizabeth walked into court it was as if the sun had emerged from clouds. Everyone admired her. Since my wife's employer and the great friend of my own employer had married, I now saw Hannah in the imperial household, although we were rarely able to speak.

"It happened one morning that she emerged into the courtyard as I was bringing out the car, and I saw the young Princess Elizabeth heading our way. When members of the monarchy appear, all employees are required to make themselves scarce, and after a while you become used to halting whatever you are doing and dropping into the nearest doorway. The royals like to move through a world of stillness, uninterrupted by the chaos of life. Hannah saw that the Princess was coming and swiftly found an arch support, stepping behind it, but there was nowhere for me to go.

"In this situation, we are required to simply become statues. I froze and waited for her to pass. But she stopped and smiled at me. What could I do but look back?

"Hannah was a jealous woman, and hated the fact that there

had been other girls before her. That night, she accused me of flirting with Elizabeth! I told her not to be so absurd, but she would not be consoled, and cried her way to bed. I see now, looking back, that this irrational behaviour was a symptom of some surfacing mental derangement.

"The next morning I discovered that Leopold, the Archduke's chauffeur, had not appeared for work. Nobody knew where he was, so I was asked to take his place. It was well-known that the Archduke liked and respected his chauffeur, so I was asked to do this without informing anyone of the change in personnel; for fear that people should think the Archduke capricious in his favourites. I was to accompany him to Sarajevo, where he would inspect the imperial garrison. I would be required to drive a beautiful automobile, a black 1911 Graf & Stift 'Bois De Bologne' Tourer.

"The night before I left, I bought a bottle of perfume for Hannah, *Atar of Roses*, her favourite. I meant it as a reconciliation gift, but I found her in a worsened state. She had somehow convinced herself that I was about to leave her for a member of the royal family. I tried to explain the outright absurdity of this idea, but she only grew angrier. I had left the perfume on her dresser while I tried on the chauffeur uniform that had been arranged for me. There was a problem with the shoes – the soles were of new leather, and extremely slippery.

"Hannah opened my gift and, with a scream, smashed the perfume bottle on the floor. I ran in and saw the mess; broken glass everywhere, the overpowering scent of roses, and my beloved wife rending her nightdress and slapping her own face between sobs of anger. Fearful that she might cause further injury to herself if she tried to clear up the glass, I began to pick up the pieces. In doing so, the rose oil covered my right shoe. I removed the shoe and left it to air in the corridor, then retired to bed.

"Hannah refused to sleep in the same room, and removed herself to another bedchamber. At six a.m. the next morning I looked in on her, but she had already dressed and left. I was upset and wished I had been able to say goodbye to her. I did not know that morning that we would never see each other again.

"I admit, as our retinue set off on the state visit, I had guilty thoughts of Elizabeth's glance. Is it man's vanity alone that encourages him to think he may attract the eye of a beautiful girl, even if she is far above his station in life? Stranger things had happened. The Archduke himself had fallen in love with a woman who was said to be far removed from his social class.

"Now we come to the fateful moment that tore my very soul apart."

Fritz looked like a man made haggard by his past. He had trouble continuing until I laid a placatory hand on his shoulder. "Please," I said, "you must reveal the nature of your burden to me."

"Very well – where was I?"

"The Archduke's state visit."

"That's right. The Archduke met me from the train in his blue-grey tunic with the red piping and gold buttons, his moustaches freshly waxed. I held the door open for him and he entered the vehicle in great style. Although there were many who opposed him in the city, there were an equal number of ardent admirers. But I had little knowledge of the city and its factions. I had no idea it was a powder-keg waiting to be ignited.

"While we were waiting to set off I heard him say, 'There is an extraordinary scent of roses in here. Are we near a garden?' I looked down and guiltily noted that my right shoe was still covered in rose oil.

"The Archduke had been warned not to travel to Sarajevo. I understand little of politics – to me; the mechanics of an automobile could teach me more about the world than the rifts and alliances of the Balkan states. I knew that Bosnia-Herzegovina had been declared a part of the Austro-Hungarian Empire by the Emperor, and that it had caused unrest among the Slavic people and the Russian Tsar who opposed it. What I did not know was that assassins lay in wait for us upon our route that day.

"There were six automobiles in our procession, and there were six assassins spread out along the Appel Quay that ran beside the river. These assassins belonged to an organisation called the Black Hand, and each was under instructions to attack us when they saw us approach. Following a request from the Archduke, I rolled back the roof of the car so that the crowds could get a better look at him and his wife, Countess Sophie.

"At around ten a.m. the first of the protestors struck, although we did not find this out until later, because it transpired that this man had turned coward and failed to throw his bomb at the procession. Supposedly, there had been a suspicious policeman standing close by who had unnerved him.

"Fifteen minutes after this, the second assassin hurled a grenade at our motorcade. I saw the small grey object flying toward the windscreen of the car and accelerated, watching as the bomb flew over our heads. It bounced upon the rear of our vehicle and disappeared under the car behind, the third in the procession. The grenade had a ten second fuse, and exploded beneath the wheels of the automobile, wounding its occupants and peppering a number of bystanders with shrapnel.

"We were travelling at a fairly high speed, and the route was thronged with a heavy volume of spectators who, we were to discover, slowed down the progress of the conspirators. The bomb-thrower tried to take his own life by swallowing a cyanide capsule, but the chemical was out of date and merely caused him to vomit.

"Panicked, he jumped into the river Miljacka, beside which we were travelling, but the muddy water was a mere four inches deep, and so the police were able to pull him out and arrest him.

"A few minutes before eleven, the Archduke decided that we should head for the hospital to visit the victims of the bombing. General Potiorek, the governor who was travelling with us, said that we would need to avoid the city centre to do so. I understood later that he had a plan that we should continue along the quay all the way to the hospital. Unfortunately, he did not inform me of this idea, and I turned right into Franz Josef Street.

"There was a run-down café there, where a small, sickly lad of nineteen who had been turned down for membership of the Black Hand sat, disappointed and embittered. This boy, Princip by name, thought that the death of the Archduke would magically release the shackles that bound his people to the empire. He had missed his chance to attack our convoy, and had all but given up when he saw our automobile turn into the street.

"The second I realised that we had made a wrong turn, I put my foot on the brake and began to back up. I admit I was disturbed that there might be another attack, and in my rush I stalled the car's engine, locking the gears. From the corner of my eye I saw the sickly fellow rise to his feet and raise his right arm toward us. He was holding a pistol, and used it now to knock a fellow bystander out of his way. I saw all this as if time itself had suddenly slowed down.

"I attempted to reverse more quickly, but the rose oil on my shoe had made the leather sole slippery, and my foot slid off the accelerator. In that brief moment while the automobile was stilled, the lad took aim and fired twice.

"His bullets found their mark; both the Archduke and his wife were shot. Franz Ferdinand's neck was pierced and gushed scarlet. Count Harrach's face was splashed. The Count put a white handkerchief on the Archduke's jugular vein to stem the flow of blood. I heard his wife call out, 'For Heaven's sake, what happened to you?' but she had been shot in the stomach, and fell from her seat. We thought she must have fainted, but the Archduke knew what had happened and begged her not to die, for the sake of her children. His ceremonial hat slid from his head – I remember there were iridescent sapphire feathers on the floor of the car.

"I pulled to the side of the road and we tried to remove Franz Ferdinand's tight blue tunic, but we could not find a pair of scissors with which to cut it open. He died before we could get to the wound. The crowd rushed forward, and in the process my leg was crushed.

"When I returned home, I discovered that my beloved Hannah was dead. She had walked into an ornamental lake and lain in it, breathing the water down into her lungs to take her own life. No-one could tell me if she had heard about the Archduke's assassination before she died, or if her wits had simply wandered after fearing that I would stray.

"The Archduke's chauffeur, Leopold, had miraculously reappeared – there seemed to be some mystery in his absence to which I was not privy – and I was asked to stand down. Later, I understood that all despatches would suggest he was with the Archduke when he died, and I, little more than a lowly mechanic raised up for a day, was erased from history. You see now, sir, the burden I carry."

"I think I understand perfectly," I said.

"I am responsible for nothing less than the deaths of thousands – millions for all I know – for just two months after Franz Ferdinand's death, Austria-Hungary declared war against Serbia, and this great conflict in which we now find ourselves began, and it seems it may never stop until all the world is dead."

"My dear fellow, you could argue that the Archduke's assassination was not the only starting pistol for the war in which we are now engulfed. I believe there were other causes for the commencement of the conflict: nationalism, imperialism, militarism," I said, hoping to assuage his guilt.

"No sir, I will not be absolved so easily. The fact remains that if the Archduke Franz Ferdinand had not been struck down, we would not have declared war on Serbia when we did, and thereby set into motion a chain of disastrous alliances that spilt Europe in twain. And his death could have been avoided."

"I sympathise with your fatal role," I told him. "You saw the day's events reversing themselves, your foot not slipping from the accelerator, the perfume bottle not spreading oil across the sole of your shoe, the glance from the Princess not incensing your wife. A single look was all it took, and now the world has been shifted on its axis. It has taken the road to Hell and damnation."

"You read my mind," said Fritz, looking down at his shaking hands. "I have suffered with this pain for two long years. With each passing day the death toll rises, and I think to myself that it could all have so easily been avoided."

"But that is what fate always makes you think," said I. "That is the role of destiny."

"Be that as it may, I now find that this is no longer a burden with which I wish to live."

"The world does not know that you are responsible for its greatest tragedy," I said. "Unless you plan to tell them?"

Fritz felt inside his jacket and removed an envelope. "You have the ability to read my mind. I have taken the time to write down my true version of the events. Can you make sure that it reaches the right authorities?"

I took the envelope from him. "You know there is nothing you can do, no piece of paper you can write that will change what people will think," I said. "But there is a way for you to be absolved." I studied his face with tenderness. "You cannot change what will now be, for the wheels of history have continued in motion, bearing events away from you. All you can do is bring your own misery to an end."

"Yes," he agreed, looking down. "I belong with the innocent dead."

"The innocent dead," I repeated, smiling gently. "You know who I am, of course."

"Yes sir, I believe I do. You are the scent of roses."

I stood and stepped behind his chair, taking his thin warm neck in my grey-gloved hands. He felt no pain. His head dipped forward until his chin pressed against his chest, and he looked for the entire world like any other man enjoying the sleepy afternoon sun in the square.

I dropped a few coins in the saucer on the table and went to catch my train.

I was needed in Germany.

On the Side of the Angels

Mary Pletsch

Our R.E.8 biplane fell from the sky like the morning star from heaven.

The two-seater aircraft's radial engine streamed tongues of flame as we plummeted to earth. I clung to the observer's chair, as though if I held on tightly enough I might halt our descent, or at least preserve myself.

I hoped that Sam was alive and working the controls; prayed he was diving on purpose, to put out the flames. At any second, I told myself, he might pull out of the fall. Building g-forces whispered in my ear, warning me it was already too late – we would rip off our wings if we tried to level out.

The jagged lines of the trenches spun in dizzying circles far below, growing larger before my eyes. The side of my face burned from relentless gusts of hot air. I wrenched my gaze away from the rapidly approaching ground and saw fire on the wing beside me, fire on the fuselage.

The fabric covering the R.E.8's skeleton was treated with dope to stiffen it, and the stuff was highly flammable. We would go up like a torch.

We could be roasted to cinders before we ever hit the earth.

And the pilot's seat was in front of mine, closer to the engine.

I lifted my head though I did not want to, though I knew my eyes would behold horrors, and I imagined a grinning skeleton in Sam's seat, or worse yet, a blackened lump of meat.

I looked against my will and there was Sam, looking back over his shoulder and smirking at me, while all around him a corona of flames crackled like hellfire. I could smell my own hair scorching as the forward fuselage blazed, and yet he reclined in his chair with regal majesty.

"Daniel. Do you want to live?" Sam shouted, and somehow I heard him over the shriek of the wind and the guttural roar of the furnace.

Of course, of course I did.

I should have prayed to Jesus for my deliverance, but I sat as one struck dumb. Then Sam held out his hand to me, and I … I reached out and clasped it, in hopes that Sam could save me.

*

The Western Front was no place for a minister's son.

Five of us went to war together from my small Ontario town; five of us who had been too young the first time the recruiters came calling.

Two of our number were good-for-nothings and sinners: Joshua stole liquor from his father's cabinet, and Matthew had gotten the neighbour girl in trouble. She'd gone to stay with relatives, her family said, but from Joshua's jests I had guessed the truth. Both of them had tormented me as a child, pushing me into the mud, jeering at me because I wouldn't curse. I turned the other cheek as the Saviour taught and they struck me on it all the harder. It did not surprise me that they joined the army. They went to France to kill.

Timothy and Peter were friends of mine, and together we protected each other. The three of us were good boys: we joined to guard our country.

Every Sunday my father, a patriot, told his congregation that the Lord was on our side. It is not the role of a good Christian to wait to be conscripted.

I volunteered for the army of my Lord.

*

I thought I remembered my hand in Sam's, and the sudden scourging lash of flame that sublimated my very cells, converting my body to vapour in an instant.

I thought I had caught a glimpse of the mysteries of transfiguration, and I flinched, aghast, at the recollection of that terrible conversion.

I thought I recalled screaming into the burning skies, my

soul wracked with agony, until mortal flesh fell silent.

I thought my eyes had seen the glory…

I flinched again as stinking water covered my nostrils.

I jerked my head upright and found myself sitting in the bottom of a shell-hole, up to my neck in soupy mud. A glove that I suspected still contained the better part of a hand was floating in the muddy water not too far away from my lips.

Sam perched on a crate on the other side of the hole, squatting on his heels, up out of the water and the muck. He was grinning, as though he hadn't a care in the world, though surely he knew as well as I that at any instant a German patrol might appear over the lip of the crater, or an artillery shell might fall in here with us and blow us to kingdom come.

"Where's the plane?" I spluttered.

Sam gestured back over his shoulder. "A write-off, I fear. The old man won't be happy."

I could not care less what our commanding officer thought. I wallowed like a pig, trying to separate my body from the muck, my reality from dream.

"You there! Flyers!" Outside the crater, someone was calling us.

I'd heard of German soldiers calling out in English, baiting downed airmen to come out into the open where they could be shot, but I couldn't bear sitting here any longer, not down in this hole with filth and rotten flesh, not after facing the impossible choice between burning to death and falling to death and then realising even that choice had been taken from me.

I scrabbled out of the mud, mindful to avoid the bobbing hand, and clambered up the far side of the hole. Carefully, I eased the top of my head over the lip of the crater.

Three British Tommies crouched behind the splintered remains of a fencepost, as though it could provide any shield should the Huns start shooting. "Are you all right?" asked the lead man, a corporal.

"We're fine," I said, with a glance over my shoulder at Sam. That smug bastard, he was more than fine, while I was still … I didn't know. I looked down at my body. Under the mud and despite the tremors in my hands I seemed to be physically intact. I pushed away the shadow looming at the corner of my mind. I just wanted to get back to the squadron, for a hearty meal and a soft bed.

The Tommies guided us through a tangle of barbed wire and then down into trenches. They were better than the shell crater, but not by much: duckboards kept our feet out of the mud some of the time, and sandbags kept the sides of the trench shored up, but as I walked past, I saw the gleam of white bone protruding from the trench wall.

I had the uncanny feeling of walking through a graveyard, and my morbid imagination thrust upon me the idea that I might be a ghost, leaving my own body behind.

Too late, I jumped onto a nearby ladder and climbed until I could stick my head over the top of the trench, to see if the R.E.8 was really a pile of ashes as I recalled. We had to have been too far away; I could see no sign of the aircraft anywhere.

Sam and I followed the corporal through a labyrinth of support trenches until we finally climbed up another ladder and into the open air. Nearby, a platoon of soldiers took turns lifting the last artillery shells out of a horse-drawn cart. As though from a distance, I heard the corporal talking to Sam, assuring him that the drayman would deliver us back to the squadron, neat as you please, once the shells were unloaded.

My hands were still shaking from our near miss as I climbed into the cart, and they continued to shake the whole way back to No. 7 Squadron headquarters.

The wagon bounced over the rutted earth, rattling my teeth and jouncing my bones, but I felt no pain at all. The ride took hours, and left me with nothing to do but wonder why I had no memory of the landing, of jumping out of the crashed plane or slithering to cover in the shell hole. I remembered only Sam – *trust me* – and how instinctively, intuitively, I had put my hand in his.

Yes, I wanted to live.

And the whole way home, Sam watched me intently. I wanted to believe he was making sure I was all right, and by the time we arrived back at our airfield, I had almost convinced myself.

But when I was eight years old, my father had taken me to the zoo, and I had seen the look on Sam's face before, in the hooded eyes of a cobra that held its prey in thrall.

*

During our training, Timothy, Peter and I stayed behind in the barracks while Joshua, Matthew and the rest of our division spent their leave time in bars, getting drunk and chasing loose women. We let them go and ignored their taunts; we had tickets to the Kingdom of Heaven, and they would envy us if they ever understood our blessings. We studied our Bibles, wrote letters home and, on occasion, played chess or backgammon.

Our friendship persisted until we went to France, into the mud and fire of the Front Lines.

There I beheld horrors that were beyond my imagination. To look upon No Man's Land was to peer through a portal into Hell. Here were the scourges of my father's sermons ripped from the hereafter into the living, breathing world. The earth thrown up by explosive shells, all greenery stripped away, replaced by puddles of stagnant, befouled water that teemed with disease.

Bodies, bloated, fly-blown, left lying about to rot. Clouds of lethal gas caused us to cough up chunks of our own lungs if we failed to get our masks on in time. Human misery surrounded us – pain and terror and grief and worry, every conceivable form of suffering.

Peter whispered to me, in the dark of the night, of the terror of the grave. Most of all how he feared to die without ever knowing the touch of a woman, the joys of the flesh. I counselled him to stay strong, to keep his feet in the ways of the Lord.

Then Timothy took a bullet to the eye.

Timothy went over the top between Peter and I. My attention had been fixed on the corporal ahead of us when all of a sudden I felt something wet on my face, Peter let out a cry and Timothy went down.

I let the others charge ahead as I knelt down, turning

Timothy's body over; then I shoved him away in horror, as though by my denial I could force the brains back into the skull, the eye back into its socket.

It occurred to me then that Peter was screaming, and my cheek was sticky. I reached up with my glove and brought it away with Timothy's viscera dripping from my fingers.

On our next leave I went to church alone. Peter staggered into town, flanked by Joshua and Matthew, and I knew I had lost both my friends. Timothy, at least, I might see someday in Heaven. Peter, I feared, was bound for Hell.

I did not know how I could survive alone down in the stinking rot of the trenches, surrounded by the company of sinners. I was the righteous one – I did not belong in this Hades on Earth.

I prayed to the Lord to deliver me, and the Lord heard my prayer.

As I stepped out of the church, I heard a throbbing whine overhead, and as I raised my eyes to the sky I saw a two-seater biplane flying in rings above the steeple, like a divine messenger.

That afternoon I tendered my application to the Royal Flying Corps.

*

I woke up the next morning and stared at the canvas roof of my tent, wondering why impossible memories still clung to my thoughts like a faint whisper of smoke.

I had survived three months of training as an aircraft observer, and, as of today, I had lived through sixteen days as a member of No.7 Squadron. I had heard the mechanics muttering about the median survival rate, whether it was down to seventeen days now or whether it was still holding at eighteen; when they thought we flyers weren't looking, they tallied the statistics on their chalkboards.

That had to be why I was nervous. I was almost at that eighteenth day, and I'd just had my closest call yet.

I got out of bed and examined my body, carefully, knowing a hard landing like that was certain to leave bruises. The smell of my own singed hair still lingered in my nostrils, and I leaned against the mirror in the bathroom, examining my cheek, my hairline. I found nothing amiss. I was as fit as I had been the day I went to the recruiting office to join up.

Had the crash been so terrible, then? Had there been any crash at all? Perhaps the horrific recollections lingering in my mind were nothing more than the vestiges of a remarkably persistent nightmare.

For a moment, I considered asking Sam what he remembered of the previous day, but I quickly thought better of it. Sam would not want to fly with a blithering madman, and I was not inclined to gamble my only friend.

I said my prayers, took my breakfast alone, and as I went outside to the hangars, I passed one of my fellow airmen, a fellow named Paul Sykes.

"'Morning, Father," Sykes said with a smirk, and I held my head up high and ignored him. I hated my nickname – Father Daniel – not because I was ashamed, not because I was Baptist and not Catholic, but because of the scorn with which the name was spoken. My fellow airmen would have done well to spend more time learning the Gospel, and less time on drink and idle entertainments.

The sun had not yet burned off the fog, which smothered the ground like a thick blanket, wrapping its tendrils around the distant hedgerows and the sides of the hangars.

In front of No.1 Hangar, Sam stood next to an R.E.8, carefully painting an image under the cockpit. He held an old piece of scrap lumber upon which he had placed dollops of different-coloured paint, using it as a palette.

Our High Command frowned on unauthorised modifications, unlike the Huns who decorated their aircraft in the gaudiest of patterns and colours they could conceive of. Still, some of our men broke the rules – and Sam was always chief among them.

A ray of sun lanced down through the morning clouds as Sam turned to me, hair glowing golden in the light, and I could see what he'd painted on the biplane: a hideous lion-headed serpent, its lip drawn back in a snarl, its tail wound about the staff of a pointed spear.

It was the same horrible heraldic device that had decorated the last plane, and though I wasn't familiar with the pagan mythology that had conceived of such an ugly beast, it did offer me the opportunity to inquire after our previous aircraft.

"Given us a new machine, have they?"

"There's a push on," Sam replied with a disarming grin, "and High Command wants all airworthy craft in the air, blinding the Hun's eyes in the sky."

Our R.E.8 two-seater was not a fighter plane. "Sounds like they're counting us out," I said. Our work ran more towards reconnaissance and bombing.

"H.Q. wants pictures of Rassicot," Sam responded, naming a little French village just a few miles behind the Front Lines. "I think they're hoping our boys will be drinking victory toasts in the streets come nightfall."

"Why do they bother?" I spat with frustration. "The British have been at this for three years; we know what's going to happen. Our push will peter out once our boys no longer have trenches to take cover in. Then the Huns will push back. We'll dig a few more trenches, and so will the Huns, and both sides will slightly adjust the curve of the Front Lines on their maps and *that will be it*. Why even bother fighting at all?"

"To show you still can." Sam didn't look at me; his gaze was fixed on the sky, eyes focused on something beyond the clouds. "To stop fighting is to indicate your acceptance of the way things are."

*

I had hoped that the R.F.C. would offer me a chance to start over. Much to my disappointment, the Royal Flying Corps was crewed by the same sort of perverts, drunkards and blasphemers who populated the army.

Before my first night was over, I was dubbed "Father Daniel" and the other trainees had been swept under the wings of squadron pilots and hauled off into town for various earthly delights, while I sat alone on the stoop of the mess and wondered where I could find a godly man in all of France to call my friend.

That, I think, was the start of it: Sam's insistence on keeping me company. I was put off by his casual profanity and flagrant disrespect for authority, but he persisted, taking his meals with me in the mess, asking me to fly as his observer.

Most of all he did not laugh at me, and when I was in his company, neither did anyone else. No one dared. He had the stern countenance of a judge – and the cold smile of an executioner.

He did not speak of religion and I did not press him. That, above all else, was my undoing.

*

Sam and I took off into the bloody dawn, circling higher and higher until we crossed the Front Lines on our way to Rassicot.

We flew slow circuits of the town as I worked the camera in my cockpit, and in between photographs I checked the air around me for any sign of German aircraft, but there were none to be found.

I entertained the fanciful notion that we had been rewarded with particular good luck in reaction to yesterday's horror. My good humour lasted until we were on our way home, when suddenly, without warning, the R.E.8. nosed down into a dive.

I looked ahead through the tangle of struts and bracing wires between the wings and saw what Sam had seen: a line of German soldiers and horses and carts travelling along the road on their way to the Front Lines. A handful of fence posts remained standing at the side of the road, indicating what had once been a farmer's field.

I watched the little figures below stop, raise their heads, lift their guns – then scatter like leaves before a whirlwind. Sam was laughing, his head thrown back and his fingers on the trigger of the forward guns, chuckling like a maniac as he rained down fire onto the Germans below.

With the sun behind us, our shadow on the ground overtook the fleeing Germans. Men fell before our onslaught as our black wings passed over. I bore witness, with impossible clarity of vision, as they marked the fence posts with their blood.

A handful of their number had the presence of mind to aim, and bullet holes bloomed in the R.E.8's fabric. It was only a matter of time before a bullet cracked the wood of our airframe, or worse, struck our engine and set us afire. I worked my machine gun like a madman, pouring a stream of ordnance into the German trenches.

Then I beheld the cratered purgatory of No Man's Land below us, and I knew we would soon cross over the British trenches. Sam just kept on firing, strafing trench after trench, and so, God help me, did I. Swept up in a strange exultation, I sang out a fierce and wordless psalm.

Only when I saw a figure in green clutch his chest and fall to his knees did I realise what I had done – *was still doing*. I recoiled from my gun and clasped my hands together, and in the back seat of the R.E.8 I begged for God's forgiveness, that the Lord might have mercy upon me, poor miserable sinner.

When we landed at the aerodrome I had transmuted my horror into outrage, for it was Sam who had led me astray, Sam who had started it and who had dragged me into this mess. I leapt from the cockpit the instant the R.E.8 taxied to a halt, and my anger overrode my fear. I grabbed hold of Sam's coat as he climbed from the plane and hauled him bodily to the earth.

"You're bloody daft," I spat. "We could have died."

"Therefore put on the full armour of God," Sam quipped as he wrenched himself free of my grip, "with the breastplate of righteousness in place."

I narrowed my eyes at him; almost certain he was mocking me. Sam never came to church, though I had invited him numerous times, and here he was quoting Ephesians.

"What were you thinking?" I demanded, and Sam's face took on the icy cast of a judge and he answered me thusly: "Lieutenant Franz Schlosser, adulterer. Private Ludwig Preis, disrespectful son. Private Karl Zweifel, liar who bears false witness. Corporal Hans Lindenschmidt, who does not keep the Sabbath day..."

I lost track of the names he listed, but three stood out: "Corporal Matthew MacDonald, fornicator. Private Joshua Churchill, thief. Private Peter Loughlin, coveter. Sinners, the lot of them, unworthy of the glory of the Lord, now delivered unto their inheritance in Hell."

As he spoke I felt his righteous indignation, and I could not disagree, if Sam's words were true, that those men were deserving of their punishments. But we … I opened my mouth to voice my concern, that terrible chill in my breast at the thought of the fifth commandment, and Sam silenced me.

"Daniel," he said, "we are the ones the Pharisees called *the severity of God*." In his eyes I could see the great wheels turning and the wings and the tongues of fire, and, God help me, I remember.

*

I remember the impact, the R.E.8's engine driven back through the pilot's cockpit, crushing Sam into a pulp. I remember pin-wheeling, flipping end-over-end when the front of the plane caught on some object, a rock or a tree or something, and the back end just kept going. I remember the blazing conflagration, my eyelids pulling back from eyes shrivelling in their sockets, their moisture evaporating in the heat, and yet, without my eyes, I see.

I see Sam in a wreath of flames, his uniform burning away, like some pagan demigod robed in terrible beauty. He reaches out to me, a wing, an arm, and my vision doubles, triples, or perhaps he truly is watching me through a legion of eyes, a multiplicity of faces and wings and trumpet mouths in endless wheels turning through fire.

I stare at him in infinite horror, and yet I keep my sight affixed upon him, for as long as I behold him, I cannot look upon myself. I know that I too stand in those same flames, and they do not burn me; and while the sight of Lieutenant Sam Smith brings me to the very edge of madness, to comprehend what I myself have become will push me over the brink.

After endless aeons the flames die down to embers, and Sam clothes himself once more in mortal flesh, no more wings and wheels, a single face, just an ordinary man standing in the burned-out hulk of an aircraft, with his observer at his side.

At long last I dare look down, and I see only myself, whole and undamaged as I had been on the day I went down to the recruiting office, four months and a lifetime ago. I stand dressed in flying leathers; invulnerable, perhaps immortal, knowing my humanity has receded on an otherworldly tide.

In desperate pursuit of that humanity, I drive the forbidden knowledge from my mind.

*

"What have you done?" I mouth the words with barely any strength, wrapping my arms across my chest in search of a comfort I cannot find.

"You said you wanted to live." Sam leans back against the aircraft and looks at me with a secret smile and, God help me, I cannot deny the truth in his words.

I can hear my father's voice, as though from a great distance, as though even now he is in the pulpit, reading from the Bible: *For whosoever will save his life shall lose it: but whosoever will lose his life for my sake, the same shall save it.*

I ... I had not had any time to think it through, as the heat charred my hair and the R.E.8 plummeted towards oblivion.

"Now," pronounces Sam, "we will do the work of our Lord, you and I."

Fernackerpan

Peter Mark May

The world was dark, the weather was winter cold and the night lit occasionally with manmade starbursts of bitter confusion.

A graveyard mist clung to the Western Front near Flanders with its fields of frozen mud and sporadic sods of grass. It was the eve before Christmas Day and no movement could be seen of man or mouse from either the German or British trenches. Everyone had hunkered down for the night seeking any warmth that they could muster from the cold Belgium earth.

The only respite the cold snap had brought was from the oozing mud and watery trenches that rotted the men's feet. For even calf-high mud had frozen solid and the puddles between them had become mini-ice rinks.

Apart from those unlucky enough to be on guard, most of 6 Platoon, C Company of the 1st Battalion the Middlesex Regiment, were squeezed together in a twelve by eleven feet underground room carved out of the hard earth, planked and boarded from top to bottom in wood. A small burner stood in the centre of this mud and wood dwelling. Its stove pipe going up through the ground to a shuttered chimney top, so no light could escape for the enemy to see.

Huddled around the stove, crouched six of the twelve men present. The other half dozen taking turns to lie in alcove bunks off the dirt covered floor. It gave them a chance to ease their boots off in dry, albeit freezing conditions.

The two men nearest the open door of the stove were trying to turn their hard mouldy bread into something that resembled toast, or at least burn out the maggots that hid inside. The other four men crouched with peeled back layers of mud encrusted coats, scarves and battledresses trying to feel any of the warm of the small burner on their dirt engrained skin.

One of the men, a private by rank moved away from the warmth. Heading towards the makeshift door they had found on patrol three months ago, beside a shell devastated farm house.

"Where you going off to on a fine Christmas Eve night then Mustard?" asked one of the vertical bunk slackers: an Irishman by the name of O'Hare.

"Away from the smell of your socks Paddy," was Private Mustard's reply as he moved closer to the door.

"'Tis not the socks that be making your eyes weep son, 'tis the mangy remains of me feet inside I'll tell ya," O'Hare chortled back in his usual reboant manner.

"I need the latrine okay," Mustard finally gave in, his gloved hands grasping the looped rope that served as a makeshift door handle. Bracing himself for the cold inrush, which he could already feel seeping through the gaps in the door.

"Hurry along then mate and don't let old Fritz Fernackerpan get you," urged Corporal Sayers from his prime toasting position in front of the timid little burner.

Mustard mumbled something incoherent, as he has raised his scarf up over his nose and mouth. Opening the door he exited the underground room as quickly as he could. Even so, the freezing night air circled in around the small room, causing all to shiver, but at least it fumigated the funk for a small while.

"Who is Fritz Fernackerpan then?" asked a timid voiced young teen soldier, who hadn't even started shaving yet. He had only been on the line for a week. "Is he a bit like Fred Fernackerpan, my old ma used to go on about?"

"Fritz is like the Hun version of our Fred. A sort of nasty inbred, sister-raping cousin so to speak," Corporal Sayers's remarked back to the green private, before munching down on his toast.

"But who is he?" the young soldier enquired again, "Me ma used to warn me not to stay out too late after dark or Fred Fernackerpan would get me."

"Fritz is like Fred, only worse. He's a walking corpse with

no face and only one eye they say and kills Tommys for fun," Lance-Corporal Bacon said adding his tuppence worth from a cot behind the young private.

"And Fred is a masculine version, I do believe, of Fanny Fernackerpan nee Ferguson a music hall girl who was one of the victims of Jack the Ripper, no less," said Lance-Corporal Pendleton from his bunk next to his fellow lance-corporal, yet in a plumier voice.

"There goes the Prof with his swear words again and him an heducated man," Bacon laughed and began to try to roll a fag with shaking cold fingers.

"I've seen the scary fella in the cold flesh so to speak. He is a frightening wicked tormented soul and worse than any living foe you'll find here," O'Hare's voice shivered as he spoke, but not from the unrelenting cold.

"Shut up the lot of ya," Corporal Sayers barked and then lowered his voice to a whisper. "Now do you want to hear about the true legend of old Fritz Fernackerpan? Cos I'm the only bloody man living that knows the full tale of it and how the fiend came about?"

"By all means continue," said Pendleton with a regal wave of his right hand.

"Tell us again Corp. I'm having trouble drifting off tonight anyway," said Bacon from his loft bunk.

"Well, it all begins," Sayers started with a brief pause to ramp up the. "On a cold winter's night, much like this. I was only a one-stripe shag of a lad and sent out on patrol with the evilest hardest bastard raises under an English sun, Sergeant Harry Herbert."

"Phew old H-H, now that was one scary toss-pot, I'd never want to meet in a darkened alley after the hour of midnight," interrupted O'Hare, rubbing the lice out of his hairline.

"Oi it's my story, so no interruptions from the floor please gents." Corporal Sayers's eyes looked from man-to-man in the ill lit smelly room until all were compliant in their silence.

"Well we had our masks on because of the Mustard gas attacks the night before and it seemed to linger like piss-coloured mists in the shell holes. We had not gotten half a mile or so into a small wood, when this fog comes up and suddenly it's like we were standing inside a bleedin' cloud from the heavens. Me and the other lads were all for heading back towards our lines, but old Harry Herbert soon squashed that notion and we heads further into the foggy woods.

"All of a sudden out of nowhere it seemed a shape appears in front of us probably not more than ten feet away, but we can't tell if the blighter is friend or foe. *Stand to and identify yourself*, cries old Harry Herbert, his rifle raised to his brawny shoulders. Now I swear on my life the figure replies in an English accent and saying to my ears the words, *Nine*, like the number. But old Harry, who was always a bit Mutt and Jeff because of his shouting orders all the time, hears the German word 'Nein' and opens fire. Four of the other chaps also start shooting and the figure goes down, disappearing into the fog. Old Harry grinning like a cat who's bagged the cream runs up on his own, ordering the rest of us to stay put; while he heads forwards to have a gander. But me being a silly beggar and urged on by my mates in the patrol, goes to have a look-see."

"What did you find, Corporal?" the timid new recruit asked, as Sayers paused for dramatic effect.

"Well I edged around to the left keeping a tree between me and the sarge, who has his back to me kneeling on the forest floor. Then I notice a lot of dead Hun, taken out by shell fire. Looked like the corpses had been there a week or so. Anyways old Harry threw something behind him which landed next to me as he worked away. I crept over to pick up and find it's a British officer's cap and inside it has a name badge: 2nd Lt R.W. Nine, Lt Shrops. I dropped the cap and heads back to me mates without old Harry noticing me. *What you see?* Me mates ask, but I keep me mouth shut and rightly so. Five minutes later old Harry Herbert calls us forward and we walk past him to see a dead body lying on the foggy forest floor. He has a German uniform on, one of their spiked helmets, but the man has no face left. It was like his skin had been peeled off his face and only one eye was left in its blood covered socket. A green eye staring up into the fog, the corpse had no lips, just lots of teeth showing and it looked ungodly. *We bagged ourselves a Hun,* bellows Harry Herbert, *now let's get back to our lines.*

"We headed back to our lines, but those wounds on the face of that corpse looked like a butcher had filleted it and didn't look like any gunshot wounds I'd ever seen before or since."

"Didn't you say something to your Commanding Officer?" the green young private asked from the shadows.

"What and go against old Harry Herbert with some cock-n-bull story and no evidence? I'd be lined up before a firing squad before I'd known what had hit me." Corporal Sayers reeled in his neck at the idea. "You don't tell tales on people like that son."

"Where is old Harry Herbert now then?" asked Jenkins crouching next to the corporal. He'd been with the platoon only three months and hadn't heard the tale before.

"Dead, like all the rest of the patrol see. They found Harry standing at his post a month later a fag still clenched in his teeth. Yet the poor bastard had no face to speak of, it had been stripped clean, white as chalk, yet still standing like on sentry duty. "

"How did the others in the patrol die?" the young private asked from the shadows of the raw earthy smelling room as the fire in the stove began to wane.

"Two of em died normal enough during the big push eight months ago. Tommy Hearn they never found him. Went out for a piss and never came back. Algie Green had his face blown off by a shell a month after Paddy joined the platoon."

"Was an awful sight to behold, face totally gone, his eyes were like two fried eggs in his sockets, nasty." Private O'Hare turned over in his bunk to speak and noticed the shadows in the room had grown deeper and the cold more prevalent.

"Kenneth Tomkins, now I was with the patrol led by Captain Carstairs who found him dead in the field. The captain led the way and in the mist covered muddy field we found the faceless corpse of old Kenny Tomkins with some Hun standing over him. The captain shoots the Hun five times in the chest, but the Hun just turns and walks off into the mist of battle and vanishes. Old Captain Carstairs was sent home after that, shell-shock they say; I know otherwise, he saw old Fritz

Fernackerpan." Corporal Sayers said, rubbing his limbs as the cold was beginning to bite.

"So you are the sole survivor of the patrol then?" the green private asked. Only the vaguest outlines of his shape could be seen in the lengthening shadows, as the stove flickered low.

"Yes," Corporal Sayers nodded, trying to stoke more life and light out of the failing burner. "What was your name again, Private?" Sayers never bothered to learn any replacement's name until they had been on the line a month, it saved time.

"Ronald William Nine," the young man replied moving out of the shadows so Corporal Sayers's could see his plaid bony countenance now. One green eye blazed with vengeance under the spiked helm upon his head.

*

"See didn't get me, did he, old Fred or Fritz," Private Mustard said as he scratched his ear with one finger as he pushed the makeshift door in with the other hand half an hour later. The dawn of Christmas Day was breaking over the broken earth of once fertile Flanders' fields.

The grey morning light shone into the charnel house to reveal the bodies of ten of his fellow C Company men. None of the ten had any skin left upon their faces and each had had an eye plucked out. There was no blood, nor any sign of a struggle. The bleached white skulls sat upon flesh and uniformed cadavers, and shone bright in the first rays of the most holy day of the year.

Private Mustard screamed out every inch of air from his lungs as his fellow officers and men came charging over to see what the racket was about. Mustard could only fix his eyes on the spiked German helmet that sat upon the cold stove. While all around it, his dead friends and fellow soldiers lay. Of the missing young private no trace was ever found, nor were there any records of him being transferred to the front line to serve in 6 Platoon.

Unknown Soldier

Nancy Hayden

"The black labour battalions ... manned three main divisions
that supplied the front... One of the worst details was Graves
Registration, to find, record, and rebury the dead."

From *The Unknown Soldiers: Black
American Troops in World War I*
*

Paul and his squad mates – Silas, Muncie, and Hank – stared at
the dead soldier they'd just thrown into the chalky earth.

The men wore helmets and gas mask satchels, but they'd
stripped off their service coats to their sweat-soaked shirts
beneath. White dust caked the back of their necks.

No one spoke.

Flies buzzed around their heads and faces, occasionally
landing on their sweaty noses and foreheads. They'd stopped
swatting at flies weeks ago.

Paul looked over the shell scorched and pock-marked
terrain shadowed by dark clouds. The remnants of broken
machines stood amidst blackened tree stubs and zigzagging
trenches. Worse than any hurricane aftermath he'd ever seen,
and he should know being from the Louisiana Bayou.

Sergeant Phelps and the rest of the squad worked down
slope and toward the west. *Like ants*, he thought. *Ants pick up
their dead too.*

Far away, artillery boomed and the land exploded. The
action near Paul came from the rats and crows and flies
competing for corpses.

They'd been on graves registration for two weeks now,
following behind the infantry, searching for the dead among
the soon-to-be dead, watching men gasp their last breath,

listening to their screams and cries and pleas. Paul had seen every stage of human decomposition.

He'd dreamed of death and dead men every night, and every day he hated the war more than the day before.

That first day, he and Silas put a dead German soldier on the stretcher. Paul took the feet end and Silas, the head. Paul had never seen a white man so close before except Stem Dawkins from back home, and he was a grizzled man, almost as brown as Paul, not white and smooth like this boy. As they started walking, the soldier's eyelids fluttered and then opened wide. Paul dropped the stretcher.

"What the Hell?" Silas said dropping his own end as he turned toward Paul.

"Mir helfen," the man on the stretcher moaned and pain shone in the blue eyes that stared at Paul, a stare Paul had seen in Stem's dying eyes.

Paul bent down to check on the man. Then he saw a knife flash in the soldier's hand. He lifted it toward Paul and for a moment, Paul was back in the Bayou – Stem Dawkins waving his knife in Paul's face, jabbing it toward Paul, "I'm gonna kill you, nigger. I'm gonna kill you."

Paul grabbed the arm, resisted the thrust aimed at his stomach, twisted the hand toward Stem, pushed it hard, plunging the knife deep. Only it wasn't Stem, and he wasn't back in the backwater Bayou.

He was in France, and he'd just killed a man, an unknown German soldier.

"Shit," Silas said and then a slow smile grew on his bony face. He winked at Paul. "Looks like you just killed your first Hun."

Paul stood up and staggered back. He closed his eyes and felt the pain of killing again. He buried his face into his bloody hands. He didn't mean it. God knows, he didn't mean it.

"Get a hold of yourself," Silas said putting his hand on Paul's shoulder. "You done right. That bastard wanted to kill you. Here, take a sip of water."

Paul wiped his eyes with his sleeve and took the canteen from Silas. He drank a long swallow and tried not to look at the

German, his staring blue eyes. Silas uncurled the dead fingers and yanked out the knife. He wiped it on the soldier's coat.

"You want it?" Silas asked.

Paul shook his head, turned away.

"Then I'm gonna keep it," he said.

The burying started on July 18th 1918, when under the cover of a rolling barrage, French and American divisions led a counter-offensive against the Germans near the Marne River in the Champagne region of France.

The Germans dug in though, and the advance stalled a few days later and only crept along after that.

Paul's squad, one of many burial details made up of black soldiers, worked sixteen, seventeen, eighteen hour days finding and burying the dead. So many bodies. With the hot days of July, it didn't take long before the bodies bloated and stunk so bad that even the infantry started puking up their slum.

And the flies.

Everywhere.

Then the shits hit.

Orders were to bury the dead as quickly as possible and throw in some quicklime for good measure. The newly dead were brought to the rear for burial in make-shift cemeteries. The long dead, the ones that didn't hold together, the bits and pieces, and the enemy were buried in out of the way patches of ground.

First, the burial team poked around to find the two metal tags each soldier wore around his neck. They'd snip the string of one and leave the other with the body. They checked for papers and personal items, and then they scooped the bones and spongy or dried flesh, depending on how long they'd been dead, into the hole.

A wooden grave marker with the dead man's ID stamped on a tin tag was nailed to the wood. Paul was the only member of his squad who could read and write. He helped the others learn their numbers and letters by copying the IDs onto the tags. All personal items went to the company officer back at camp. Sergeant Phelps was adamant about that.

Today they didn't check for tags; they were burying the

enemy. German soldiers – no longer white and fresh like that dying blue-eyed boy Paul killed. Maybe they'd been like that, crying out for help.

They had dreams and families and sisters.

They wanted to live.

Paul saw that German boy whenever he rolled the dead soldiers over, when he checked the pockets, when he dropped their remains in the hole.

"All right, let's go," Silas ordered pushing on Hank who was nearest to him. Silas was in charge of the crew and liked it. "Let's get those other Hun bastards and shovel them into the hole with their buddies."

"Hank. That's me," Hank said and giggled. He mumbled something no one could understand and giggled again. A chill went down Paul's back.

Muncie, big strong Muncie, who used to sing those old slave songs that so riled Silas, picked up the stained canvas used for hauling the dead; he wasn't singing anymore. A rat scurried out from underneath the tarp. Muncie kicked at it but missed.

"I hate rats," he said. "I hate 'em."

"Rats," Hank said and laughed.

Paul grabbed the other end of the canvas and started leading the way. Anything to get away from Hank.

"Hank, you just take a nice rest," Muncie said. He'd looked after Hank ever since training. Hank was the youngest member of the squad and didn't talk to anyone but Muncie. He was sickly too. Paul wondered why the Army would send somebody like that into war. "'Cause they's the Army," Silas explained which he said for just about everything that happened.

Hank looked up at Muncie and sat down on the edge of the hole. When the three men had gone a few paces, Hank started giggling.

"Christ. That sonofabitch is gone loony on us," Silas said shaking his head. "Loony."

Paul thought maybe they were all going loony, himself included. Every night since it'd happened, he dreamed about that German boy he'd killed, and about Stem Dawkins. Paul had received a letter from his sister before they went on burial detail. He'd burned it a week ago, hoping it would make the dreams stop, but it hadn't worked.

He remembered her words and her warning.

They found Stem Dawkin's body yesterday with a knife shoved in what was left of his belly which wasn't much. They came around asking after you but I see they have killing on their minds. I got my things together and with the help of Jonas left in the middle of the night cause I know that if they can't get the Negro they looking for they take someone else instead even a girl. I don't know if it was you or not but they think it was so don't you come back to the Bayou. Ever.

She'd written in the French Creole, the only thing she could write in. Their Grandmother had taught them both. Maybe that was why it had taken so long to get through the censors. Maybe that's why it made it through at all.

Paul looked back at Muncie and forced a smile at him. He wasn't the same since Hank started going crazy. Muncie didn't smile back. As rain clouds threatened, Paul trudged ahead. Maybe rain would cool things off, although it never did in the Bayou.

A shadow with a German helmet slunk behind the rocks. Paul stopped and stared; blood pounded in his ears. Muncie walked into Paul. Silas came hurrying up.

"What's wrong?" Silas asked.

Paul pointed in the direction he'd seen the shadow. His body froze. Silas ran over to the rock pile Paul had indicated. He looked around before walking back to the others.

"What'd you see?" he said.

"I," Paul tried to speak, but his mouth had dried up.

Silas pushed him. "What?"

Paul let the chill run down and out of him back into the earth. "I thought I saw someone."

"Who?" Silas said.

Paul took a deep breath. "A German soldier, his shadow maybe."

Muncie and Silas glanced around.

"A shadow?" Silas said.

"Probably just a trick of the light," Paul said. He looked at Muncie and Silas. "Just my eyes playing tricks." He swallowed. *Just tricks*, he thought.

Silas narrowed his eyes at Paul.

"I didn't see nobody," Muncie said and looked around again.

"What's going on around here?" Silas asked. "First Hank with his giggling, then Muncie won't sing, and now you seeing things. Christamighty."

Silas looked all around again and back at Hank who was still sitting on the side of the hole.

"Let's get on with it," Silas said.

They turned beyond a pile of rubble, walked further up the slope, and stopped next to three decaying and half-buried bodies and a wrecked Maxim machine gun. Shell blast. Paul kicked some of the rocks away.

They'd been dead for a while.

Over a week.

Bones shone white against blackened flesh.

"Good," Silas said as he looked down at the corpses. "Nicely aged. They won't stink so bad as some of 'em. Looks like someone was here before us though; their boots is gone. Probably nothing in their pockets for us neither."

Silas bent over and checked the pockets of their coat, finding a few papers, but coins, watches, knives, chains, all of the usual items were gone. He used a stick to check for gold teeth.

"Yep, must be those infantry sonsabitches was here," Silas said. "They done picked these bastards clean."

"Let's load them up," Muncie said. "Got to get the job done."

"We ain't never going to get this job done," Silas said. "We keep burying 'em, and each side keep killing 'em."

Paul nodded. As long as the troops were advancing and the Germans were fighting back, the dead kept piling up. They were just one squad, and they'd already buried over a hundred bodies and a few horses too. Sergeant Phelps said the French and Americans had the Germans on the run. If they did, they weren't running very fast.

Paul and Muncie always used their shovels to roll the bodies onto the tarp. That way the clothes kept the bones together for the most part. As soon as they moved the first one, they stepped back from the stink. Paul coughed. Muncie gagged. Silas laughed.

"No surprise there," Silas said. "At this stage in the game, it's always the underside that stinks worst."

They rolled the other two onto the tarp, stepping back after each one to let some of the smell dissipate, staring at wriggling maggots underneath. The last soldier's head fell off. Silas kicked it on to the tarp.

"Yep. We's experts on decaying bodies now," Silas said. "That's what we done learned in this man's army. Some guys learned how to shoot guns, load artillery shells, or fly airplanes. But us, well we learned how long it takes a man to bloat up after he's killed. And how long it takes for the meat to fall off the bones. And how to tell how long some bastard's been dead by the tang of the stench he gives off and the black beetles eating the maggots in his belly."

"Come on, Silas." Muncie never did like Silas's speeches. "Hurry up and grab the other end with Paul. I want to check on Hank. I'm worried about him."

"He's beyond worrying," Silas said and picked up his end.

As they walked back to the grave, Paul saw it again. The shadow with the German helmet, moving in front of them.

"Look," he said to the others. Too late; it slipped over the rocks.

"Not again," Silas said looking around. Then rolled his eyes. "Christamighty."

Paul looked down.

"I can't wait to tell the folks back home what I did in the war," Silas said as they stumbled across a shell hole. "My girl is going to ask me if I fought the Hun and made the world safe for democracy. I'm gonna say, Hon," he started laughing at that. "Get it? Hon, like Hun."

Neither Paul nor Muncie answered.

"No? You don't think that's funny?" Silas looked over at Paul.

"Okay. Okay," Silas said still smiling. "Let me finish. I'd say, Hon, I didn't fight and kill those Boche swine; I just buried 'em."

Silas laughed again. Paul didn't feel like laughing. He felt like walking and never coming back. If he were brave, he thought, he'd get out of this war right now with either a bullet or a prison term. He wasn't brave.

"Damn," Muncie said when they were a dozen or so paces from the hole. He dropped his end of the tarp and looked around. "Where'd that Hank run off to? Hank!" He turned around, a worried look on his face.

"Hank," Silas called out. "Hank, you loony bastard."

Paul's stomach tightened when he saw the German shadow, this time creeping into the open grave.

Muncie and Silas hurried toward Hank's voice coming from the hole. Paul followed. What he saw when he looked down made his whole body stiff. Hank sat on one of the bodies, wearing a German helmet and jacket, bending low and whispering in the dead man's ear.

Hank ignored Paul and the others; his face was turned away, just his cheek and chin visible. It looked white.

"Come on now, Hank," Muncie said in a voice to coax a small child. "Come out of that hole. A grave's no place for you. I'll put my hand down for you to grab."

Muncie knelt down and extended his hand. Hank still hadn't turned around; he was rummaging through the inside of the dead man's trousers. He started laughing and talking.

"Come on, Hank," Muncie said. Muncie's coddling had always annoyed Paul. If the boy wouldn't get out of the damn hole, then Paul would just go down and haul him up.

"Wait!" Silas said grabbing Paul's arm to keep him from going forward. Paul looked at Silas's face, wide eyed and rigid. Another chill crept down Paul's back.

"Listen," Silas whispered. "Listen. Hank's talking German."

Paul didn't know any German but he'd heard prisoners before, and it sure sounded like German. Silas reached over to Muncie, but too late. Muncie stepped into the hole at the same time Hank turned.

Silas stepped back, pulling Paul with him. "No!"

Paul stared at Hank's face that didn't look like Hank's face anymore. That looked white and chiseled like the German boy Paul had killed. Muncie yelled, "Hank," at the same time Paul saw the Lugar in the boy's hand, the same moment Silas pulled him back, the same moment Hank let out a flurry of German.

The gun shot shocked Paul into motion.

"Those rocks," Silas said, pulling on Paul, stumbling for footing. "Got to get behind those rocks."

Paul grabbed onto Silas as the two ran up the slope toward cover. When they reached the rocks, Paul turned and saw Hank, but it wasn't Hank, emerging from the grave.

"Muncie," Paul asked. "What about Muncie?"

"Muncie's dead," Silas said. "Hank shot him right in the chest."

"Not Hank," Paul stared at Silas. "Didn't you see his face?"

"I was looking at the goddamn gun, but it was Hank. Who else you think it was?"

"It wasn't Hank. I saw him. It was a German soldier." Paul was sure of it. That boy he'd killed; he'd seen the white skin, the blue eyes.

"Christamighty," Silas groaned. "Don't you go crazy on me? Not now."

Paul leaned back. Maybe he was going crazy. Seeing a German face on a black kid. Got to be strong. Silas was looking at him.

"What we going to do, Silas?"

"That's better."

Silas stuck his head up a little to get a look. Another gunshot and ping, a bullet hitting the rock. He dropped down.

"Hank's coming after us. We got to make a run back up to the machine gun post before he gets any closer. There's good cover there."

"Sarge and the squad will have heard the gun shots," Paul said. "They'll be coming up."

"Hell, we be dead by the time they get here." Silas poked his head up. "Let's go."

Paul crouched and ran. Gasping for breath, he stumbled

over rubble and rocks as he followed Silas up the hill. He slammed his knee and elbow as he landed at Silas's feet behind a rubble wall. Silas stared at him for a minute like he didn't know him. Then he helped him sit up.

"I wish we had a gun," Silas said, when he got his breath back. "I wonder where he got the Lugar. Huh? Must a been hidden on that German soldier. How many bullets in a German gun, I wonder? Hmm. Damn, I wish we had a gun. We're just like bandits holed up in one of those westerns we seen on the boat. They had guns though. I wish we had guns."

Paul could hardly listen to Silas though. The cries of the German soldier filled his ears, "Mir helfen, mir helfen." Paul tried to block out the noise with his hands.

"What you doing?" Silas said pulling Paul's hands from his ears. He held them tight as Paul tried to pull away. "Stop it, Paul. What's wrong with you? I can't deal with you and Hank at the same time for Chrissakes"

Paul stared at Silas's face, wet and dirty, but he couldn't speak. Silas pushed back Paul's helmet and slapped him.

"Shit," Silas said, shaking his hand. "Don't make me do that again."

Silas worked his way up to look over the rocks.

"He's taking his sweet time. Look like he's having a hard time walking."

Silas crouched down next to Paul, grabbed the straps of the gas mask satchel and twisted. "Now out with it, you sonofabitch."

Paul cringed. Silas twisted harder.

"Say something, boy."

Paul coughed. Silas loosed his grip a little.

"That German boy. He's coming after me."

"What you talking about?"

"The one I killed."

"I'm gonna slap you again less you start making sense."

"That blue-eyed soldier I killed the first day of burial detail. He's after me."

"Christamighty," Silas said letting go of the straps. "Another loony."

Paul stared at Silas. "You ever kill a man?"

"No," Silas said and eased himself up again to look. "Not yet anyway."

"I killed that German boy cause when he was waving that knife at me, I saw a man from home. A white man who waved a knife in my face. Who was gonna kill me." Paul stopped. He closed his eyes against the tears. "I stuck him too."

"Shit!" Silas said then grabbed Paul's shoulders and pushed him back against the rocks. "Now you listen to me. Hank's coming to kill us. Not no German soldier. That's your imagination. It's crazy Hank we got to deal with."

Paul tried to listen to Silas. He couldn't think. The soldier's pleas rang in his ears.

"Can't you hear it? He's calling out to us in German."

Silas shook him again. "Stop it. I need you with me."

"I'll try," Paul said and closed his eyes. They snapped open when Silas punched him in the chest.

"Stop it, you loony sonofabitch."

Paul held his knees. Silas took a deep breath, wiped the sweat from his face.

"Listen, Paul. You got to get a hold on yourself."

Paul looked at Silas's head nodding up and down.

"Okay?" Silas said. "Okay?"

"Okay," Paul said. "Just my imagination."

"Good. Now, here's the plan. I'm going over there without Hank seeing me. Then I'll come up from behind him. You stick your helmet up so he keeps heading toward you. He ain't that bright. I'll take him down when I can. Got it?"

Paul stared.

"Mir helfen, mir helfen."

"Silas?"

"Got it?" Silas yelled.

Paul nodded. He eased up to look over the rocks. The soldier was still thirty paces away, one of his legs twisted. That was slowing him down. Paul crouched back down.

"Got it," he said.

Silas moved off to the left and was gone.

"Mir helfen."

"Just my imagination," Paul said and crept up again to look. With the sun behind him, the German soldier looked like he stepped off one of those war posters from home, the face hidden in shadow. The man raised his gun and pointed in Paul's direction. Paul crouched down as the gun fired, chunks of rock flying off when the bullet hit.

"That ain't no imagination."

Paul eased up again and quickly dropped down. The soldier had moved closer. The gun fired again. Where was Silas? Another dozen steps and the German would climb over the rocks and shoot. Paul grabbed some rubble, raised up a little and made ready to launch it and run when Silas jumped behind the man, a piece of the machine gun tripod in his hands. He cracked the German on the back of the neck. The gun fired. The soldier crumpled and fell.

Silas knelt next to the body. Paul scrambled over the rocks and grabbed the gun out of the soldier's hand, just in case he wasn't dead.

"Give me that gun, you loony," Silas ordered as he reached over and yanked the gun from Paul. He clicked on the safety and put it in the waistband of his trousers.

"Is he dead?" Paul asked. Silas checked the neck. It was a bloody mess. Paul looked in the direction of shouting; Sergeant Phelps and the others were hurrying up the hill.

Silas turned the body over. It was Hank's face now, but the eyes, wide open and staring straight ahead, weren't.

"Blue eyes," Paul choked out. He couldn't breathe. "Silas, don't you see?"

Silas used his fingers to close Hank's eyes. He looked back toward the approaching sergeant and then toward Paul.

"Now you listen to me," he said, his face hard. "Everything happened just like it did. Hank went crazy. He found a gun on the German soldier and shot Muncie, then came after us. I went behind him and hit him on the back of the head. I guess I hit him too hard, didn't mean to but had to stop him."

Silas leaned closer to Paul; his dark eyes narrowed.

"And here's what didn't happen. Hank didn't speak German. Shit, he never spoke German in his life. And," Silas looked at Hank's face and back to Paul. "And, there weren't no blue eyes. Right?"

Paul nodded as he stared at the German shadow now kneeling next to Hank.

"No blue eyes," he said and laughed.

The Blinds

Thomas Strømsholt

The November day retreated into sombre tranquil dusk. A chill breeze blew from the west, stirring the few leaves left in the small copse that hid a detachment of ten men under the command of Hauptmann Lipschitz. One of the men, Leopold Herbst, was brooding over the content of a letter when he was distracted by a nudge.

"Leo, got a cigarette to spare?" asked Ernst in a low voice.

"Geh zum Teufel!" Leopold retorted, smiling all the same at the banter. They were friends from the university back in Emden and had volunteered together. They were nineteen years old. Like so many other young men, Ernst and Leopold were swept up in the general jubilation that followed the outbreak of the War; they were hungry for danger and heroic glory too. The carefree life at university seemed a thing of the past now, almost unreal. So far though, it'd all been chores and endless marches, thin pea soup and long uneasy nights. They'd grown restless and were happy to have been chosen for the night's reconnaissance mission. It was rumoured that an advance for Bixshoote was drawing near, and it was reasonable to surmise that the mission was part of the preparations.

Leopold carefully folded the letter back in the envelope and placed it in his breast pocket. The letter was from Erich, his big brother who was a lieutenant attached to the Eighth Army at Galicia. Erich normally wrote long and detailed letters, but this one, written on September the 1st, was but a single sheet containing a poem:

Dead lies in my breast
every vain desire;

and dead too my hatred
of evil's empire,
and for my own and other's
grief, I care not a breath:
But one thing lives on – Death.

He'd asked Unteroffizier Cotta about the poem. Cotta, who'd been a school-teacher and was known for his love of poetry, said it was *On Departing* by Heine in one of the poet's gloomier moods. Leopold still didn't understand the reason why his brother had written him that poem, nor why he was silent about the victory at Tanneberg.

The evening star was a faint misty glimmer on a cloudy sky, and the level country beyond the copse lay quiet in darkening shades of blue. It reminded Leopold of his East Frisia except that here the crops were yet to be harvested; but then the War would soon be over, he reflected, and life would return to normal with all its petty worries and all its ennui.

The content of Erich's letter continued to oppress his thoughts, and he shifted his legs uneasily while staring into the deepening dusk. The tension was relieved, however, as Cotta began to sing a saucy ditty to the tune of *Heil dir im Siegerkranz.* They all giggled, except Lipschitz who merely uttered an amused grunt.

Leopold cast a sideway glance at Lipschitz. He looked hard as rock, his eyes like dark slits in a face of grey sleet, but he was barely twenty-five years old. In addition to earning his rank at the siege of Liège, he'd been awarded the Iron Cross after the Battle of Mons. He didn't wear this distinction though, and unlike some of the other experienced soldiers he was never heard talking of his exploits. Leopold wasn't sure what to make of the hauptmann but felt that he was a man to trust one's life with.

The clouds thickened, obscuring even Venus, and soon Lipschitz gave orders for breakup. The soldiers walked in a single file along a dirt road that winded through the fields. They were unprotected but for the deepening darkness, and for the first time since arriving at the Front, Leopold felt real fear.

The fear iced his belly and crept over his skin, but at the same time it sharpened his senses to a marvellous degree. He thought with certainty that nothing out there in the darkness could move without escaping his eyes or ears. The *genius loci* of the landscape seemed to reveal itself to him, not as a visible entity but as a breath that enveloped his very being.

They hadn't gone far from the copse before Lipschitz raised a hand and stopped dead in his tracks. Almost instantaneously, the men behind came to a halt. Leopold peered into the encroaching darkness but could detect nothing. His belly fluttered, and he clutched hard at his Mauser. As the seconds trailed off, the tension became unbearable. He half turned to look at Ernst who merely shrugged his shoulders and grinned.

All of a sudden there was a burst of lights. Leopold looked up to see a profusion of silvery star shells floating serenely across the smoky sky. The men before him cast long shadows along the ground, shadows stretching out as if in an attempt to detach themselves and flee from their fleshy forms. The magnesium flares endowed the plain with a ghastly beauty which reminded Leopold of an altar piece he'd once seen of angels descending in an aura of flames, hills made of skulls, a ground strewn with writhing naked bodies: it was the world consumed by illumination and made infinite. Awed by this vision, he was unable to move, and the rifle hung limp in his hands.

But an instant later the lights faded, and the vision was replaced by confusion and noise. Lipschitz was gesticulating wildly and shouting, though the words drowned in an inferno of white whizzes and dark rumbling. The ground shook; jets of mud and dirt were spewed high in the air leaving columns of white smoke. Leopold, hearing a scream close to his ear, slowly turned to see Ernst drop to his knees, a puzzled look on the remaining half of his face.

Then, as if by an invisible fist, Leopold was knocked off his feet, and the world went away in a thunderous turmoil of smoke and blackness.

*

"Auf wiedersehen, all you pretty Emden girls," hollered Ernst drunkenly, circling round Leopold who lay sprawled on the wet cobble, too inebriated to do anything else but laugh and gaze at the swirling stars above Emden.

He closed his eyes, and when he looked again he was in Flanders, alone in a damp field of tall grass without his rifle, field cap and knapsack. And the night sky was starless, clouded over by either clouds or gun smoke.

He'd no idea where exactly he was, or how he'd got there, he didn't even remember regaining consciousness. Every now and then a flotsam of images washed up on the banks of his stunned consciousness only to be mercifully washed away again by the black waves of Lethe. His ears still ringed with explosions, and his body felt strangely light. It was the sickening airiness one experiences from a wild carousel ride, the after-effect of great exhilaration or of great fear.

The country lay calm and cold. Leopold shivered and tightened the coat about him. Three buttons were missing, and there was a large tear in his trousers just above the left knee where a burning sensation told of a flesh wound. He supposed that he was lucky to be in one piece.

It occurred to him that if he should meet a superior officer, he would be punished for being in such a poor and unworthy state. With a momentary sense of shame he feared that his absence might even be viewed as cowardice or desertion. He'd hardly finished the thought before feeling absolutely ridiculous for worrying about such trifles.

He patted his breast pocket for a pack of cigarettes, but apart from a small envelope it was empty. He recalled how he'd lost the cigarettes in a game of cards earlier in the day, and a terrifying image of Ernst presented itself to his mind. He lurched and vomited. It was tempting to just lie down in the tall grass, curl up and wait for the oblivion of sleep to come. And yet he kept on his feet. The night encompassed him with a dank hostility. The threat was vague like the shadows in one's bedroom when one awakens from a nightmare only to realise that the horrors are still there, lurking and waiting for their prey.

The pain from the wound grew worse for each step, and although Leopold walked slowly, carefully, he often stumbled and fell. Rumblings were heard in the distance, but from which direction he couldn't tell. He feared that he was going in circles and would be lost forever in this pitch-dark nothingness. The twin emotions of desperation and dejection fought in his mind, but just as the latter seemed on the point of wining, aided by inevitable exhaustion, gravel crunched beneath his weary feet.

Somewhere in the far distance, a red mist glowed hellishly upon the black sky. It was a sign of battle, or perhaps of the aftermath of battle; either way, the red glow was a fixed point in the otherwise vast nothingness surrounding him. He'd not gone far along the gravel path, though, before realising that his legs wouldn't even carry him close to the desired point. Further up the path, however, the darkness thickened into the black silhouette of a village – friendly or not, he didn't care.

The path led to an uneven road, but as Leopold neared the first few scattered dwellings, he became conscious of something amiss. Even at this time of night the low farm houses were too quiet and too dark. The whole scenery, in fact, emanated an eerie desolation that made his heart sink. Closer to the village, the road was riddled with shell craters, and felled birch trees lay strewn on the ground like great Mikado pick-up sticks.

The village itself was a heap of ruins. Here and there towers and spires loomed against the sky, but most of the buildings were reduced to rubble. The houses that lined the main street were outer walls only, their windows gaping with black emptiness. Somewhere, a dog began to utter a series of barks and yelps that cut through the sad silence that ruled the village. The air smelled faintly acrid, but as Leopold moved through the ravine-like street, he noticed a heavy stench that he couldn't immediately identify. The stench, laced with sweetish shades, brought to his mind how one morning many years ago he'd seen a stable full of dead cows left to rot, and suddenly, sickeningly, he knew what it was...

A flicker of light drew his attention to one of the upper windows of a one-storey building. He thought he saw a woman holding a candle against the night, her face a white oval whose features were condensed into the sharp characteristics of a skull. But the next second, the light was gone as if it had never been there.

The house seemed miraculously unharmed by the destruction that had befallen the rest of the village. Located next to the shelled remains of a church, it was perhaps the parsonage. In this desert of ruins, the house appeared to Leopold to be an oasis or a mirage.

Some of the windows were shuttered, the rest were dark, and he hardly dared hope that the walls would prove to be more than a coulisse screening a void. And yet, believing he'd seen a sign of life from within that house, he climbed the pile of rubble that lay in front of the entrance. The painful exertion drained him of his last powers. He fell against the door which yielded with a loud splintering noise, and inside the house he tumbled, unconscious.

*

Leopold found Erich in the copse.

His big brother had climbed a tree almost to the top, and he waved his arms at him. What was he saying? Leopold started climbing the tree but halted midways. It wasn't Erich, as he'd thought, but a woman whose eyes seemed to have been gorged out. As Leopold, strangely entranced, looked into the woman's empty eye sockets, cold blackness starred back at him. Then he was in the field, blinded by a silvery light. He called for the hauptmann, and at once the figure of Lipschitz rose up before him, tall, dark and reassuring.

"What are my orders, Herr Hauptmann?"

But Lipschitz, looking more stern than ever, merely gestured at the ground where Ernst was kneeling, his face in profile. Slowly, ever so slowly, he turned round to face Leopold and asked for a cigarette.

Leopold cried out in horror and almost fell from the arm-chair. It was pitch-dark, and for a moment he thought he was at home in the attic room overlooking the Rathaus, but by gradations it all came back to him. He found a box of matches in his pocket, however, his hands were shaking violently, and it took three tries before he managed to light a match. Next to the chair, there was a round table with a half empty glass of water and an oil lamp. He'd almost used up all his matches before a steady flame appeared.

The first thing he noticed was that his wound had been dressed with pieces of cloth. It was clumsily done, but at least the bleeding appeared to have stopped. Next he noticed was the books. Most of the volumes lay in piles on the floor, fallen from the collapsed shelves that had blanketed most of the walls. Ugly cracks ran through the stuccoed ceiling, some turning into regular fissures that continued down the brick wall, and the floor was covered by a fine layer of white dust. The window blinds were drawn, and the door was ajar. Though the windows had withstood the shelling, the room was very cold.

Leopold supposed that he must've dragged himself into the library and somehow tended to his wound before finally passing out. He reached for the glass of water and it was only after he'd swallowed the contents in two greedy gulps that he realised that he couldn't possibly have had the strength to crawl in there, tend to the wound and pour himself a glass of water. The image of the woman in the window flashed before him and he winced at her skull-like countenance. But, recollecting himself, he assumed it must've been her who'd nursed him and provided him with water. Besides, it'd merely been the candlelight that'd made her appear so ghastly, so like a warning.

Leopold got to his feet, picked up the lamp, and limped a couple of steps towards the door before uttering a cautious "Hello?" but only silence answered him. The door led out to a corridor that communicated with a large living room, kitchen and larder, all empty and in various states of disarray. A staircase with a broken banister led to the first floor.

A hasty search of the larder failed to come up with any food; he did, however, locate a bottle of green liqueur stashed away in the back of a corner closet. While in the larder, he thought he heard the upstairs floorboards creak, but he wasn't sure. Returning to the corridor, he looked up the staircase and called out once more. Again he received no answer, but straining his ears he did hear something that sounded like a scurry of little feet. Rats, he thought with a repulsed shiver, of course the house was infested with rats.

Back in the library, he sat down and poured himself a glass of the green liqueur. He told himself that he was merely postponing a search of the rest of the house until he'd regained some of his strength, but he had to admit that he felt uneasy. It wasn't the rats. Although the mere thought of rats bothered him, he supposed he could tolerate them for a night. What made him uneasy was the presence of the woman who must surely be hiding somewhere upstairs. Why didn't she make herself known? Most likely she was afraid. After all, she lived in this house and would regard him, a stranger and a German soldier, as a threat. And yet she'd taken care of him.

Outside, a dog began to howl, and distant thunder rolled. Leopold, trembling and feeling simultaneously cold and hot, poured himself another glass and pulled out the letter, now greased and slightly soiled. He fingered the soiled envelope absentmindedly, his thoughts drifting off to his native country. He tried to remember a happier time, the days before the War, but all his memories were as nebulous and immaterial as Fata Morganas. But this night, this present was imbued with a certain unrealness too, as if he'd been transported to a place that belonged to neither waking nor dreaming, and he asked himself, *What kind of future can possibly arise from this twilight realm?*

Leopold was segueing into sleep when a loud bang reverberated through the lonely house. He jumped up from the chair and was instantly punished by a sharp stab of pain that made him cry out. With the indifference of a fatigued mind, he registered that the poorly applied bandages was soaked with blood.

He limped to the foot of the staircase and held out the lamp while he called out, saying he meant no harm, there was nothing to be afraid of, adding that he was grateful for all she'd done for him. But as before, only silence ensued. Then, haltingly, he began to climb the stairs, one step at a time.

Small picture frames, loosened from their hangings by the drumfire, lay face down on the landing. He paused to turn them over. The pictures appeared to be crude family portraits, one depicting a young woman and another showing an elderly man, but in the half-light it was difficult to make out any details, and the canvasses were torn besides.

He proceeded to mount the remaining stairs, but a creaking sound made him halt and peer into the darkness. It could have been rats or even the old house settling; or it could have been the timid movements of a frightened woman; it could have been any number of things, but for some unknown reason the sound made his hairs stand on end. He lowered the lamp, turned around slowly and descended the stairs without looking back.

The thought of the woman hiding somewhere in the dark house was becoming unbearable. He wasn't even sure anymore that she was really there at all.

He poured another drink and drowned it swiftly, enjoying the warm sensation of the liqueur flowing out in his body. But he remained restless, casting furtive glances at the door, the ceiling, and the murky crevices. He browsed the dishevelled piles of books at random. Many of the titles were concerned with theological matters, but there were also sturdy volumes of poetry and modern novels, including a *Winnetou* novel by Karl May that his mother had read to him in a time long before the War.

"Cowboys and Indians," he murmured to himself, "how ridiculous!" He went back to the table for another drink, but picked up the letter instead. There was no reason to open the envelope, for he knew the contents by heart. But only now he understood, although dimly, the meaning of poem.

"'But one thing lives on...'" he murmured. The last syllable stuck on his tongue and for a while he just stared into vacancy.

The dog had finally ceased to howl, but from the window Leopold heard the first faint quaver of birds: a new day was dawning. As he approached he thought he discerned the upstairs floorboards creak. He imagined how, like any ordinary morning, she would pull back the blinds to let in the early dawn light, dispersing the gloom. But he didn't reach for the blinds. He halted, and it seemed to him the ghostly woman upstairs had halted too. For them there could be no dawn, and the blinds of this empty house would stay drawn.

The Iron Shovel

Amberle L. Husbands

Axel woke up, but his brain got caught in the barbed-wire between 'asleep' and 'awake'. He shivered against himself, waiting for it to catch up, but it slipped backward instead, leaving him as brain-dead as the shell-shocked bastards they saw every day in the fields.

Even in his dreams, Axel Stein had been burying bodies. After ten hours of doing it whilst awake, that could only be expected. Perhaps it wasn't reasonable – war had never been reasonable or considerate in dealing with the men involved – but it was to be expected.

For one clear, bright moment, the dream took him to a well-lit world. There was sweetness in the air, and after a moment, he realised it was the forget-me-nots in his mother's garden.

He could see the black, tilled earth, the low fence of brightly painted pickets, the single larch tree at the corner. Behind the fence, he saw her; her hair tucked up beneath the old sun hat, her face beaming up at him as he bent to touch the earth with her ... but that was only a moment out of a night full of restless dreams.

Too soon, he was back to the fields.

Come back in one piece, she'd said: her only words on the matter of his leaving.

He didn't know how many they'd buried, that last day. Burial was a terrible job. Most men were only too glad not to keep a count in mind as they went. Axel did as the others; collecting IDs and whatever personal effects were easy to spot. A watch, a wedding ring, a pay book. They all went into little bags; each tied up and marked with one ID disk while its twin remained on the body.

The smells were by far the worst part of the job.

Eventually, his fingers had grown callous to the clay-like softness of cold flesh. His eyes had grown used to the sight of mud where organs should have been, and blood where flowers should have bloomed.

But he never could get used to the reek of it.

The smell clung like a ghost around him, lingering in his hair and clothes and in the dirty creases of his hands. It got into his mouth when he tried to eat. It got between the sheets with him, when he should have been alone with the phantasy of Evelyn Nesbit.

When he closed his eyes to conjure up her face, it was as if he was sharing her with all of *them*, the hundreds of men cold in their graves. And what was worse than *that*, even, was when he realised that they all had *different* smells, and that he could distinguish between them.

German bodies rotted faster, probably because of the leather.

The French smelled sweeter, a little bit like the native soil they were going down into.

I've become a connoisseur of the dead, Axel thought, and groaned to shake off the nightmare born of that image.

Lastly, they'd been told to remove the boots. Those weren't given any identification, as though it would be easier for living soldiers to accept dead men's shoes if they were anonymously donated.

And then, finally, the bodies were buried.

Axel had put each little bag with all the others, and carried each body over to the holes. Digging the pits was the coveted job on grave duty, aching backs, frozen feet and all. Axel carried each body to the edge of the hole, jealous of the men who only wielded shovels. Each pit was supposed to hold thirty bodies.

But it was someone else's job to keep count.

He dropped in corpse after shattered corpse.

Good God, he felt sick.

The first hour had been enough to insure that, but then, at the end of ten hours, when the shell exploded…

Axel Stein's eyes shot open, sleep shredding apart like a rotten piece of skin.

He remembered the shell exploding in detail that seemed unfairly vivid; too vivid to be a nightmare. It had been buried loosely in the mud, where they had already begun to dig the third pit. Someone's shovel must have struck it just right.

He remembered the flash first, then feeling the cold bundle of corpse he was carrying torn from his arms. Cold, rushing air came next, stinging his face, and then the taste of mud and blood.

But he didn't remember ever hearing the sound.

He'd seen the earth convulse, and the two already filled-in pits had exploded outward again, spewing up all the bare-foot soldiers they'd held. But he couldn't remember the *noise*, the sound of it, because ... because...

"*Mein Gott*," he whispered, and pulled aside the unbuttoned front of his coat to reveal the livid, puckered line of stitches marching across his stomach where...

Where things were put back in, he realised.

He didn't remember the noise of the explosion because it had come after his death.

"*Mein Gott...*"

With two shaking fingers, he touched the red flesh and angry black-thread stitches. The flesh was fever hot, and pain shot universally through his body at the contact.

Still, the memory would not be rebuked.

"I died," he whispered; everything he knew about how the world worked confirmed it. "I did die."

Axel looked around, at the stone-walled, dirt-floored and windowless room around him, with no way to explain it to himself.

There was a ladder and a trap-door above him ... so he was in a cellar. And since his last days had been spent with his unit near Lille, it was reasonable to assume he was in a cellar somewhere in northern France.

But reason might have very little to do with it, he told himself.

On a whim, he raised his fingers to his face and breathed in;

he could smell nothing. For the first time in months he smelled clean.

But not alive, he realised, his stomach turning cold.

A sudden noise overhead – like a chair scuffling over the wooden floor – drew his attention, and he could have laughed when his hands flew immediately to take stock of his weapons.

What do the dead need with rifles, he thought, but still cursed to find his was missing. So was his personal revolver. All he could find was the trench knife strapped securely, still, alongside his right ankle, inside the boot. He held it close to his chest and tentatively, through explosions of pain, raised himself into a crouch. His eyes were already well-adjusted to the cellar-darkness.

The wooden scuffling above him gave way to a softer shuffling. Then, he heard humming.

It was a woman's voice, and not an especially melodious one. But he knew the song. It was *Sous Les Ponts De Paris*. He seemed to hear the sickening and infectious tune everywhere he turned, lately.

So, he *was* still in France, at least. Probably.

The humming stopped. He heard something porcelain being set on a counter top, and then water was poured. As Axel listened the humming started over again, taking up the song's beginning.

With the knife clenched securely in his right hand, he moved across the dirt floor to the ladder. The pain originating deep inside his abdomen and chest dulled surprisingly quickly, but refused to fade away altogether. It lingered as a mildly burning, leaden lump against his guts.

He took hold and put one foot on the ladder, shifting his weight slowly and waiting with bated breath for a betraying creak from the old wood. But none came. One rung after another, he climbed until he was stooped against the ceiling, ready any minute to fling up the trap door and confront his captor.

Or course, he thought, there could be chains and a padlock, or heavy furniture, or any number of other surprises on the other side of that door. There could be a roomful of enemy

British or French infantry. There could be peasant shotguns. One woman humming badly didn't prove anything.

Still, Axel couldn't see what other choice he had. He squared his shoulders an inch below the door and gathered his legs beneath him, waiting until he heard the humming grow distant, until the slipper-shuffles sounded like they were across the room. Then, he sprang up the last few steps, knife ready before him; the heavy door giving way and falling backward with a thud.

A woman shrieked and he heard the heavy *gong* as something cast iron clattered to the floor. Axel spun around, stepping quickly off the ladder. He made sure the sunlight caught his knife's blade, waiting until the metallic ringing faded and he was sure he had the woman's attention.

She remained exactly where she'd stood when he surprised her, with a cupboard's shelf pressed into the small of her back, her hands clasping its edge rigidly, her eyes wide with shock. Axel waited, but her shriek hadn't brought anyone running from another room.

The woman wasn't bad-looking, was his first thought. But she was no Evelyn Nesbit, either. Her features had the same quality as her singing had; they were pleasant enough without being in the least appealing. Then, Axel saw the steel-gray strands mixed in her dark curls, and the lines around her sapphire eyes. She must have been a good thirty years older than what he'd originally believed.

So that was it, he thought. She *had* been good-looking, and now was only not-bad-looking.

Her eyes lost their initial fear quickly, though her cheeks remained flushed. He thought she was probably always quick to become frightened. With the war on, that wasn't necessarily a bad thing.

She bent slowly to pick up the enamelled iron bowl she'd dropped. "Good Lord, you don't know how you startled me," she mumbled in French.

"Are you alone here?" Axel asked. He repeated the words in his scattered, halting French, jabbing the air with the point of his knife for emphasis.

"Except for you, yes." The woman scowled at the blade in his hand, looking more annoyed than frightened, now. "You put that away."

Axel feinted again, instead, watching her jump slightly. "Who are you? Are you alone here?"

"See for yourself," she said, shrugging, and gestured with one hand.

Tentatively, Axel let his eyes dart from her in quick, careful forays. Aside from the central room they were in – holding the cupboard and a table and hearth, a churn and two chairs, nothing else – there was only a narrow bedroom with open door to one side, and windows out onto a small, bleak yard on the other. On the table between them was one dead rabbit, winter-thin and sad-looking. Holding the knife before him still, he backed up and quickly checked out the bedroom. It was even emptier than the kitchen.

The best place in the little cabin to hide would have been the cellar, and he knew already that it was empty.

Empty except for us ghosts, he thought, but the lingering pain in his chest refuted that. He was no ghost, yet.

"Who are you?" he asked the woman again, more calmly now and in slightly clearer French. She continued watching him with narrowed eyes.

"Put your knife away before we talk, young man."

"Answer what I ask, and I may put my knife away."

Shaking her head, the woman almost smiled before answering. "Ungrateful ... I am Collette Tillart. I am the person who unburied your stinking corpse, carted it here, and returned you to it. Now, put your knife away. Then we talk."

Axel felt each word like a new punch in his already aching gut. Even though she'd done little more than to confirm his own nightmarish suspicions, the reality of it coming from another person was almost more of a strain than his mind could bear.

It was all he could do to keep from dropping his trench knife, but he somehow kept a hold of it, and kept it pointed at her breast bone.

Collette shrugged again, throwing her dark hair over one

shoulder.

"Good. Suit yourself. Keep your knife, but you must not keep me from work, if either of us is to eat tonight."

She took the bowl and a knife from the cupboard behind her. At the sight of the blade, Axel jumped into a ready stance, but she didn't so much as blink. He watched her sit at the table, take up the rabbit, and begin skilfully to slice the fur and skin from its long body.

"I suppose it would be asking too much, to request you introduce yourself, as well."

Axel did not move, but licked his lips and took his first deep breath since leaving the cellar. Pain shot into his lungs as a dark reminder.

"I am *soldat* Axel Stein. I am ... I was."

She raised her eyes, a little softness there now.

"My corpse, you said ... you unburied my corpse ... you said that you..."

"Right. Your poor, muddy body..." She shook her head. "So young, I could not stand it. And strong, too, it showed, and I needed the help, and so, I brought it home. And returned you to it."

"You ... you did what?"

"Oh, I got everything out of the mud, and washed and poked and sewed. Everything important, anyway. And of course..."

"You brought me back to life?" Axel asked, putting words together carefully, sidestepping any ambiguity of translation.

Her words and pantomimes had already brought too many sickening images to mind – his comrades, fallen in the dark mud, their faces obliterated, their bodies shattered, organs exposed and strewn about, or their eyes flashing sickly pale as they choked on last breaths.

Or the watery, *unflashing* eyes of the long-dead, who rolled so loosely and sprawled in his arms on the way to their graves ... he could feel rage rising inside him, along with bile.

"But of course, yes, that is what I've been saying." She set the rabbit and knife aside and spoke directly to him, as she might have spoken to a small, slow child. "I took you and your pieces from the mud. Tied everything back together. Then, I brought *you* back to it. You understand?"

Axel did understand, but still he shook his head, not wanting to believe.

He had begun to shake, and the images of the battlefield, of thirty man graves, still haunted his mind's eye.

"Why?" he finally asked. "There were … I mean, there were so many of us there, that there must have been more ... there were *so many* dead, there. Why only me? Why did you do this to me?"

Collette frowned at him a little, as if in amusement.

"That's the way we've always done it," she said. "I need help but, I couldn't feed a whole army, could I? And you, you were strong, not too badly torn ... and fresh. What more is there to say? So many of the others were…"

Axel had moved before he knew he meant to, with a cloud of black rage blinding him; the woman barely had time to look surprised before his knife was buried in her throat.

He could feel its point nicking bone as her blood, hot and thick, blossomed out to cover his fist.

Collette's hand moved only after it was over, going in an almost gentle, perfunctory movement to her own kitchen knife. Axel watched her fingers settle over its handle softly, a moment after the light of life had left her eyes.

*

Afterward, when both the woman's body and his own mind had cooled, he regretted it.

Axel carried her awkwardly down the ladder, wondering how such a small woman had managed to get *his* inert body down there.

"Probably dropped me in like a sack of potatoes," he mumbled, almost using French but reverting to German when he remembered that it didn't matter anymore.

Outside, near a roped-off yard that he assumed had until recently held a cow or two, he found a shovel.

Not far from that, he found a stand of holly, its red berries gleaming in the fading light of day. The days were growing impossibly short, now, he noted.

He left a bound bouquet of holly on the mound that remained, after he had buried Collette Tillart in the cabin's cellar.

What's one more grave in a land made of graves, he wondered. At least Collette's body had been intact, and even mostly clean, when he carried her to her hole. Those were luxurious details of death he was unused to.

Now seated at the kitchen table, Axel's fingers went back to the warm, puckered flesh of his stomach. Whatever she had done to him, he was no cannibal, flesh-hungry ghoul, the like of which had filled his childhood folklore and haunted his early nightmares. No, he was a true living being, again ... at least, he thought he was.

Just to be sure, he pricked the skin of one index finger with the same knife he'd used earlier in rage.

A dark, glossy bead of blood rose there when summoned, and slid lazily down his dusty finger.

Well, he thought, standing up, *if I'm a living human being, then I should be with my fellow men ... my brothers among the living.*

"We living have to stick together," he said aloud, and grinned foolishly at the thought. Of late, he had seen far too much fraternization between the living and the dead to really believe that.

He searched the cabin for his guns, but they must have been among the 'unimportant' parts Collette had left in the mud. He found cigarettes, though, and two mummified apples.

With a sigh he shifted his trench knife to his belt, where it would be easier to access, took the cigarettes, ate both apples, and set off, pulling the cabin door firmly closed behind him.

The road out front had looked vaguely familiar, earlier in the day light. Axel believed if he walked west and slightly north long enough, and was cautious enough, he could be back with whatever remained of his comrades within three days.

But it was a moonless, frigid December night.

The first thicket of brambles he stumbled into put an end to his night-walking. Pulling his filthy coat around him, the soldier huddled down beneath the next thick shrub he came across, to wait out the dawn.

*

He slept in brief snatches, each filled with a different image of death.

Axel didn't know if these scenes were images from the afterlife he had been severed from, or merely the product of a brain that had been supersaturated by blood and gore.

In one scene, he waited in a yellow-walled kitchen with other mutilated, dead soldiers, while one after another they walked up to a steaming pot with bowls in hand.

But each one, after peering into that cauldron, shook their heads and retreated, starving rather than eat what they saw there.

When his turn came, Axel took up the great ladle, stirred the pot, peered in, and awoke choking on a scream.

Wish as he might, the dream of home, of his mother and her quiet, bright garden, would not repeat itself. He recalled the images to his waking mind, in the darkness after each nightmare, and squeezed the juice from them until he cried.

*

The rotting began the next day.

"Just trench-foot," Axel told himself, wriggling his numb, necrotic toes. But it wasn't only there; he'd found patches of mould growing beneath his fingernails.

When he'd cleaned it away with the tip of his knife, pieces of skin came away, too.

"Ring-worm," he muttered, lighting the day's first cigarette.

One day, Axel thought, trying to still his mind, *I must come back here in the spring*.

The sun was slow to rise, and the low clouds had turned grey and pink long before any real light touched the land. The German soldier sat cross-legged, slumped beneath his shrub, and smoked as it came slowly along. He allowed himself and the world to be quiet and at peace until the end of that cigarette. Then, he climbed achingly to his feet and began walking away from the rising sun.

He went carefully, trying his best to remain vigilant, scanning the terrain and horizon around him constantly. But it wasn't easy. Every muscle in his body screamed in pain at

being forced into motion – *Death'll do that to you,* he thought
grimly – he was hungry, and one more insomniac night
listening to the dogs of war howl hadn't helped. The
nightmares left him aching.

And it was even worse than ever, he thought. Now, the
dreams were even more vivid. He'd gained an even more
intimate knowledge of the material at hand, since awaking in
the cellar.

The sound of distant guns occasionally broke the early
morning peace, reminding him of the living world at hand.
Axel wasn't terribly surprised to creep over the crest of one hill
and find himself almost on top of a stack of bodies. It seemed
like the next logical step in this waking-dreaming, living-dead,
hell-world he moved through. He descended, looked them over
once, and went to work with a sigh.

There was no-one living in sight.

Axel analysed the scene quickly, identifying bodies both by
uniform and by smell.

The men, four Brits, two Germans, and a Frenchman, had
been dead for probably only two days; no more than three.
They had been collected and stacked neatly together and their
single pit-grave had been half-way dug. But the work had been
abandoned at that point.

He didn't have the energy to really wonder why.

Axel explored the two Germans first, seeking and finding
their ID disks still in place. He took one from each. It was
already noon, but they were still cold; all seven of them already
had the soft, doughy feel of a few days in the mud. Touching
the Frenchman, Axel's hand slid into a gaping hole he hadn't
seen in the man's chest. He would have retched, but there was
nothing left inside him.

The sudden image of France in the spring, when all these
graves began to grow things and the dirt sagged in above its
rotting harvest, came suddenly to his mind. Except there were
no daisies or tulips or even grass – he foresaw only bones and
grave mold sprouting.

Cursing, nearly crying, Axel pulled his hand from the dead
soldier's chest and wiped it on the man's pants leg. He groped

blindly for some form of ID and then left the rest; he didn't have the heart to go through any more pockets.

The half-dug hole wasn't long enough, but someone – perhaps one of the dead men himself – had thoughtfully left a shovel at the bottom.

"Is this it then?" Axel raged at the sky as he worked, chopping big, wet shovelfuls of black mud from the earth. "Is this why You left me here!? To go around on grave duty forever? To go around digging holes in a world already damned full of them!?"

He was heaving air in and out of his chest between thrusts into the earth, and the stitches in his gut twisted like an angry, biting mouth with every move he made.

One final stab at the dark muck and his feet skidded out from under him. All the air hammered out of his lungs as he landed hard on his back. Not a bird sang anywhere. Not a breath of wind bothered to stir even a hair of the landscape, up above him. The low brown clouds looked like the palm of an angry god's hand, bending to smother the world.

It all might as well be dead, he thought, lying breathless at the bottom of the grave. *All the world, in a single pit.*

It was growing dark again, by the time he had the hole filled in and sat down irreverently on the mound to rest. He was down to two cigarettes and recklessly used one of them now.

Putting the other away gently, he felt something shift inside his own shirt; his own upon-death identification. He almost added his to the growing collection in his coat pocket, but then came to his senses.

"I'll report you seven to the counting men, when I get to them," he whispered to the earth.

Then what, it seemed to whisper back. *Report fresh for grave duty, again?*

The earth and clay were laughing at him.

*

By the third evening, Axel Stein was mentally and emotionally dead; from time to time, he pulled out his trench knife and cut a tiny line into one of his forearms, to see whether or not he still bled.

He did ... but it seemed awfully slow.

At least the cutting kept his mind off the cigarette he was saving, he told himself. But really it didn't. And it didn't keep his mind off the steady blackening of his fingers, or the four disconnected toes he'd found hung up in the wet fibres of his socks, or the six teeth he'd lost since dawn that day.

Nothing succeeded in taking his mind off those things.

Steadily, his world had become one pounding, driving imperative; he had to make it back in one piece, more or less. He just had to get there, and then the doctors...

But whether he could make it home in one piece or not, as *she'd* asked him to ... he was beginning to taste doubt in the bloody wells of his missing teeth.

He had seen landmarks, so at least he knew he was moving in the right direction. Still, he couldn't help thinking that it would be so much easier to just lie down in a hole and wait for fate – the enemy, or a blind bombshell, or just a flash-flood rainstorm – to carry him back to where he now belonged.

He was passing so many bodies, that it was ridiculous to even think of stopping to bury them all; their number was one of the landmarks that let him know he was getting closer to the fighting. But he still carried the shovel he'd dragged along since the first day, when he'd dug the seven-body-pit. It was equal parts weapon, standard, and trophy now. He did stop to collect identification, though. His collection was growing impressive.

I wonder if they give out medals for that? Record Number of Deaths Recorded. In recognition of superior hole-digging. Above and beyond the call of duty. The Iron Shovel.

Night came on, still with no living men in sight. Axel began to seriously wonder whether there *were* any more living men. Perhaps something bigger than a single unexploded shell had happened. Perhaps he'd somehow slept through the end of the world, and had woken up on the other side.

Maybe he really *had* been brought back, just to be the clean-up crew.

A high, bone-white moon peeked occasionally from between the rolling clouds, and he kept walking by its light. Another body lay in the mud ahead of him; one hand clutching at what was now unrecognizable as a face and head, and one thrown out to the side, grabbing at the air desperately.

Axel dropped to his knees beside the mess, immune now to any gruesomeness.

No, he thought. *Not really immune. Just too smart now to let myself look too deep.*

This particular boy, he noticed instead, had been fairly torn to shreds by bullets and later by crows. There was hardly a uniform left, even. Perhaps a stray dog or two had come through this way, too, Axel thought.

He felt a terrible, throbbing ache all through his body, where his flesh longed to be dead. It had taken the place of revulsion. He fumbled in the dark, fingers blindly refusing to recognise anything they touched that wasn't an identification tag. Then, they searched again. Then, his mind rebelling, Axel forced himself to really look at the body for the first time. The bile in the back of his throat made his head spin.

For a horrible second, it was his own face staring back. But then, the hallucination faded, and only the pitiful boy lay before him.

He searched once more.

Still nothing.

There wasn't even the remaining single ID to show that this one's death was already catalogued. Simply nothing. No letter yet to be mailed home. No pay book. No pictures of girlfriends. Nothing at all.

Axel went on searching, growing inexplicably frantic. There had to be a name, he thought illogically. There *had* to be *something!*

Nothing.

In fury as helpless tears began to spill down his cheeks, his fists began beating at the torn body, catching in the shredded clothing and leaving ugly depressions in the dead man's clay-like skin. He felt the rotten bones of his knuckles crack and splinter.

"You have to have a name!"

He beat at the poor, obliterated head even, cursing its faceless grin. "Damn you, you bastard, you must! *You must!*

Who are you!? Who *are* you!?"

Only silence answered him.

Once more, Axel slammed a fist into the mess – and withdrew it missing three fingers.

The dead man, nearly lying across Axel's lap, now, went on grinning with his non-head and single row of shattered teeth.

Before he could stop himself, Axel pulled out his last cigarette and lit it with shaking hands.

He closed his eyes as the tears continued to leak down his face and pulled smoke deep into his lungs.

The world went slowly quiet, again, around him.

No, he realised, not completely quiet.

There was a human voice carried on the breeze. He could only catch scattered words, and those were in English, but it was undeniably a living, breathing, human voice.

He must have been closer to the trenches than he'd thought.

But the words ... even from the snatches he caught, Axel could tell the voice was raised, no matter how mournfully, in song.

"Silent night ... holy night ... all is bright..."

The words drifted to him broken and sad, but as he listened other voices joined in, and the song hung completed in the air. It was surreal, and Axel could do nothing but freeze beneath it and listen, the cigarette glowing, forgotten between his lips.

And all too soon, the song ended.

It was only a short one. He felt like crying again; it was short, and so achingly sweet.

"O du frohliche, o du selige, gnadenbringnde..."

Axel nearly dropped his cigarette. The new voices were closer, German, and lifting up a song he knew. It was as poignant and familiar to him as the scents of his mother's garden had been.

"It's Christmas," he breathed, looking around in the dark for any sign of where the others might be. But he could see nothing. There were only the songs, wafting on a sporadic breeze, and the smell of his own tobacco.

"Christmas Eve."

Soon, another English carol answered the German one. Axel

was ready to laugh at the absurdity of it. He slapped the nameless body in the mud beside him familiarly. "It's Christmas Eve, friend! Smile!"

Then, he realised what he was about to do.

Axel let one hand – the whole one – dig and sift through the dark mud around him. He could almost feel things waiting for their chance in the sun; lilacs and forget-me-nots. And yes, grave mould too.

It was too much to ask, Mama. There is no returning from a land of holes without a few to show for yourself.

The cigarette burned his lips and he threw it into the mud. Without giving himself time to think, he took out his entire collection of individual ID tags and placed them in the dead man's rigid fist. The cold fingers curled tightly back in around them.

"Merry Christmas, my friend," he whispered, and placed his own identification tags – both of them – into the dead man's torn shirt pocket.

Now unafraid to be seen, he stood up and turned around, walking away from the singing, back over the corpse-strewn field, with his shovel thrown over one shoulder.

Where the Long White Roadway Lies

Mike Chinn

The road was quiet – even for close on midnight. No weary squads being marched either away from or back to the Front; no shiny new replacements, eyes ablaze with misplaced eagerness, singing their way to the mud and death that awaited most of them. No trucks; no ambulances; no munitions trains. He didn't expect birdsong: but the odd owl hoot; a few desperate frogs screeching from filthy puddles; crickets?

It was as silent as it was cold. Even his boots sounded muffled: as though they were swaddled in his faded puttees.

There wasn't a cloud to be seen, either. The moon hung full in a black sky, giving both the road and the pocked devastation which radiated to every horizon a silvery glow.

It lit his way brighter than a searchlight.

He began to whistle, a tuneless warble which at first just kept pace with his footsteps – anything was better than the gaunt silence. After a while it turned into a recognisable tune: a slow, gentle melody. A waltz, almost. He began singing along, his mind barely focussing on the words.

"Roses are shining in Picardy, in the hush of the silver dew,

"Roses are flowering in Picardy, but there's never a rose like you…"

He had a good voice: once a boy treble in the church choir, then an alto when his voice broke. Even out here, in this godless wilderness, a subaltern had picked him to lead the lads during church parade.

But where was that subaltern now, eh? Hanging on the old barbed wire, like as not – along with everyone else…

He shrugged his rifle strap back into position – the dam' thing kept slipping. His old drill sergeant would have had plenty to say if he let the Lee Enfield drop – not that it could get much shabbier. The years had left the gun as muddy and scarred as No Man's Land; it was a wonder it could fire at all.

"And she sees the road by the poplars,
"Where they met in the bygone years,
"For the first little song of the roses
"Is the last little song she hears…"

He imagined he saw those poplars, too: standing tall and narrow: pale against the sky, picked out by moonlight. A smile warmed his face, cracking the dried mud which still clung to his unshaven whiskers, and he enjoyed the lie for as long as he could.

But all too soon the illusion faded: not slender poplars, but the shattered stumps of trees, clawing like the ghosts they were at the black sky. Stripped and brought low by artillery fire. It was a miracle that even these remnants stood, defying men and their shells.

He could just make out the corpse of a building to his left: its roof long gone, walls crumbling. Naked windows stared like a skull's sockets.

Something hung from one of the trees: shreds of cloth, a tangle of wooden spars; speared through by jagged stakes of trunk, pinned by toothpicks of fragmented branch.

A downed aeroplane – its remains barely enough to make a child's kite. As he approached, he could just make out part of a black cross on a strip of pale linen. Not one of ours, then, he thought. Of the crew there was no sign; in fact what was crucified on this particular Calvary was little more than part of a wing – as far as he could tell. You never got much of a close-up look at the aeroplanes when you were head down in a trench. The rest of it would be spread across the ground somewhere else, or cleared away by one side or the other.

He shrugged his Lee Enfield back in place again and continued on his way. His blokes were out here somewhere, and if he couldn't find them it would be jankers – or worse. The moon seemed to be lower in the sky – dipping slowly towards the horizon before him. It looked bigger, too.

The cluster of splintered trees passed him by, along with the shell of a building – but a colourless wall grew up parallel to the road, on his left. From the ground it stepped up – stone by shattered stone – until it reached the height of his shoulders.

What looked like limestone wash had been splashed carelessly over it – chipped and fallen away in parts – and it was peppered with the scars of bullets or shrapnel. A dark shape was piled against the base, no more than fifty yards from where the wall started.

He paused, not sure how to proceed; eventually curiosity overcame his caution. He hurried towards the shape – which swiftly resolved into a figure: sitting against the wall, bent forward in a position he knew only too well. An injured man – most likely in the gut or chest – curled up against the gnawing pain. He knelt by the figure's feet, slipping off his rifle and lying it down carelessly on a crust of dried mud. He bent forward himself, trying to see into the figure's slumped features.

"You all right, chum?" his voice sounded distant – yet shockingly loud against the quiet. It drifted out across the landscape and died there, shorn of any echo or resonance.

The figure stirred; the head raised a little. It muttered softly in a guttural tongue, the alien words absorbed into the battered wall.

"Boche, eh?" he straightened a little, fingers inching towards his bayonet scabbard. From the downed aircraft, he imagined. Taking a better look it was obvious the Hun's clothing was of a higher peg than his own khaki rags: a thick leather coat with fur collar, fancy britches, and tall boots that gleamed in the moonlight.

The flier slumped again, as though those few incomprehensible words had exhausted him. He began to shiver.

"Well, you might be a filthy 'un – but I'm guessin' you're still a Christian," his hand drew back from his bayonet, unslinging a canteen instead. It felt heavy and sloshed encouragingly. He unscrewed the deep cap and poured in a little water. "Here," he held it under the bowed head.

The Hun stirred again, head raised gradually once more.

Eyes that were colourless in the silver light flickered from the cup, up to his benefactor's face and down again – torn between thirst and suspicion.

"Nah – don't be like that!" He took back the cup, raised it to his own dry lips and drained it: the water was surprisingly cool and fresh. Like the first pint after a long day's grind. He poured himself another, drinking it gratefully. "Don't know what you're missing, Fritzy…"

He filled the cup a third time and pressed it close to the Hun's mouth. This time, after the briefest of hesitations, the flier drank: noisy and careless. More than half spilled, but what little the Boche took seemed to revive him. Lifting his head, he rested it against the battered wall, eyes closing. *"Danke…"* It was little more than a sigh.

"Danke? That means thank you, don't it? Well, think nothing of it, me old comrade."

He went to pour more water into the cup, but changed his mind and drank straight from the canteen. "Thy need is greater than mine, as the Good Book 'as it." He screwed the cap back on and placed the canteen next to his rifle. He took the opportunity to take a proper look at the Hun's wounds, now the man was sitting a little straighter. The shiny leather coat glistened more than it should, right about where the flier's stomach would be. "Reckon you got a Blighty one there, mate. Or whatever you lot call it."

The flier groaned several more meaningless words: they spat like a machine gun through chattering teeth…

"Sorry, old son – don't speak a word of Boche." He opened one of his pouches and drew out a pad of gauze and lint. "Here we are … let's see if we can't patch you up like one of yer planes, eh? My lads are out 'ere: once we all join up proper, they can take care o'yer…"

He went to unbutton the leather coat – but a feebly-swung hand and what was likely a stream of cuss words stayed him. He held up the wadded bandage before the Hun's pain-etched face.

"I'm tryin' to help – understandee? Make you feel a bit more comfortable. I've seen enough blokes 'ad their insides blown out ... bleedin' to death ain't the worst that can 'appen, but if we can stop it..." he gestured towards the blood-slicked coat with one hand, raising the bandage again with the other. "Yes...?"

After a moment, the flier's eyes flickered, and he nodded slowly.

"Good man." Gently, he unbuttoned the coat, peeling it back from the soaked tunic underneath. He began to sing again, timing his movements with the words:

"Kaiser Bill is feeling ill,
"The Crown Prince, he's gone barmy.
"We don't give a cluck for old von Fluck
"And all his bleedin' army."

The tunic and whatever was underneath – shirt or vest – was sliced cleanly open as if a great blade had sheared through, exposing the flesh below. There was a hole the size of his fist which showed far too much muscle, bone and sinew.

"Well now, that ain't so bad. I've 'ad splinters worse than that." Carefully he pressed the wadded material against the wound. "And if you could just hold that for me, cocky...," he took the Hun's right hand and placed it over the crude dressing. "...Ta."

Sitting back on his heels he wiped his fingers on his own battle-dress; a drop more blood wouldn't change matters. "Now what you need, Fritz me boy, is someone what's a dab 'and with a needle and thread. And ain't this your lucky day! Just so 'appens I cut me teeth darnin' up the soppy animals what caught themselves on the wire down on my Uncle Fred's farm."

Which was close to the truth – except the poor sods laid open by barbed wire hadn't been animals, and the land in question had never been worked by anyone with a name like Fred...

He produced another wad from his pouch: this time a large darning needle and length of twine packed in crusted cotton wool. He held the needle up, and made sewing motions so the Hun would understand what was going to happen – and be ready.

"This ain't going to be Florence Nightingale standards, Fritz
– but needs must."

Carefully, he moved the other's hand away and peeled back
the dressing. "We could do with a bottle – for both the pain and
the germs – but we ain't got one … so…"

He set to work, unconsciously singing again, under his
breath, to distance himself from the work before him.

"The bells of hell go ting-a-ling-a-ling,
"For you but not for me,
"And the little devils how they sing-a-ling-a-ling,
"For you but not for me."

The Hun, for his part, remained heroically still and quiet –
even the shivering quietened – just hissing as the needle first
slid in.

"Oh death, where is thy sting-a-ling-a-ling,
"Oh grave, thy victory?
"The bells of hell go ting-a-ling-a-ling
"For you but not for me…"

Eventually it was done. It wasn't a neat job: bunched and
puckered; the Boche flier was going to have an ugly scar to
show the girls. But most of the bleeding had stopped. He took
the Hun's hand again, once more pressing the bloody dressing
against the stitched wound.

"Just keep that held in place, Fritzy, and you'll be right as
nine-pence. They'll be along soon – when it's morning, like as
not – and they can cart yer off to hospital. Have all them pretty
nurses fussin' over yer. Some of 'em are French, I 'ear…" He
rummaged around in his pockets for his cigarettes tin. "You'll
like that. *Don't you know that over here, lad, they like it best like
this…!* Here we are…"

He snapped the tin open and removed two roll-ups, lighting
both. He offered one to the Hun – placing it between the pale
lips when it was obvious the other couldn't take it. The flier
muttered something: it might have been a form of agreement;
perhaps he understood a bit of English, after all.

"We'll just smoke our fags, like gentlemen, and then see
how the land lies, eh?"

He settled himself on the Hun's left side, back comfortably

against the splintered wall. He glanced at the moon again: it was within ten degrees of the horizon, pale and huge.

He thought he could make out every feature on its cratered face. "Looks like they're 'avin' a bit of a war up there too, Fritzy: see all them shell 'oles? Blimey – something bigger than a six-pounder, wouldn't you say?" He'd been walking in the chilly hush for so long that now he had an audience, he felt he had to keep talking: to hold the silence back, fill it with his voice.

"Wouldn't volunteer for that one, though – not for a thousand pound. No more than you'd get me up in one of your aeroplanes. Ain't natural," he chuckled. "If God had meant us to fly, 'E'd 'ave shoved a whizz-bang up our arses..."

The Boche laughed too: a quiet, wheezy sound – though it wasn't obvious what he was laughing at. Some private joke? An automatic response to his rescuer's amusement?

"You know any songs, Fritz? Other than all them boozin' songs... You lot are fair stuck on yer boozin' songs..." He glanced at the Hun, who seemed to be half-asleep, head resting against the wall; a network of fine cracks radiated out from under it. The cigarette hung off his bottom lip, twitching in time to each shiver. "Here's one for yer:

"There's a long, long trail a winding,
"Into the land of my dreams.
"Where the nightingales are singing,
"And a white moon beams.
"There's a long, long night of waiting ,
"Until all my dreams come true.
"Till the day when I'll be going down,
"That long, long trail with you."

He flicked his cigarette butt away, suddenly feeling low. "There's a white moon beamin', all right, Fritz – for all the good it does either of us. The Zeppelins liked it, though, when they bombed London. Bastards!" He smiled again. "No offense, Fritz..."

The Boche flier grunted, and his head tipped bonelessly to one side. The cigarette dropped from his mouth, bounced off a coat sleeve, and lay on the dried mud.

"Fritz?" he got back onto his knees, looking intently at the Boche's features. The muscles were slack, lips drooping; the shivering had stopped. "Fritzy?" he leaned in close, putting his cheek up against the still lips.

He felt no breath.

His left hand, resting on the ground to steady himself, was suddenly overwhelmed by warm ooze that flowed between his fingers. Swearing up a storm, he pulled back, jerking the hand away. Glancing down to see what he'd leant in, he saw the black puddle, spreading by degrees from under the tails of the Hun's leather coat. Blood. Pints of it. The poor sod must have been ripped up inside – bleeding away even as the outer wound had been stitched up.

"Sorry, Fritzy. Did me best," he sighed, taking the sticky dressing out of limp fingers and tried to clean up his own dripping hand. "Just wasn't meant to be…"

He wasted some of his precious water cleaning up his hands: just wiping at the drying blood didn't work. He felt dirty – infected, somehow.

Like it would never come off.

Then what to do with the body … he could simply leave it as it was – but that didn't feel right. Sacrilegious, somehow. In the end he laid the dead Hun out: straightening the body as best he could, folding the hands across the fine leather coat. To be honest, he was tempted – for a moment – to have the coat for himself; Fritzy wouldn't be needing it any longer, and his own uniform wasn't keeping him all that warm. Ultimately, he left it. He told himself that swagged up in the black leather he might get mistaken for a Hun himself, and shot on sight. Some of the lads didn't have his Samaritan temperament.

In truth, he would have felt like a grave-robber…

He draped himself with the canteen and Lee Enfield once more, stood a moment over the corpse, head bowed – though no prayers came to mind – then set off again towards the setting moon. The lads would come past, by and by; they could give Fritzy a decent burial. In the morning, like.

The moon was on the horizon now; a tiny sliver had already been shaved off its base. The satellite was a vast, silver face –

bright as the sun, he thought – gazing straight at him across the destroyed landscape; gaping in dismay.

The silence descended again, broken only by the deadened thump of his boots on the road. No birdsong struck up to greet the dawn he was certain must only be an hour or two away; no guns, no screams. The world had died – that Boche had been the last living soul – now all that remained was himself: walking down a long, white road.

The moon sank until it was a hemisphere, its circumference widening with every degree it dropped. It was a white hole in the black sky: reversed like a negative photographic plate. He wondered: if he kept on walking, would he eventually pass through that looming gateway? The thought made him pause, suddenly terrified.

He took out his fag tin and lit up, to disguise what that subaltern would have called a blue funk. As he shook the match out he saw figures on the road behind him; they seemed to be passing by the wall where he'd laid Fritzy out. None of them so much as paused, though, or even slowed. He'd found them at last; or rather, they'd found him.

He waited for them to reach him, relieved; hoping none of them would ask what he was doing out here all alone. In silence they approached, and in silence they filed past, their tramping boots no louder than a breeze through tall grass. Each pale face acknowledged him mutely – but no one spoke, or seemed surprised to see him. The line wound on forever: figures so caked in pale mud that he didn't know if they were friend or foe. Down the road they marched, faces bleached of thought and emotion, made pallid by the bloated moon.

Eventually the end of the line reached him; the last rank of men passed by. One of them waved: a tall figure in a long coat. Waving back, he stepped into line, glad to be reunited with them all. He matched his soundless pace with Fritzy's, and together they kept perfect time: marching towards the bright, patient light.

The Wire

Stephanie Ellis

He could see the barbs glinting in the moonlight; jagged blades that waited hungrily as they had done every night since he'd been ordered to this God-forsaken place. The grim landscape of No Man's Land: this deadly snake wound its way across the disputed territory, ready to snare the cannon fodder that was sent relentlessly into its midst.

Jenks could still see the body of his pal, Fred Jones, hanging on the wire in mock crucifixion, some two weeks since he had been shot. They had been prevented from recovering his corpse by the incessant shellfire and even though that had ceased in recent days, it was still deemed too dangerous.

This had made the men angry and there had been mutterings bordering on the mutinous but so far no one had broken ranks and gone over the top. And so there Fred stayed, his body silently accusing his former comrades for their negligence. Now they had been moved back but Jenks had stayed in position.

He had been on duty for well over twelve hours, expecting someone to come and relieve him on his watch but no replacements had been forthcoming. This wasn't the first time that this had happened in recent days and he had had to fight hard to keep his exhaustion at bay. To fall asleep on watch would have been a certain ticket to a more permanent kind of rest.

On this particular night, he was finding it harder than usual to keep his eyes open; he needed something to help him focus his mind. The sounds of war that erupted intermittently around him had become mere background noise. A fatal state of affairs but something he could not fight. To jump at the crack of every whizz-bang or burst of rifle fire would have resulted in a complete mental breakdown. He needed to preserve his sanity and if that meant becoming indifferent to the death and destruction around him then so be it. This did not apply, however, to Fred and the wire – these had become the focus of his attention.

He could see the metal serpent coiled around his pal, holding him up in proud boastfulness at its power over life and death, taunting Jenks at his helplessness, goading him for his inaction.

He looked at its barbs again. He had been counting the spikes that now seemed to point at him but had kept losing count as they merged and blurred, increasing in number before his tired eyes.

Heavy clouds had been in the sky all day, swept across the battlefield as a howling squall but as evening had set in, the winds eased and the clouds slowly dispersed. Now, for a brief moment, the moon was allowed to peep out, illuminating Fred as it did so, bathing him in its ethereal light. To Jenks it felt like a sign, a message. He had to get his pal out of there. As if in agreement, the moon slid back beneath the night sky, casting the area once more into shadow, providing him with the cover that he would surely need.

The war that he knew was still going on somewhere around him seemed totally separate. He and Fred and the wire existed in their own isolated world. He made up his mind. Tonight he would retrieve the body, bring him back into the fold of the British Army to receive the honours which were due to him, even if it was posthumously.

With a decisiveness that had long been absent from his behaviour, Jenks stirred himself, forcing his numbed fingers to slide the wire-cutters into his pocket and a pistol into his belt. He left his rifle behind. Something told him he would not have much use for it. He took a last swig from his hip flask, the brandy warming his chilled bones and giving much-needed strength to his resolution and climbed towards the parapet.

Cautiously he peered over the top. German voices could be heard calling to each other in the trench that he knew wasn't that far from them. Yet that sense of separateness that he had started to feel continued to envelope him and he ignored the threat of their presence.

He cast his eyes along his own trench; his only company the bodies of his fallen comrades and the rats that had now come out to dine. He found it hard to recall the names of the men, if he tried it brought back memories not just of their lives but of their deaths. He did not wish to recall their end, its savagery and barbarity, and so pushed his knowledge of them from his mind. Yet they still lay there, unclaimed and unburied as, like the watch, the medics and stretcher-bearers had failed to come to their aid. His and Fred's abandonment seemed to be complete. He wondered if they existed in anyone's memory anymore apart from as a name and rank that had disappeared into the mud.

He stood on the bottom rung of the ladder remembering the last time he had gone over the top. There would be no blast of a whistle this time. His captain lay behind him, the whistle still between his lips where it had been when he was shot. He hadn't even made it up the ladder. Their sergeant had taken charge then, forcing them on despite the death of their captain.

He had been prepared to shoot anyone who refused. Bullets to the front, bullets at the back. There had been no choice. When he had made it back to the trench he had discovered that the sergeant too was lying dead in the trench although his demise had been caused by a bullet in the back. This had given him no concern.

The sergeant had been no friend to the men and his bullying behaviour had created many enemies. He did not give any thought as to who had fired that fatal bullet, the dead man, he felt, deserved it. Now, to his own astonishment, he was going over the top of his own free will.

He carefully made his way up the ladder, pausing to gaze across the blasted landscape in front of him, at the darkness which hid treacherous craters and unexploded mines, and the wire that commanded everything around it.

He breathed deeply and then slowly, inch by inch, started to crawl over the edge and through the mud towards the savage steel that had been the cause of so much loss of life.

Like the worm that he felt he had become, he wriggled across the ground, nerves tense as he listened for something that might halt his progress but there was nothing apart from a strange air of tranquillity that currently hung over everything. Ahead of him, he could see a gap in the barricade; he would not need his cutters yet. A good sign.

With relief he edged his way through to find that there were other gaps conveniently placed to help him on his forward path. He continued to crawl commando style through these tooth-wreathed holes, his confidence growing as he did so. At this rate of progress he would have Fred cut down and back behind their own lines in absolutely no time. There couldn't be far to go now.

He paused and decided to risk using his torch. He shone it low on the ground in the direction he had been expecting to take. Something shimmered briefly, there was a slight movement, and the wire that had previously been so accommodating had suddenly become a tightly coiled barrier preventing any further advance towards his goal.

This didn't worry him too much though, it was easy to veer off course in the grey light that now hung over them, a sign that dawn was on its way. The movement of the fence he put down to tremors vibrating through the earth in response to the pounding of guns that registered dimly on his periphery.

For the present he was in a clear patch and so risked standing up to take a look around, his confidence increasing as he saw a path that would allow him to pass on unhindered.

He walked down this avenue of bristling spikes which shimmered as he passed by before fading back to their more usual rusted appearance. In this light the muddy brown resembled the scabrous colour of congealed blood.

If Jenks had turned around he would have seen a bleeding fence, droplets falling from its teeth to merge with the blood that already nourished the soil, a stream that was slowly wending its way towards him.

But Jenks did not turn around. His unhindered progress meant that his mind had begun to wander, meaning that at first he didn't register the tug on his coat.

He took another step forward and this time the pull made him pause. Looking down, he realised his coat had become snagged on the steel fangs. He prised the material off carefully, he had a good thick coat which he hoped to make last the winter.

Despite his care, a spasm of pain shot through him as he worked the material away from the barbs, he examined his throbbing hand and saw that he had sliced his finger open on the wire which now accepted the drops of blood that flowed onto it, silver becoming red.

As it did so he noticed a change in the air around him, a growing tension electrically charged with an expectancy he couldn't quite comprehend. Another movement: a twitch in the corner of his eye. The fence moved.

Jenks dismissed the sight. He knew he was tired. His mind was playing tricks on him. The pain in his finger was good, it would keep him alert. He wrapped his hand in a rag and continued to ease the coat from its saw-toothed captor. Free once more, he continued towards Fred, the dead man's shape now a darkened shadow ahead of him.

Not much further.

Another tug.

With irritation he noticed that it was his sleeve that was caught. He stopped to free himself, this time without mishap. Metal mouths whispered behind him, a noise he disregarded, dismissing it as a disturbance caused by the mortars that fell somewhere in the rest of the war.

He continued to walk again. It felt as if he was going in the wrong direction but still Fred loomed ahead. Jenks shook his head to clear his thoughts. Rip. The lining of the bottom of his coat had caught on the razor edges that decorated the wire. He bent down and started to carefully release the material from the barbs that held it.

So it continued.

Another step, another tug, another stab of pain.

This time it was his leg. Somehow he had stepped into the midst of a coil and become imprisoned. He pulled out the wire-cutters and snipped the offending strands away. They slithered off into the darkness and Jenks did not notice.

He cast his light around him once more to find that his path ahead no longer existed. Rolls of wire writhed and rippled, surrounding him, snaking its way towards where he stood.

Finally, he registered that things were not as they should be.

A cold trickle of sweat ran down his spine, he could feel the hairs on the back of his neck prickle. The fear that he remembered from his first days in the trenches returned. It had immobilised him then, turning his feet and his thoughts to lead as he sought to make sense of the horrors that surrounded him, horrors to which he had slowly become immune. Now he felt the full weight of his fear once more. He was in the middle of a sea of rippling spines, a tide that was rolling in towards him, preparing to engulf him beneath its waves. A trap that he had willingly walked into. Had he been that keen to die?

Somehow he had to find a way out, but first he had to gain his bearings.

Fred.

He pictured his friend as he had seen him from the vantage point of the trench.

Fred had died nearer to the enemy lines than their own – he had almost made it across.

If Jenks could get to his pal, it would be an easy matter to get to the other side. He would surrender; raise his arms as soon as he was in the range of the Germans. Being their prisoner of war could only be preferable to attempting to return to his own lines.

He had to move quickly. His eyes sought out Fred once more. Even in death his friend would help him. He saw his shape and began to move towards his comrade.

A coil of wire started to unravel alongside him turning into a single silver strand that suddenly whipped up into the sky above him with a crack that sent sparks showering down. A few landed on his coat and started to smoulder. He batted these out with hands that found themselves grabbed by spikes and metal claws. In terror he jerked his hands back, ripping flesh as he did so. He fought to push pain to the back of his mind as his hands became slick with blood.

He ran through a gap that had suddenly opened up only to find his way blocked and the strand that had lashed the night sky speeding towards him, a deadly tentacle searching him out, twitching as it tasted the blood that dripped behind him. He searched round frantically, looked again for Fred.

The earth started to shake and a blast sent him flying. A mortar had made its way into his little pocket of hell, blasting the wire as it did so. For once, Jenks was thankful for the artillery bombardment. He didn't care which side had fired it, it had provided him with a brief but welcome respite.

The force of the explosion threw him into the bottom of a crater, free of the wire which had previously enveloped him. Dazed and deafened, he lay there looking up at the night sky watching the stars in bafflement, the clouds had gone and now they were revealed in all their heavenly glory, looking just the same as they did back home.

How could something so beautiful shine down on such horrors and not be affected by what it saw. Was the universe so oblivious towards such suffering? This truly was the Devil's Playground and he a mere toy, a broken soldier to be cast aside at the whim of his superiors.

Well, to the devil with them all, he thought.

He looked around the rest of the crater, noted the unidentified mounds as well as some things which were only too identifiable. He averted his eyes and considered his next move. He could not stay there. Should rain begin to fall again it would become a quagmire and he would never escape.

He had to climb back up into the clinging embrace of the waiting wire. Around him, tiny strands of steel lay scattered. He chose to ignore them, assuming, wrongly, that they had become harmless. If he had watched them closely he would have noticed that they now they sought each other out, metallic slivers that writhed like maggots across the mud, twining themselves together when they met so that once more they would become whole.

He scrambled up the side of the crater, finding it difficult to get any purchase in the mud but with some effort he soon found he was at its brim. He looked over towards Fred. He was very near his friend.

Behind him, the newly reformed strand wriggled after him, gliding over disturbed soil and bleached bones that had resurfaced on the mortar's impact. It soon caught up with him and started to wind itself around his feet. Feeling the sudden pressure on his boots, he looked down – horror ripping through him as easily as the wire barbs that had sliced at his skin.

He jerked himself free and ran but still the strand pursued him until, just as he reached Fred's side, it coiled itself once more into a tight spring and then launched itself at him, lassoing him with ease. The loop tightened around his arms, its vice-like grip cutting into him as he fought against it, its movement easing when he stopped fighting, becoming tighter when he struggled again.

It swung him to the ground and he was dragged onwards through razor-tipped wire that slashed and cut at him as it tore away his clothes, ripping through to the skin beneath which now glistened wetly with sweat and blood.

He tried to close his eyes but the lids were immediately ripped open so that he could see the forest of metal weaving itself above him. For a moment it reminded him of a winter's drive not long ago when he had travelled through ancient woods and looked up at the night sky to see the bare arms of silver birch reach their fingers up into the night sky.

A comforting memory that was however stolen as swiftly as it had come to him, replaced by the sight of metal shards gleaming against the velvet blackness in a terrible parody of his earlier vision. These fingers weren't reaching up however; they were stretching down, extending their talons towards him, pinching and nipping viciously at him with a terrier-like tenacity as he passed.

His body was in agony as he continued to be dragged along the serrated ground. He didn't even begin to wonder if he was still whole, if he retained all his limbs, he had no comprehension of what was happening any more. All he knew was that every nerve ending in his body was alive to his pain, every muscle ached, every inch of skin burned.

He had descended to the seventh circle of Hell.

On through the labyrinth of wire he went, the pace slowing slightly but which only served to increase the depth of his suffering. How long this continued he had no conception, time had ceased to exist for him, his agony now his only focus. Then suddenly he was still. The wire that had born him along loosened its grip and withdrew. Through blood-filled eyes he could see that he was now upright and facing the German lines.

His arms were stretched out at his sides, pierced by the wire as it supported him. From the stigmata on his hands he watched the blood flow, a steady trickle that bathed the wire and washed away the rust; his tears followed, their salt stinging his open wounds. His feet were likewise pinioned to the ground, serrated edges grasping his boots, rendering him immobile.

The only part of him that could move was his head but when he tried the pain was too great, the horror too much.

Yet he was not on his own. He had managed at last to reach Fred. The figure of his friend hung next to him but now Jenks had no chance of helping him, let alone helping himself.

"You know the first few days are the worst," said Fred.

Now I'm hearing things, thought Jenks.

"No," replied Fred. "I'm alive – I think. I've not always been sure. When a bullet's ripped through me or mounds of earth blown up in my face, I've felt its force, felt pain. How can I be dead if I can feel that?"

No, thought Jenks. *He's speaking my words, my mind. I've watched him hang here day-after-day without any sound or movement coming from him. If he had been alive I would have come for him.*

"Would you? You didn't make much of an effort before."

"It was orders," explained Jenks giving himself up to the idea of a conversation with a corpse. He sensed he was dying and that his brain was helping him through his ordeal albeit in bizarre fashion. He wanted it to be over; he would just go along with whatever happened.

"Orders? Or just fear? Or apathy?"

"Apathy?"

"Your orders were to return. You've been in that trench for days. You didn't follow your comrades when they went back you just stayed there. You gave up."

He had not given up! He had stood watch just like he'd been ordered. He had done his duty.

"No, you gave the *appearance* of doing your duty. You just couldn't face it any more could you?"

It was coming.

He knew it would eventually, that moment of shame when he had to finally admit the truth to himself, face reality at last. His unit had been destroyed; he had been the only one left, watching Fred every night for the past fortnight.

Part of him had known Fred was still alive when he became trapped on the wire but the other part of his brain refused to acknowledge this and so he had stopped in his trench, caught in a No Man's Land of his own making.

Painfully he turned his head towards Fred again. He could see no life there. The man's face was grey; flesh was falling away from bone. He was dead. Then Fred lifted his head and grinned at Jenks, a mockery of the smile that he remembered.

From his mouth erupted strands of wire, pushing their way through skin and cloth like plants pushing their way up through the soil to reach the sun-light. Barbs coiled out from him in never-ending strands, steel vines that merged with those that held both his and Fred's bodies.

"You can keep watch here, Jenks," said Fred. "With me."

Jenks nodded in surrender. What other choice did he have? He turned his face towards the enemy.

From the German trench, the soldiers looked on as the Tommy clambered over the razor-wire oblivious to their presence and their calls to surrender. At first they thought he was going to collect his compatriot's helmet and identity tags which they had left hanging on the wire and held back on their gunfire. Then he had stopped moving and faced them, his skin deathly white and his eyes staring blindly ahead.

One of their number crawled out over the top and made his way to the wire, a short and relatively safe journey on this particular night. He stood up in front of the man and moved a hand from side-to-side but the soldier showed no sign that he registered the man's presence.

The German took the man's wrist to feel for a pulse but again there was nothing. He could cut him down he thought but then he would have to bury the body, just like he had had to do with that other Tommy who had died in the same place a fortnight ago.

It had been a hard job and had resulted in the disturbance of other corpses whose decomposing remains had given him nightmares for several nights running. He did not want that duty again and no one else would volunteer. As the youngest, the work usually fell to him. No, he would leave Tommy there.

The German returned to the trench and reported that the man had died but that to release him from the wire would be a time-consuming job, time which their recent orders did not allow them.

They shrugged their shoulders and continued to dismantle their armaments and pack up their supplies. The tramp of the soldiers' feet faded into the distance as they marched off into the night to join battle elsewhere. The Tommy on the wire was forgotten.

The trenches on both sides had fallen quiet as the theatre of battle moved away to the east leaving No Man's Land silent and deserted, save for the remnants, human and otherwise that remained as mute witnesses to the slaughter that had occurred.

The coils of steel that had bristled with such vibrant energy as it wove its tortuous path across the land seemed to shrivel and die as the soldiers on both sides moved away, becoming mere rusted heaps of metal, brittle to the touch and more nuisance than danger.

It still had a role to play however and was even now sending fresh tendrils through the soil to find the soldiers on which it could continue to feed, like it had on the body that it now left behind.

There would be plenty of other toys to play within the Devil's Playground.

Yugen

David Thomas

Well it all happened to me lads on my birthday!

That morning I had been assigned by my sergeant for map making duties as punishment for not singing *God Save The King* the night before. I would have to go into the nearby woods and draw out the lay of the land for the battalion and if I should happen to run into any Germans who might be hiding there, then that was my tough shit.

I took it on the chin as you do and trudged off into a section of woods that was almost untouched by the shelling. Early sunrise was always the safest time to go; the Hun were usually laying low, filling their bellies for the upcoming slaughter, but then weren't we all? All I had with me was a pistol; a leather bound notebook and pencil.

My sergeant called out to me as I left: "And don't lie in a ditch somewhere and make it up, Private. I'll be checking it all against the aerial photographs." The red of the rising sun cast him in a deep hue, never did I see such a devil of a man as him; I nodded and made my way in along a dusty trail.

All I could really think about after that was a word that was very special to me, something that had stuck with me since reading it on a cold winter's day as a child. A word which perhaps only children can understand and that helped a lot when I could feel the pressure building up inside.

Yugen.

An old Japanese word that has no real English translation, but like the lice in my hair it had managed to stay with me throughout this war, many a time it felt like the only thing worth keeping.

Anyway, as I began walking through the woods I couldn't

help but notice the first of the morning light flooding through the branches above my head. It reminded me of that funny feeling you get when you go into a cathedral or museum, and I think for the first time I began to understand what that word, Yugen, really meant.

It was as if at that precise moment I had caught a glimpse of its deeper meaning, or more importantly its deeper joy.

But that sense of happiness which was waking within me also made me feel awkward. You have to understand lads; I'd been on the front line for five months. It had been a long time since I felt myself smile, like a human being, and not like a pawn that's every move were controlled by unseen hands.

A mile in I finally decided to work on sketching out the hills and gullies, yet with each stroke of the pencil I could feel the emotion of that word drift away from me and leave in its place the usual sadness and revulsion that had been building up ever since I'd stepped foot into this war.

After a few more pages of sketching I decided to wash my face in a nearby stream. The reality of war always made me feel unclean, it still does, but as I cupped my hands in the water a headless soldier floated by me like driftwood. I watched as the poor bastard got tangled up in the lily beds.

How could such beauty be so close to such death?

I tried hard not to think about it, my head was already overflowing with the daily horrors of battle, but then as I went back to wash my face I caught a sniff of an old familiar smell blowing in the breeze. In the trenches I used to joke and call it *Hague's Perfume*. I always like giving wrong names to wrong things; to me it was the only thing that made sense, at a time when there was so little *too* make sense.

I tucked the pencil and book into my inside pocket and took out my gun and decided to follow the stench. Why I don't know, maybe out of curiosity, maybe out of some hidden death wish, I really don't know.

It didn't take long before I saw what made that terrible smell. There were at least a hundred dead bodies scattered in a clearing deep in the woods, while all around them dozens of hungrily squeaking rats picked and nibbled at their rotting flesh.

Right there and then as I saw the blood of those wasted men ooze into the leafy ground, I felt like tearing up the pages I had drawn and ramming them down my sergeant's throat.

But instead, things took a turn for the worse; a lot worse – something in fact I would never have imagined or wanted.

A dead solider nearby raised his half missing head towards me and lisped through shattered teeth: "Don't worry son, you're not mad."

Its funny looking back on it now, you'd think I would have screamed wouldn't you? But this war had taken so much out of me; scarred me so deeply, that all I could do was stare.

I knew I hadn't gone mad though because I had seen men go mad before, some whilst reading a letter from a farewell lover, or others on their first day of duty, or even worse on their last day of duty.

No I wasn't insane. What I was I didn't exactly know exactly, but it wasn't madness.

Another dead soldier who was propped up against a tree close by opened his eyes as I stood there in silence and said to me in a thick cockney accent: "You're just a puppet whose strings haven't been cut yet. That's all, sunshine."

A rat nearby scuttled up onto his chest and pushed and shoved its way into his mouth before slipping gently down his throat. I watched as he hungrily sucked up its tail like spaghetti and said with an air of cockney bravado. "We're all going to die someday mate, why fret about when and where?" I felt my stomach lurch as he gave out a piggish burp.

His eyes then glanced nervously at me. In them I could see the shame of a man holding onto his own death. He knew as well as I did it wasn't right. I licked my dry lips and said numbly: "If I haven't gone mad my friend then why am I seeing you like this?"

He rubbed his belly and whispered: "I guess it's because she likes you," and turned his head towards the thing that had been watching us both.

Don't get me wrong lads I knew I was speaking to a corpse and one that I pitied. But that wasn't what was concerning me:

it was the fact that I knew who he was talking about!

There had been some discrete whispers along the front the last couple of weeks. Men had seen something late at night in No Man's Land, a figure moving amongst the dead and the silver moonlight.

The brass up top of course, after getting wind of it, had sent out search parties to try and catch what they thought was a spy, but no-one was ever found.

Then one morning we had all been ordered not to say another word about it.

A young soldier, no more than a boy in fact, had hanged himself the night before after apparently seeing something.

Morale had to be kept you know, lives could be thrown away, but morale had to be kept no matter the price.

I considered praying, but what was the point? In the trenches, if there's one thing that's never there when you need it most lads, its God, so I just turned round and faced the thing. What was there to lose?

In a way I wasn't surprised at all by what I saw.

She was sitting on a tree stump not far from me – the first of the morning light silhouetted her outline. She was wearing a brightly coloured dress and green shawl, at her bare feet a rat stared up at her in silent awe.

For a moment there was nothing but the sound of the wind hissing through the trees before I felt my gun slip smoothly from my fingers and slap to the ground.

She looked at the weapon, then me and said: "Hello," casually sucked on a thin clay pipe, as if she had all the time in the world. I smelt its rich spices twirling in the air. Nice. The rat on the other hand, gave a questioning twitch of its nose and scuttled away to join his mates as they feasted.

I knew who she was all right, everyone along the front knew her, but believe me lads no one ever dare say her name out loud – it was a sure sign of bad luck – because, as you might have already worked out, she was Death and no one ever speaks about her when there on the front line do they?

Anyhow, as she sat there, her dark eyes narrowed at me and slowly looked me up and down. In them, I could see the prickly fear that crawls across a man's chest just before he goes over the top. She blinked and they slowly turned to a soft green that reminded me of the untouched fields back home.

"Can we talk?" she asked and blew out a thin blue line of smoke. It slowly rolled like an ocean wave across the rays of the morning light.

A hand tapped my dirty boot as I stood there wondering if I had a choice. I glanced down and saw a soldier with missing legs staring back at me – the rat that had been looking at her was now nibbling one of his bollocks.

"Don't fuck this up boy," he said wearily. The rat then sank its sharp white teeth into his ball-sack. I felt my stomach lurch again.

I turned my head away. I'd seen plenty of blood and guts before don't get me wrong, but it was their eyes that got me every time. I couldn't stand it lads, because he, like the other soldier, knew he was dead. He knew that his time had passed and it scared the shit out of me to see that kind of despair in a man's eyes.

I bit my lip and turned back to her. She reminded me of a fortune teller I once saw on Brighton beach, but only thinner and a lot younger and maybe a little bit more … well you know what I'm getting at don't you?

She chuckled, a smokers' laugh, as she saw my eyes betray my thoughts. "What did you expect?" she asked with a twirl of her hand. "Mata Hari?"

My face blushed as the soldier again tapped my boot. "Talk to her boy, she doesn't bite." The rat was now working on the rest of his scrotum.

I know what you might be thinking, but I tell you lads there really wasn't any point in running away. Death wanted to talk to me and that felt like it meant something.

It's funny sometimes how you can easily accept the impossible when you see it face to face. "What do you want?" I eventually asked.

Puffing on her pipe she gave me a wink, the kind that says *it's okay.* "You seemed so happy a little while ago, why was that?"

The question took me aback, I'll be honest.

What the hell could I know that she didn't already?! She was Death; I was just a man who'd been manipulated into hating others. I knew nothing.

So I just did what you do when you're out of your depth: I kept my mouth shut.

Placing a hand on her knee she leant towards me. "I asked you a question. All this bloodshed, yet I saw a look on your face that was *different*?"

Warm embarrassment began to well up inside me. Even when facing Death square in the face, you have to understand something's still yours and yours alone, even if it's just a made-up word from a children's book.

We all have secrets, don't we? Little things that will never see the light of day and this one was mine. You see it had been there for me too many times. I was not prepared to give it away so easily.

But that was the problem right there, because as I looked away thinking of a clever way not to tell her, I could see that all the soldiers were staring at me. In their dead eyes I could see a longing that meant only one thing: they wanted confirmation of their lives, wanted meaning to all this insanity and I guess the pressure I'd been feeling, meant I did too.

Rubbing my face as hard as I could, I let the embarrassment turn to surrender. What could I do? She was Death, they were dead, and I was a long way from home. Luckily enough the words poured out of me easier than I thought. All it took was a deep breath and a leap of faith. But then if you think about it, that's all it ever really takes.

So I told her straight.

"I felt Yugen, it means..."

She cut me short with a flick of her pipe. "I know what it means young man. Why did you feel it here though, of all places?"

"Because," I took another deep breath and let the secret fall out of me like a catholic. "Because I long for it, because it keeps me sane, it keeps my inner love from turning to hate."

The soldier at my feet gave out a sad groan of reflection.

She looked around puzzled. "And you see it here?"

I glanced over at the rats as they picked and clawed their way through the bodies of the men.

"I see it when things like that can't be seen."

A soldier nearby shouted out from a tangle of legs and arms. "You're fucking telling me boyo."

A leg gave him a quick boot to quiet him down.

She folded her arms like my mother did when I had done something wrong and gave me a scowl. "Then what are you doing in such a place as this, if you can feel things like that?"

The question as you can imagine, was just too big to answer, and let's be honest: can any soldier truly answer that one? I took another deep breath and tried to make sense of it all. "Why are you doing this to me?"

"Yugen, you daft twat!" shouted a soldier who was hanging upside down from a tree. "Tell the people what connects us all; what joins us together – so that no mother can feel like my mother's gonna feel when she finds out what happened to me!"

He finished his last word with a whimper of despair that I knew all too well.

"Don't you realise," the soldier at my feet said. "You felt something we never had the chance to feel." His voice then burnt with a frustration that only the dead know. "Prove the bastards wrong."

From the scattered bodies came a cry of approval, a cry of demand.

I looked down into his face and said something stupid, something thoughtless. "This *is* a dream isn't it?"

With a snort of contempt he glared with those dead eyes and snarled. "We should be so fucking lucky."

Sensing the bitterness she stood and walked over to me, standing so close that I could have reached out and touched her.

"Whichever way you look at it," she whispered. "I am Death and I'm sick of doing my job for all the wrong reasons." She leaned closer, whispered in my ear. "There are many reasons to come to me."

I could smell soil and ungodly things on her cold still

breath. A shiver went up my spine.

Her eyes widened (thankfully though they remained green and not that darker nightmare stuff). "There's always a right way to die. But believe me, this isn't it."

"Why me?" was all I could think of to ask.

"It's not just you." she replied with a click of her tongue. "I've been trying to tell you foolish men this since you first started murdering each other."

She gestured with her pipe towards the rats. "But still you want this banquet." She then looked at the bodies of the soldiers with a sadness that made me think she was going to burst into tears.

"Surely a single word can't change all this?" I rubbed my forehead I felt confused at my own contradiction. Hadn't it managed to help me through though? Wasn't it powerful...?

"Yes it can," she snapped. "And there are other words too: Love. Peace. You shouldn't be afraid of using them. They won't hurt you."

"Unlike other words," said the soldier at my feet. "The ones they tricked us with: Hate. Fear."

He then finally slapped the rat away and composed himself. "And you know the biggest one of them all?"

She pointed a finger towards the horizon and screamed: "War!"

In the far distance the first shell barrage of the day rumbled its way across the shattered landscape. She gave a nervous flinch and turned to me. "It's up to you now young man."

Beneath my feet the ground began to shake. A sudden rush of questions flooded my mind. I knew I would have to run soon, run for my life, but I had to know while there was still a little time left.

"What is this then, if I'm not mad or dreaming, what is this?" I motioned to the carnage around me.

Giving a small shrug of her shoulders she pulled her shawl tightly around herself. "Two worlds that got too close."

The barrage moved nearer, she flicked her head towards the way I had come. "You'd better go."

Picking up my gun, I stepped away and headed back as fast

as I could.

As I ran I didn't feel like looking back. Some things are best left as they are, especially when Death does you a favour.

But do you know something lads?

I actually started to understand how she felt about having to take those men and take them by the thousands. Day in and day out.

It wasn't right for her to be used like that. Like a whore.

I met up with my sergeant back in the trenches; the bastard had been waiting for me. He spied the pages I had drawn out. "Is this all you did, Private?!"

His eyes lingered on mine, he was hungry to punish me some more.

"Yes sir," I said as I tried to catch my breath. "The Hun's barrage started to come in before I could finish."

He gave a grunt and sent me to shovel out a new latrine. As I walked away he sneered that it would be good for my singing voice. In my mind's eye I pictured him smirking to himself, thinking he was close to breaking me, grinding what little I had left into dust. I just ignored him and walked on.

As I set to work, my thoughts went straight back to what had just happened. I rolled it around my head all day, but as I shovelled and shovelled, I still had the same old familiar feelings sloshing around inside.

I still felt like me.

And the reason? Well, that was simple: it's because seeing Death back in those woods wasn't something special. In truth we're all going to be touched by her someday. From the moment we're born her shadow is cast. I'm not unique at all.

Later on that evening I found a quiet corner and watched the sun slowly dip over the trenches. The thought of Yugen came back into my mind like an old friend and I knew instantly what I had to do: I would honour the wishes of her and those men and give up this war. Though also to speak those words that we need to hear, those words that we *have* to hear.

But let's be honest, we all feel like we're doing something wrong don't we? And do you know why that is, why we're always feeling the pressure?

It's because we're not meant to kill each other!

And someday, as a species, we're going to work that out.

When will that happen, I don't know? Maybe in this war, maybe the next, but someday we're gonna grow sick and tired of all this bloodshed.

Peace will come, just like she will.

The one thing that makes me feel nervous right now however, is that you might think it's all just wishful thinking, or worse a pack of lies.

I tell you with all my heart that one day there won't be any more wars or armies, because why would a word like Yugen exist? Why would it if it wasn't true?

Anyway I'll end with this lads: there is a right way to die and this is mine…

*

"Is that all you have to say Private Robert Ian Patterson."

"Yes, Captain."

"Then by order of the British Army you are hereby to be executed for abandonment of duty. May God have mercy on your soul. Sergeant, kindly follow out your duty."

"With pleasure, sir. Right men! Take aim and fire on my command."

The Wolves of Vimy

David Jón Fuller

Corporal Thomas Greyeyes took the measure of his fellow captives in the weak candlelight of the German dugout. Whether the five of them would live past the next forty-five minutes depended on how their sergeant answered the following question. "Sir," said Greyeyes, "How do you feel about wolves?"

Sergeant Balfour had been leaning his head against the barred door of the dugout. They had been put there as soon as their captors had marched them back to the Stellung I line of trenches around midnight. The very Bavarian soldiers the 107th and the other Canadian battalions had been taking prisoner in the ongoing raids over the nights prior to zero hour, had now locked them up. And they were unlikely to go easy on them.

Balfour looked sharply at Greyeyes, his ear still cocked at the doorway. "Ssshh."

Greyeyes nodded, sharing a glance with the others who had survived when the raid went sour.

Private Skaptason, a Lewis gunner from Lake Winnipeg, southeast of where Greyeyes hailed from in Red Sucker Lake, Manitoba; Private Deer, who everyone just called 'Goose,' a sniper from Kahnawake, Quebec, showed he understood with the shift of his ears, as if he were sighting a shot.

Private Naytowhow, from northern Saskatchewan, who went by 'Sparky' since he could light up a trench with a Mills Bomb like nobody else, also nodded.

Greyeyes' nickname was Mahiinkan, but only to people who knew the Island Lakes dialect Ojibwe word for 'wolf.' Everyone else just called him Grey Eyes, since he never saw things in black and white, but rather the grey, shifting tints that mingled in the mud of no-man's-land.

Greyeyes leaned closer to Balfour. They had no nickname for him yet, as he'd just been assigned to the 107th – the 'Timber Wolf' Battalion, raised in Winnipeg – from the 69th Battalion out of Montreal. They didn't know him, really. It was the main reason they hadn't gotten free yet.

Greyeyes went to check his watch, then remembered it had been confiscated.

Les allemandes had taken everything of use from them but their shirts, trousers, puttees and boots, leaving them shivering in the early spring air. Greyeyes hoped one of them was unlucky enough to use his Ross rifle, that piece of garbage. If he made it out – *when* he made it out – maybe he'd finally get a good Lee-Enfield like Skaptason. Goose swore by his Ross for sniping, but then he spent a lot of time keeping the damn thing clean and dry.

His wrist felt bare, but Greyeyes estimated they had forty-three minutes. When you lived every day with your waking hours sliced up by endless fatigues, you knew how long every second lasted.

Balfour turned to them. "All right. I think there is only one outside. Private..." he pointed at Skaptason. "Ask him for some water."

Skaptason frowned, but rose. "I don't speak Boche, sir."

Balfour shook his head. "Norwegian, German, they are similar, no?"

Skaptason shrugged. "I speak Icelandic..."

"Just try. If we can get him to come in," here he glanced sharply at Greyeyes, Goose and Naytowhow, "you all know what to do."

Greyeyes cleared his throat. "Sir..."

"A moment, Corporal."

Skaptason thumped on the door.

"*Was?*" came a high-pitched voice from the other side.

"*Vatn,*" said Skaptason. "*Vatn.*"

There was a moment when the five men shivered silently in the near-dark, before the door opened. Two soldiers, in their long, muck-spattered trench-coats and each sporting flower-pot steel helmets, pointed their Gewehr rifles at the Canadians.

Skaptason gulped. "*Vatn?*"

The older, burlier soldier scowled. "*Wasser?*"

Skaptason nodded.

The larger soldier kept his rifle pointed at Skaptason while he spoke to the other in German. Greyeyes couldn't quite make it out but the tone was clear. The slender soldier, clearly younger, swallowed and lowered his weapon and then reached for his canteen.

Without giving any warning, Balfour sprang for the bigger soldier's rifle, pushing the muzzle up. Skaptason ducked. Naytowhow went for the younger soldier, who screamed. A gun went off and dirt pecked off the ceiling of the dugout. Goose and Greyeyes moved forward, and then two more shots rang out. Balfour flew back into Goose and Naytowhow fell onto Skaptason. Greyeyes dodged between his fellows and then froze. The big soldier's rifle pointed up and to the side but his Luger was aimed straight at Greyeyes's face.

For a second he was sure he was about to die. Out of the corner of his eye, he saw the younger soldier still gripping his weapon with trembling hands. The acrid odour of gunpowder filled the small space.

Then the larger soldier snapped at the younger one, who flinched. Both retreated out of the doorway, and the door was shut and barred. Terse shouts in German followed outside the door.

That can't be good, thought Greyeyes, before realising that was exactly the sort of thing Naytowhow would say. Except he hadn't.

Goose stood, helping Balfour up. Balfour's shoulder now had a dark red well bubbling blood through his muddy white shirt. Goose clamped a hand over the wound. "Check Sparky," he ordered. But Skaptason was already kneeling by Naytowhow. Half of Sparky's neck was missing. "Dead," said Skaptason dully, as if unwilling to admit it.

Balfour's face was pale and sweaty. "Damn it."

Greyeyes rubbed the tops of his thighs, his teeth chattering. "Do you think anyone made it back?"

Balfour opened his mouth, but Goose shook his head. His deep voice rumbled. "That wire needs more attention. They got back, we'd have heard the howitzers by now."

The others nodded. The whole point of the raid had been to ensure the preliminary bombardment that had been going on since March 20th had taken out all the barbed wire.

Artillery, of course, swore they'd done it – said the new 106 Fuze made guaranteed short work of the wire, instead of just uselessly exploding shrapnel above it.

But General Currie, bless him, hadn't wanted to send even one brigade of the massed Canadian Expeditionary Force into a stretch of intact wire, to be strung up like flies for Fritz's machine gunners like they had at the Somme. Artillery's forward observation officers couldn't verify the section was destroyed. So they'd drawn one of the platoons from the 107th Battalion – and with all the training they'd gotten for the upcoming battle, every Canadian felt he knew his way backwards, forwards, up and down Vimy Ridge.

Balfour and the others had all been sure they could ascertain whether the barbed wire in this section had been obliterated, and maybe cause Fritz some grief into the bargain.

But the wire was still up, and worse, when they'd tried to get around it, they were surprised by a patrol based in one of the craters in No Man's Land. They'd been pinned down and more a few of them killed. To be captured, especially now – it had been April 8th, but by now they were well into the small hours of the 9th – was the worst thing that could have happened.

Balfour's shoulder wound had soaked the top of his shirt deep crimson. Skaptason helped Goose support him but they had nothing to dress it with. None of them could bring themselves to remove Sparky's shirt and rip it up for bindings.

"They'll kill us now, for sure," said Skaptason.

Not if I can help it, thought Greyeyes.

Balfour shook his head raggedly. "They will try to get some answers out us first, I think. Same as we do to them. Time, Corporal?"

Greyeyes shut out the sounds of orders barked in German

outside their dugout. "Half an hour, thirty-five minutes, maybe."

Balfour licked his chapped lips and shuddered. "Then we stall them. Keep them going until ... zero hour."

The weight of what that meant sank in with a heavy silence in the cramped space.

Greyeyes thought of his wife, Clara, who sent letters with the help of a Mennonite pastor – she could neither read nor write. He hadn't been able to either, until Skaptason, whose nose was always stuck in a book or a newspaper, taught him.

He thought of his two children, sequestered at the residential school Clara could not get them out of. It was a large part of why he had enlisted – a steady job, more reliable than trapping, to show the church authorities who ran the school he was fit to take them back home.

But now, sitting in the muddy darkness of the Kaiser's occupied France, he felt perhaps the priests had hoped he would go off to war and never make it back. Like Sparky – and too many of their fellows.

He looked up and saw the others locked in similarly grim thoughts. "There's something we can try, sir."

Goose turned his sniper's stare at Greyeyes. He knew what was being suggested. Greyeyes raised a respectful hand to him. True, Balfour was white – but so was Skaptason. And that had worked out.

Balfour frowned, as if trying to wake from a nightmare. "*Eh, bien?* Let's hear it."

"You'll have to trust me. It won't be easy, especially..." Greyeyes paused. *Especially if I don't know the stories you were raised with.* His grandmother had been very specific about that, when he was younger. *But it's either this or let him die.* And newcomer to the Timber Wolf Battalion or not, Balfour was their C.O. You didn't leave a man like that behind. "Especially since we don't have much time," he said.

Balfour wheezed and shivered. "As long as it doesn't give *les allemandes*...," his voice choked in a wet, bloody, cough.

Goose's eyes seemed to bore into Greyeyes, a near-blatant challenge. *He's already dead,* Goose as much as said. But outside military rank, it was Greyeyes who held the authority in this.

Skaptason cleared his throat. "It's all right, sir. Boche will never see it coming."

Greyeyes reached for his knife, but of course it wasn't there. Grimacing, he bit the back of his hand till it bled and let his spit cover it. He motioned to Goose, who took a slick palm away from Balfour's injury. Greyeyes pressed his own fresh wound against it, mingling their blood and his saliva. Greyeyes chanted softly in Ojibwe, as his parents and grandparents had taught him. The words focused his prayer to draw strength from the earth below and pull it into Balfour's body, healing it.

That, and much more, if they could do it in time.

Balfour rallied as Greyeyes took his hand away and Goose replaced his. "Eh? What was that?"

Greyeyes raised the sergeant's chin to look him in the eye. "When we leave here, it will be as wolves. Remember that."

Balfour squinted. "*Quoi?*"

"It's not how I would have done it," said Goose.

Greyeyes bared his teeth. "He'd never make it otherwise."

"They still talk about the loups-garous in Quebec. I have a cousin in Oka, he said…"

"Ssshh!" said Skaptason.

The door was unbarred and the dugout became even more cramped as the two soldiers, rifles up, covered Greyeyes, Balfour, Goose and Skaptason.

"Hands!" said the big one.

Balfour could only raise his left; his wounded arm hung limply. Goose put his free hand up behind his head, keeping his left pressed on Balfour's shoulder; this meant turning his back to the Germans. Greyeyes and Skaptason put their hands up behind their heads and waited. Sparky's body lay as if sleeping, but for the glassy stare on its face.

The Bavarians scanned the small, musty dugout and after a moment, the big one, his jaw unshaven and face grey with mud, shouted back over his shoulder without taking his eyes off the Canadians. Greyeyes was close enough to Goose to hear him whispering to Balfour in French without giving any sign. *Wait for us to act before you try to do it. Don't be afraid. The change may happen if you think you're about to die. Just breathe, and follow us.*

The Bavarians parted to allow an officer through. From the lack of pips on his shoulder boards, he looked like a Prussian leutnant. He was clean-shaven, clear-eyed, and he had his Luger out, resting on his opposite forearm as calmly as if he were checking his pocket-watch. But there was nothing relaxed in the set of his mouth, barely-suppressed snarl, or in the clench of his jaws.

"Who is the officer among you?" he asked.

Greyeyes pointed with his face to Balfour. "Him. But he's wounded. You can talk to me."

"Name? Rank?"

"Greyeyes. Corporal."

The leutnant peered at him. "*Indian*. So, the Canadians have run out of their 'storm troops' and now send their savages and half-breeds against us?"

It was meant to goad Greyeyes into giving something up, so he tilted his head back, just as when facing down the government Indian agent who thought he could tell him where to fish and hunt, and how much of his catch he could keep.

Greyeyes was tempted to grin and say, *I'm fighting for the King, same as my grandfathers did before me. Canada didn't send me, I volunteered to help Britain.*

It was a distinction that mattered to him, and many of the 'Indian' soldiers, but he didn't think this would-be aristocrat would care. And, Greyeyes noticed, the leutnant had a stretched, harrowed look to him. Aside from the fact the 107th had earned the 'storm troop' nickname from the Germans as well as any other Canadian battalion, he suspected the Canadian and British bombardment over the last few weeks had taken more of a toll than the Germans would admit.

"My men are growing tired of your nightly harassment. This makes twenty-four raids in a row. What do you hope to accomplish with this?"

Greyeyes shrugged. "A man needs a hobby, I suppose."

The leutnant cracked a brief smile. "Yes, perhaps. Ours seems to be enduring as many shells and bullets as you can send over the godforsaken land between us. In fact, it's nearly daylight. I imagine we will have more to look forward to this morning."

Greyeyes kept his expression neutral. *More than you think, Fritz, he thought.*

But though he kept himself from looking at his confiscated watch, he marked the time.

Thirty-odd minutes. His cheek twitched.

The leutnant pursed his lips and gestured with his Luger. "When will the attack come, Corporal?"

Greyeyes permitted himself a rueful grin. "Don't ask me, friend. I'm just infantry."

"Yes, the entire force of Canadians is out there, isn't it? Helping your British masters, to save the French. How many men do you have to throw at us? We hear ninety thousand, maybe one hundred. The French tried to take this ridge from us two years ago and they *lost* half again as many as that. You can fire all you like at us but as soon as you storm our lines we will cut you to pieces."

Not with the rolling barrage we're going to hit you with, thought Greyeyes. True, he was 'only' infantry, but Currie had had them rehearsing the attack for weeks, with and without their C.O.s – Currie assumed a high officer casualty rate, as they'd seen at The Somme and Verdun – on full-scale territory mockups; and the entire infantry had been reorganised into the new platoon formation, with each soldier trained in his fellow's tasks, so if they lost their mortar man or their machine gunners another could assume their duties.

Currie was very big on training and preparation, and he had little time for the brave, pointless offensives the French seemed to adhere to. So Greyeyes felt sure this Prussian leutnant and his superiors, right up to Prince Rupprecht, might well see something unexpected this morning, in less than half an hour.

Greyeyes swallowed, and thought of his family. The leutnant was going to see something new a lot sooner than his men.

The leutnant smiled briefly again. "I know what you are thinking: 'If I simply say nothing, he will keep me until I do speak; and perhaps my friends will storm the barricades and save me.' Yes, perhaps. But you Canadians have been far too predictable in your bombardment. Always hitting the same places. The line of our defence has been very heavily hit – in fact the entrance to this room was only cleared again yesterday! So I think, if you tell me when the attack will come, I will remove you to the Swischen Stellung or the Stellung II lines. If you don't, I will leave you here and bar the door, and you can wait – as we all wait, every day – for the scream of shells and wonder whether you will be blown to pieces, or buried alive, by your countrymen. It's not much of a choice, but I don't have much to offer, I'm afraid. When is the attack?"

Greyeyes cleared his throat, curling a low growl into the sound. Goose and Skaptason coughed back. They understood.

"Do you have the time, Leutnant?" asked Greyeyes.

The leutnant's eyes widened, then glanced at his watch. He cursed in German and said: "Today...," and as his Luger pointed away from Greyeyes that was as far as he got.

Greyeyes was exhausted, hungry and cold. *I'm sorry leutnant*, he thought. *But we have to get home.* He reached down deep into the earth below to draw the power he needed to change, and it filled him with strength and speed. He grabbed the German's weapon arm and pushed hard, pinning it to his body and forcing him back.

The pistol fired, its muzzle flash punctuating the darkness. Then the deafening crack of rifle shots from the older soldier.

The younger soldier staggered and fell, yelling, into the trench. But Greyeyes was already changing, reaching for the leutnant's throat with his lupine maw. He hoped Skaptason, Goose and Balfour had not been hit.

He tore into the leutnant, fully wolf now, his shirt and trousers ripped and his puttees and boots falling loosely off his hind paws.

He wore the ancient form of the dire wolf, his shaggy smoke -grey coat proof against prehistoric cold, his limbs and neck thick and powerful, and his jaws best suited to crushing the bones of a mammoth or woolly rhino.

His teeth clamped around the high-collared neck of the

German leutnant and bit nearly clean through it.

The officer fell dead in the thick mud of the dugout doorway, pinning the bigger soldier on the left, who struggled to get his rifle into position to fire on Greyeyes point blank.

Greyeyes didn't give him the split second he needed, and the soldier died with his eyes wide in disbelief, his mouth agape. Before Greyeyes could turn to the younger soldier, he was shouldered aside by Goose, who finished him.

The four wolves stood atop the bodies of their former captors, Greyeyes thrusting his massive head out of the dugout to listen and smell for any others. Shouts called from past the next corner of the zigzag trench. The gunfire had alerted the others.

There was no time to lose. But they were free. Their wolf bodies sang with power – they would all be able to leap out of the German trench and soar over the barbed wire line before the Boche had a chance to light flares and mow them down. The craters that pocked No Man's Land with artificial valleys would give them cover until they had crossed it and could transform back into men – naked, shivering, and exhausted, but alive.

Greyeyes sprang out the doorway, a grey blur of fur and claws; Goose followed, and Skaptason herded Balfour out.

Balfour had taken the form of a brown-and-grey wolf. Once in the trench they all spent a few seconds to take his scent.

He shied, stumbling, still unfamiliar with the balance and coordination of his new body. The change had taken hold as soon as the leutnant had fired – brought on by the sudden, instinctive surge of adrenaline from fear of imminent death.

Greyeyes had hoped that much would work, and it had. But if Balfour couldn't figure out how to make his new body run and leap he'd die just the same. Greyeyes licked Balfour's muzzle in a cursory comforting manner, then gave a quick growl and yipped. He pointed his snout at the parapet of the trench, hoping Balfour would understand.

Goose surged up onto it and barked down at them, his ears flat and his tail low. All it would take was one flare and they'd be plain to see for the machine gunners, who after weeks of bombardment would be eager to shoot at anything that looked like a threat.

Four wolves, each the size of a bear, would be target enough.

Greyeyes snapped his teeth at Balfour's hindquarters, hoping to send him scurrying over the parapet after Goose. Skaptason kept guard at the north end of the trench, a low whine / growl warning them the Germans were on their way to investigate the gunfire. Still Balfour hesitated, shaking his lupine head in a parody of a man with a hangover.

Don't think about it, Greyeyes urged silently; *just go. Before they see us.* The first time changing was always hard, but they didn't have time to do this the proper way. *Grandmother, please forgive me,* he thought. *I couldn't leave him behind.*

Balfour licked his black lips as if trying to rid them of a bad taste. His fore-claws flexed and dug into the soft, sodden mud of the trench floor, and his back arched, forcing his head down. A strangled howl forced itself through his clenched teeth.

Shit, thought Greyeyes. *Goose had been right.*

In Quebec they still tell stories of the loups-garous.

Greyeyes was very careful about with whom he shared his gift. He'd been raised in the stories of his people, the Severn Ojibwe, and all the history of the Anishnaabeg.

His grandparents and parents had shown him how all people had a place in the world, and so did all the other creatures people share it with – wolf, beaver, eagle, turtle, and all the rest.

Sometimes, they shared their shapes with people, an ability carried down through the generations. But what a person's body did with that shape depended on what was in their mind. Greyeyes' grandmother had been the one to pass on the wolf's shape to him – but only after she'd been sure he knew the stories, and wouldn't fear it. So he could wear the wolf's true shape.

Greyeyes had gotten to know Goose and Naytowhow well enough to be sure how things would go when he decided to share it with them as well. Their peoples had their own stories and he'd listened to them.

In the front lines, you needed every advantage you could get, and sometimes a wolf's shape was better than a man's for reconnaissance. Skaptason he'd discounted at first – white people seemed to be afraid of animals they didn't pen up – but as the Icelander had shared stories of his ancestors, of Odin and his wise wolves, as well as a giant wolf that was no fool, Greyeyes had come to hope it might be different with him.

And it was.

But not with Balfour.

The wolf quivered, rasping and coughing, as its limbs elongated, its chest broadened, and its hind legs and paws shivered and shifted into human approximations but remained covered in fur. Balfour's head, however, stayed lupine, his forepaws not quite hands and still tipped with sharp, curved claws.

Goose leaped back down, biting Balfour's shaggy neck. Greyeyes darted at Balfour's hamstrings. They could not let him live. His mind was trying to force his body into what it thought a wolf was: a savage, rapacious monster. And anyone he bit would become the same.

Balfour spun on two legs, knocking Goose into Greyeyes and dislodging him. Then he charged south down the trench. Greyeyes howled to Skaptason and all three of them raced through the deep muck after Balfour.

Greyeyes no longer knew how much time they had left.

At zero hour, five-thirty a.m., the artillery would unleash a bombardment as it had every previous day since March 20th, to destroy the last of the German defences and keep their machine gunners and snipers in their dugouts.

But the rolling barrage would begin as well, proceeding slowly through German lines and much deeper this time, to pin the Huns down while the Canadian infantry marched to take Vimy Ridge.

What the French had been thrown back from, what the Germans considered unassailable, the Canadians meant to take in one day. And the first shells would fall right where Greyeyes and the rest of them were now.

Pistol fire erupted through the darkness and the sporadic

muzzle flash cast shadows of Balfour's monstrous form on the trench wall before they rounded the corner.

Greyeyes was the first to see Balfour tear a German soldier apart with his paw-like hands, and mingled with the odour of gunpowder and chewed-up mud he smelled fresh blood. Not just the soldier's, but the stink of Balfour's.

Balfour leaped over the falling corpse and onto the neck of the soldier behind him, who turned to flee. Greyeyes bounded high and sprawled onto Balfour's wide back, sinking his knifelike teeth into the scruff of his neck.

Only moments ago, this was how he had intended to carry his C.O. over the barbed wire, like a cub, if he couldn't jump himself; now he did it to tear him from his prey.

Balfour tried to shake him off, grasping with his long arms at the wolf on his back. Greyeyes' guts went cold when Balfour's hands found purchase on his upper forelimb and ear; this wasn't like fighting with another wolf. The loup-garou could reach farther. And no simple show of dominance would settle it. Balfour meant to kill him, too.

The German soldier staggered back, his overcoat in shreds and his neck and face bloody. He fired at them both and Greyeyes felt the bite of steel in his shoulder. Balfour made a scream-like howl and let go of him.

Goose bounded past them both and seized the German's pistol arm in his teeth. He crushed it with a single snap of his jaws, and then tore out the man's throat. They couldn't leave a single person Balfour attacked alive.

Balfour raked at Greyeyes with one of his hands, lurching off-balance as he attacked. Greyeyes, his left shoulder a sharp miasma of pain, couldn't evade him and caught the blow on his brows.

The loup-garou's claws left parallel slashes that burned across his face. But he reacted quickly enough to avoid losing an eye.

He snapped out blindly, going by scent, and his teeth took hold on Balfour's arm. He was tempted to clench his jaws and sever the hand, but that was not how wolves took down their prey. Instead, he bit and held, sinking his weight and pulling back with his hind legs.

Skaptason charged through the filth and harried Balfour's other flank. Balfour howled and kicked Skaptason in the muzzle. Greyeyes blinked through the blood running through the fine fur on his face and saw Goose dodge around, mouth open, ready to go for Balfour's throat while Greyeyes tugged him off-balance.

Then a burst of machine-gun fire from down the trench cut Goose in half.

Greyeyes let go of Balfour and Skaptason got behind the towering loup-garou. Balfour screamed, a ragged sound full of rage. He charged down the trench toward the unseen gunner. Greyeyes and Skaptason shared a low growl. *We can't let him scratch even one person.*

As they dashed after him, Greyeyes cocked his ears west. No sound yet other than the shouts from the German trench they were in. What time was it?

The staccato burst of automatic fire mixed with a monstrous howl before a sharp shriek cut it short.

Greyeyes and Skaptason caught up with Balfour, his fur thick with mud and blood, as he sank his teeth into a German rifleman. The machine gunner, his weapon mounted at a strong point along the parapet, lay in pieces strewn about the trench.

While Balfour's back was still to them, they darted in and hamstrung him. The monster fell with a panicked yelp. Then Greyeyes bit at his torso while Skaptason went for the throat. It was over in seconds.

The remaining German soldier crawled away in fits and gasps. Balfour's mouth had been on his wounds.

They killed him, as well.

After a moment to breathe and listen, Greyeyes barked. It was time to go. Skaptason picked up something from one of the fallen soldiers in his teeth and followed Greyeyes with a powerful leap over the parapet.

Shouts in German rang out from the trench they had just left. The two wolves kept low, moving slowly and using their dark fur to blend in against the cratered moonscape that spread between Vimy Ridge and the Canadian lines. If they were seen they could still be shot to pieces. Just like Goose. Greyeyes tried not to think of how much their 'escape' had already cost them.

They had nearly reached the barbed wire, Greyeyes' wounded foreleg aching, when the far-off thunder from the west began. Zero hour. The bombardment had begun.

Greyeyes barked to Skaptason. They had to get back, change into human form, and warn the platoons assigned to this section that the wire was still intact.

The infantry would already be starting their advance, now that the artillery had opened fire. And the rolling barrage, which had been harrying the German lines for short stretches for weeks, would be unleashed in full, pounding every square inch of the Stellung I, Swischen Stellung and Stellung II trenches, while the full strength of the Canadian forces advanced, before the Germans could prepare for their attack.

They'd rehearsed it endlessly. It would not be like the failed French assault. It would be trench warfare like no one had ever seen. And Greyeyes and Skaptason were right in the middle of it.

Without hesitating Greyeyes took a running start, bunched the massive muscles in his hind legs and flew over the barbed wire. He stumbled upon landing, his injury forcing his foreleg to give out.

He checked over his shoulder for Skaptason and stopped short. He was still on the other side of the wire.

He barked at him. *You fool! Can't you hear it? They've started!*

Skaptason spat out the thing in his mouth – it looked like a gun – and changed back into human form. His pale, naked skin stood out like a white flag on the battlefield. What the hell was he doing?

"They have to know!" he said hoarsely. "In case you don't make it." He picked up what he had dropped and brandished it: a flare gun.

The incoming whine of the shells grew closer. The howitzers.

"Artillery's FOOs will have to see this!" said Skaptason. "Run! You bastard. And give the Boche hell if you live." Then he stood right by the barbed wire and fired the flare straight up.

Greyeyes turned and bolted for the nearest path between craters, even as machine-gun fire erupted from German lines.

He ducked behind the lip of a crater nearly forty feet deep and sixty across, then turned to look. The machine gunners had tagged Skaptason, but he was changing back into a wolf and would heal. He was already preparing for the leap over the barbed wire when the sound of the shells seemed a deafening shriek and Greyeyes wished for a moment he had human hands to cover his ears. Then the light of the flare was obliterated in the shuddering roar of exploding earth and stone as the German line was hit.

No one had targeted Skaptason's flare yet, but he was still too close to the main barrage. Greyeyes's last sight of his friend was of his half-furred limbs being blown in all directions and his body disappearing in a spray of blood and dirt, bits of flesh and hair caught grotesquely in the barbed wire.

His keen ears still ringing from the deafening line of explosions, the pineapple reek of cordite in his nostrils, Greyeyes looked toward Canadian lines in the ashen predawn light and thought he saw an incoming shell. He fled the area, making it to the cover of another crater before a Fuze 106 landed on the barbed wire, vaporising it and opening the way for the Canadian troops heading for this section.

Canadian Lewis guns fired from behind their own lines overhead, adding to the din, a black-fly storm of steel raining down on the Stellung I.

Greyeyes knew he would have to revert to human form before being spotted by his fellow troops and shot out of fear or surprise. In the growing light of day he would be easily seen on the treeless waste. But he also knew the casualties General Currie had allowed for when planning the assault. Some of Greyeyes' fellows now marching towards him would soon no longer need their uniforms, kit, and weapons. He'd find one, say a prayer for him, then outfit himself and march back to pay Fritz another visit.

For his family, his battalion, and for the wolves of Vimy.

The Silk Angel

Christine Morgan

"Ready, kid?"

"Ready sir."

Captain Hollister grinned and clapped Augustus on the back, hard enough to stagger him in his boots. "All right, then. In you go!"

"Yes sir!" Augustus snapped a sharp salute.

He was hard-pressed to keep from grinning himself, and didn't begrudge in the least being addressed as 'kid.' True, most of the others weren't *that* much older than him, but in wartime the years between practically-sixteen and seventeen-through-nineteen could be ages.

Hard-won experience made men of boys. It gave them valour and glory, the pride to hold their heads high, having lain their lives on the line. For King and Country.

How any red-blooded chap could expect to show his face back home if he hadn't done his part...

Well, it would not be said of Augustus Arthur Michael Pearce.

With eager speed and nimble grace, he scrambled into the sturdy wicker basket. The addition of his slight weight – he was a lean, wiry youth – hardly made it sway at its moorings. Not when he'd be sharing the cramped quarters with the captain as well as the bulky equipment. Camera, radio, binoculars, the usual kit and canteen, maps and charts, everything they'd need.

Overhead, the balloon bobbed in the breeze, a great oblong cloth sausage-casing stuffed with hydrogen gas. A steel cable tethered it to a winch. The rest of the crew stood ready to loosen it up, and reel it back in at the end of the observation session.

Augustus affixed the safety lines to his waist-harness and crowded himself into the corner to make room for Captain Hollister to swing a leg in.

"Tally-ho," the captain said, buckling his own. "The blue skies await Launch us aloft, boys!"

The blue skies, Augustus decided not to point out, were rather less than exactly blue. They were, in fact, overcast with clouds, against which the various thin spirals of smoke from the battlefields blended into a grey haze. But it was a small matter, meaningless in the otherwise grander excitement of his first official mission.

That he had lucked into *this*…

Not to say that he'd protest doing anything else, to be sure. Artillery, the front, even the trenches if need be. Whatever he could do. However he could best serve.

He gripped the basket's edge, eyes wide, the grin escaping. The winch creaked, the cable unspooled, and up they went with a giddy sensation of lift-and-rise. His stomach seemed to do a not-unpleasant flip as the ground dropped away.

The perspective … their own guardian anti-aircraft guns … tents and lorries, men scurrying about in diminishing size … the broadening expanse of countryside … the landscape a patchwork of farms and pastures … to one side, the glimmering ribbon of a river curling toward the roofs of a quaint little village … to the other, the churned and muddy smear of No Man's Land, pocked with foxholes, twisted with snarls of barbed wire … beyond that…

Beyond that, the enemy.

Everything looked so small, so far-away and fragile.

"Four thousand feet, kid, how do you like it?" Captain Hollister asked.

A delighted laugh was the best reply Augustus could give, staring agog in thrilled wonder at the panorama. Hollister laughed as well. He delivered another hearty back-clap that could have toppled the youth out of the basket if he hadn't been braced and holding on.

The grey clouds remained as distant as ever. Between

clouds and land, planes swooped. Their own fighter aircraft patrolled nearby, in case any of the German pilots decided to take a chance at joining the roster of aces known as 'balloon busters.'

"Keep a particular eye out for that black-winged bastard," the captain added, a grimmer note entering his voice.

That 'black-winged bastard', as Augustus and everyone else in their regiment knew, was Oskar Luffengraf, who flew the *Sturmvogel* and had been responsible for the fiery, crashing, bullet-riddled deaths of far too many of their fellow balloonists.

"Yes sir."

They went to work spotting for troop movements and artillery emplacements, relaying their findings to the lads below. It had to be quick work, because nothing got Fritz stirred into action like the sight of a balloon heading on high to have a looksie at what they were up to over there.

Soon enough, the Germans made their move. Engines snarled as they came into view, dark silhouettes swarming against the grey. A squadron rose to meet them. Guns chattered and chuddered. Their propellers made circular, whirring blurs at their noses.

Augustus had seen aerial dogfights before, but always from *terra firma*. Never from up here, in their very midst as it were! Never as they wheeled and dived ... as clusters of bullet-holes popped open like shocked eyes ... as flames seethed and smoke spewed ... as a plane corkscrewed down in a terrible dying spiral ... as a man jerked, arms flailing, blood bursting from his shoulder in a spray...

He'd seen blood before, too. He'd seen men who'd been shot, and shelled, and shrapnel-torn. He'd seen men with limbs blown off by land mines. He'd seen men with their skin blistered, melting, sloughing off from exposure to lethal poison gas. He'd seen men kill and men die.

Now, up here, it occurred to him – as if for the first time, though he knew it wasn't – that he might have to kill. That he could be killed. That he could die. Those pilots, those gunners and navigators, they were the cream of the crop, the best of the best, flying expensive planes that were the very pinnacle of modern warfare … and they were dying.

While he was a kid hanging under a balloon! A balloon! A bag of hydrogen, a bag that could be ruptured and explode into a fireball, plummeting thousands of feet to collapse in a blazing ruin.

A kid armed with a pocketknife, and a service revolver he'd never once fired at anything more dangerous than a big brown battlefield rat.

A kid who'd fibbed about his birth-date in order to enlist. Not because it would impress the girls – not just – and not just because it sounded so much more a grand adventure than sitting in school – not just – but because … patriotism, pride, King and Country!

His fingers clenched white-knuckled on the edge of the basket, the wicker pressing ridges into his palms.

"Get a hold of yourself, Artie," he said in an under-the-breath mutter, using the pet-name bestowed by a favorite cousin without even thinking. He dug deep and found the Pearce nerve, the Pearce backbone, the Pearce discipline of body and mind.

Captain Hollister, with steely aplomb, kept peering through his binoculars while shouting his observations into the phone. He paid no attention to the chattering gunfire, the soaring, banking planes, and the dull thunder of the anti-aircraft artillery.

"Sir!" Augustus cried. "The black-winged bastard, sir! The *Sturmvogel!*"

He pointed at the aircraft, painted black with white trim and jagged yellow stripes, each wing and the tail emblazoned with the image of a bird of prey, lightning bolts clutched sparking in its talons.

At that, the captain did turn. A snarl curled his lip. Though Augustus couldn't hear him over the din, he rather suspected he could guess the following utterance.

The *Sturmvogel's* guns flashed and spat, peppering their signature along the side of an olive-green biplane with white and red markings. Then a steel tube mounted on the German plane's outboard strut belched forth a rocket. It missed, veering a smoking trail past the balloon.

For one heart-stopping moment of clarity, Augustus saw the famed and hated Luffengraf, saw his square jaw and the tight line of his mouth, and the distinctive dueling scar that sliced across one cheekbone. He could not discern Luffengraf's eyes through the goggles but a chill prickled the nape of his neck and he knew their gazes, for that split-second, met.

And what, he wondered, did the flying ace see? A boy, just a kid, just a child? A boy as blond and blue-eyed as any German himself, as Luffengraf's own younger brother might be? Or a Tommy, the enemy, hated and despised? One more faceless, nameless soldier? One more tally for his reaper's total, as he added another balloon to his record?

Luffengraf pulled the *Sturmvogel* into a steep climb. It roared, engines screaming, up and out of Augustus' sight.

"Take the charts!" Captain Hollister thrust the leather-bound and string-tied folio into his arms. "Tight to your chest!"

The men below at the winch were reeling them in, but it was much slower going, the balloon fighting the cable's insistent pull. Another German plane buzzed them, this one sporting the emblem of a war-axe wreathed in fire.

"Go," the captain's back-slap was, this time, a deliberate shove. "Jump for it, kid!"

Augustus half-sprang, half-tumbled out of the basket. Sheer terror seized him, an instant of panic, as he fell into open space, still at least two thousand feet up. He felt a hitch at his harness where he'd affixed the shroud lines and briefly prayed that he had indeed affixed them correctly.

He wanted to squeeze his eyes shut but didn't dare. Instead, he looked frantically up at the canvas bag on the side of the basket, the bag to which the shroud lines led. His descent tugged the bag open. A wadded bundle dropped after him.

Then, out of nowhere, the *Sturmvogel* returned in a barrage of bullets. Wicker flew in shredded confetti. Sparks pinged from the equipment. Blood flew into the air again as Captain Hollister was driven backward in the disintegrating basket. The steel tube mounted on the plane's other wing coughed smoke.

The parachute unfolded with a pale, silken billow. As it

blossomed out into a graceful dome, it obscured the rest of the scene above him from Augustus' view. But he didn't need to see to know that, this time, the incendiary rocket did not miss its mark.

*

Paul Ellory stood on a catwalk outside the manager's office, overlooking the main work-floor. He paused at the rail to rest, leaning on his cane. Cold, damp weather such as this pained his leg, badly broken in childhood and never properly healed.

It had kept him from the army. His mother always said that should make him thankful, as if a constant ache and stiff, clumsy gait were anything to be thankful for. Did it stop the pitying looks? Did it stop the sneering of the ladies of the White Feather brigade? As if he'd done it on purpose, perhaps. As if he'd been so prescient as to shatter his bones at the age of seven to avoid a war the likes of which no one – no one! – could possibly have foreseen?

He frowned, brows drawing together. Sarah, seeing this expression, evidently mistook it for a sign of disapproval, and scowled herself.

"I've done the best I could," she said. "I thought you'd be pleased."

Brushing the bitter dregs of memory away, he turned to her and smoothed the frown into a smile. "I am, my dear. My mind wandered a moment. No. I am quite pleased. Quite. You've done very well."

Mollified, she likewise smoothed away the scowl and favored him with a smile of her own. He'd only just returned from months in London and abroad, entrusting the running and management of the factory to his capable wife.

Below them on the work-floor, under the harsh but yellowish glare of suspended lights, rows of large industrial sewing machines buzzed and droned like a busy hive. Women in plain dresses, their hair bound under kerchiefs or caps, fed piece after piece of pattern-cut cloth through them. The jabbing needles moved too fast for the eye to behold, stitching strong double-seams.

"And they're no trouble?" Paul asked. "The workers?"

Sarah shook her head. "No trouble at all. They're glad for the work. They have children at home, a lot of mouths to feed on scarce income. They need the money. As much as that, they're glad to have something to do, some way to feel useful and contribute to the cause."

There was, these days, a shortage of able-bodied grown men across much of England. Paul had only seen a handful of beardless youths and bearded elders in New Fairchurch, and a scattering of the unfit and the idiotic and mad. The rest had enlisted to fight the dirty Hun. They left behind their wives and sisters, daughters and mothers, households needing upkeep and families looking after.

"I feed them, as well," Sarah added. She lifted her chin at him. "They're here long shifts, long hours. A hot lunch is the least we can do. Nothing fancy, mind ... soups and stews, brown bread, tea."

"Hmm." Paul rubbed his thumb over the brass-knobbed handle of his cane.

Times were hard. There were shortages, rationing. Even in the great houses and on the grand estates, he had heard, belts and budgets alike were being tightened by necessity.

He watched as younger girls trundled in laden trolleys of raw materials at one end of the long room, and other girls trundled out laden trolleys of finished product at the other. He watched the women at the sewing machines replace huge thread bobbins or bent needles with barely a disruption in their routine. They made little conversation, which would have been difficult above the steady ratchet and hum.

Later, he supposed, their weariness would show. For now they seemed tireless, dedicated, eternal.

Before the war, the Ellorys had been in the business of household linens mass-manufacture. Now, the factory made parachutes. If Paul Ellory's anticipation proved true, increasing demand would soon put New Fairchurch on the map. It might also make him a modest fortune.

"The Germans," he told Sarah, "plan to begin issuing parachutes to their pilots as well as their balloonists. It's only a matter of time before we follow suit."

"Oh, have they finally seen the value of more young men's lives?" asked his wife, with a touch of the acidic.

They had no children of their own, he and Sarah. He wondered if he should be thankful for that, just as his mother told him he should be thankful for his leg. If he'd had sons, would he want them sent off to France and Belgium? To the battlefields? To the trenches?

"What was the previous argument?" she went on. "That, if a pilot had a parachute, he'd be more likely to bail out at the first bit of damage?"

Paul nodded. "Abandon his plane and let it crash, rather than try to bring it down in repairable condition. That was their reasoning, yes."

"Their reasoning." Sarah scoffed. "Reasonable enough reasoning on the part of the pilot, if you ask me."

"Whereas, with no parachute, he'd have little other choice than to stay put and do his best ... and men, they believed, were both cheaper and easier to replace than expensive aircraft."

"It took them how long, and how many dead, to realise the contrary?"

"I still don't know if they've quite realised the contrary," he admitted, a wry tuck to the corner of his mouth, "but they are beginning to realise any number of planes do no good on the ground with no pilots to fly them."

One concern, Paul knew, was fitting the bulkiness of a parachute into a cockpit. It was easier with the balloonists; the bags were slung on the sides of the baskets, and all the observers had to do was clip their belt-harnesses to the lines.

If they had to jump, the falling weight of their bodies would yank the bundled silk folds out of the bag as they went. Some kind of accommodation would have to be made. Backpacks fitted with pull-cords had been suggested, an idea that seemed to have some potential.

Sarah moved to the end of the catwalk and clanged a loud bell. It cut through the constant din, which dwindled as women stepped back from the sewing machines and switched them off.

"Ten minutes, girls," she called.

A slight babble of conversation arose. The workers stretched, craning their necks, twisting their backs. Many headed to a side door, which let out onto a brick courtyard where they could smoke. Others made for the lavatories, or rubbed liniment into joints and medicinal cream into chapped and chafed skin.

"Who is that?" asked Paul, indicating a hitherto-unnoticed figure bent over a well-lit worktable in the far corner. Even from here, he saw that the woman was very elderly, frail and almost gaunt.

Sarah raised her chin at him again, in that manner she had when she'd made some decision or taken some action to which she worried he might object. It never stopped her from making said decisions or taking said actions, of course…

"Her name is Marlene Montgomery," she said. "She lives over in Little Kirkby, you know, the old village up Kirkallen Lane."

"And what's she doing here? She must be seventy if she's a day."

"She's working."

"Working," Paul repeated.

"She turned up here one day," Sarah said. "She said she wanted to help, to do her part for our brave boys. She told me she didn't think as how she could run one of these big newfangled machines, but her up-close vision was sharp as ever and she was still a deft hand with a needle."

"So you hired her?"

"Yes, I hired her. I felt sorry for her, a widow, childless and alone. What else could I do? Turn her away?"

"Well, but can't the local vicar…"

"Who's busy with hospital efforts," Sarah interrupted. "And she doesn't want charity, Paul. She wants to work, to earn her keep. So, yes, I hired her."

"But hired her to do what, exactly?"

"To be our final inspector." She gave another incremental lift of the chin. "Marlene checks the finished parachutes for missed or bungled stitches. If she finds any, she snips them and sets them right."

"Hmm." Paul again rubbed his thumb over the brass knob of his cane.

"Her cottage – though, to be fair and I've seen it, it's really more of a shack – is miles from here. She walks it every working day, rain or shine, with never a word of complaint. At the end of her shift, she walks back. All for meager wages and a hot lunch … which may well be the only decent meal she sees."

"Good Lord, Sarah. This won't do. This just won't do at all." He started for the stairs.

"Paul, what are you doing?" She rushed after him.

Without answering, he made his way down and crossed the much quieter and emptier work-floor in his uneven stiff-legged gait. He saw the elderly woman clearly now, saw that he'd underestimated her age if anything. Eighty, eighty at least. A tattered shawl wrapped her bony shoulders but could not conceal the dowager's hump of her back. Wisps of cobweb-fine, cobweb-white hair trailed from beneath the edges of a kerchief so faded it seemed to have no colour at all. Her wrists, poking from frayed cuffs, looked like spindly bundles of twigs wrapped in wrinkled tissue paper.

Her hands, he noticed, were not the gnarled and bunched claws he'd expected. They were of course as thin and frail as the rest of her, but her fingers were straight and limber, and they moved with nary a tremor as they drew a tiny silver needle through parachute silk.

Sarah caught at his sleeve. "Paul," she said, imploringly.

At her voice, the woman glanced up from her sewing. She must have been a fair beauty once; the ghosts of it lingered in the contours of her face. Her eyes were not clouded, but remarkably clear, and of a deep, warm brown.

"Oh, Sarah," she said. "Why this must be Mr. Ellory."

"Mrs. Montgomery." Paul inclined his head. "My wife's been telling me about the work you've been doing."

"It's my privilege and pleasure, Mr. Ellory."

Sarah said nothing, but her gaze pleaded.

"They may be silly, I know," the elderly woman went on. "Still, they are meant well, and it does my heart good to hope that they might bring those dear boys at least some luck."

He had no idea what she meant, some non-sequitur of her dotage perhaps. "We'll likely be taking on considerably more business in the near future," he said. "I want to be sure the factory weathers these coming cold winter months well. I'd hate to have everyone arrive in the morning only to find a water pipe had frozen and burst, or some such other calamity."

"Goodness, that would be dreadful, yes!" Marlene agreed.

"To that end, Sarah and I were discussing finding someone to stay on of nights, to sleep here and keep an eye on things."

From the corner of his eye, he saw Sarah's anxious look melt into one of understanding and affection.

"It wouldn't be much, I'm afraid," Paul continued. "Just a cot in one of the storerooms. But, it would be, I daresay, comfortable enough, and it would include a small pay rise. Might you be interested?"

*

"…no apparent physical injuries…"

"…promise not to disturb or upset him; I only want to…"

"…possible concussion, or signs of shell-shock…"

They whispered at the foot of his bed so as not to wake him, but he already was awake. Hadn't been sleeping. Only resting, and only that under grudging duress as per doctor's orders. He felt fine. This was ridiculous.

"…won't take much time. You'll hardly know I'm here."

"Well…"

"Pretty please?"

"I … I do have other patients to check on. You can have a few minutes."

"Thank you. Nurse Renard, was it? Thank you so much, Nurse Renard."

"…Collette."

"Collette."

The soft squeak of her shoes indicated her moving away, so Emmerson opened his eyes. The uniformed young man still standing at the foot of his bed was about his own age, seventeen, maybe eighteen. He sported a lieutenant's insignia and an RFC balloonist's badge, thick blond hair, and the kind of dimpled smile that made girls giddy.

Emmerson sat up, hiking himself higher on the pillow. "Sir?"

The lieutenant shushed him and waved at him to take it easy, darting a glance after the departing nurse. She peeked back once over her shoulder, an auburn lock that had escaped from her pinned white cap curling winsomely against a rosy cheek ... a cheek which went rosier as she averted her gaze and went out.

They both, it must be said, couldn't help watching and enjoying in silence the roll of her hips. Then the lieutenant cleared his throat, turning again to Emmerson.

"Private Whitte? Emmerson Whitte?"

"Yes sir."

"Lieutenant Augustus Pearce." He hitched a chair around to sit backwards on it at the bedside. "Don't stir yourself, unless you want to earn us both a scolding." The smile became a grin. "Not, in her case that I think I'd mind..."

"No sir, me neither, sir."

"They're treating you all right, then, I take it?"

"Treating me like an invalid, if that's what you mean, sir."

"After that crash, I shouldn't wonder. They can't believe you came away without a scratch. At the very least, they suppose your brains must have been given a rattle."

"That, or the shell-shock," Emmerson said. "But I haven't, sir, I swear. Not a bit. No nightmares, no shakes, no clammy sweats, none of it."

"You do remember what happened, though?"

"Oh, yes sir," he gulped. "Never forget it. Might wish I could."

"Some men would turn to hard drink for that very reason." Pearce looked around the hospital ward, rows of metal-framed beds. A few were crisply-made, empty and awaiting future occupants. Most were already taken. "One of many reasons a lot of us will have, no doubt."

"Yes sir. I mean to say, no sir, I don't plan to turn to drink."

"Can you tell me about it? Your last flight?"

"There isn't that much to tell. We spotted a squadron of German planes, and moved to engage. The usual firefight, at first. Our bird took a peppering to the tail. Didn't damage the rudder. Billy – the pilot, Second Lieutenant Darby – laughed and shouted back to me something about how the Krauts were lucky to hit the piss-pot twice out of three, not to worry."

The lieutenant's sigh said that he'd heard similar ironic statements before. "His last words, I presume."

"Next I knew, one of them strafed us crosswise from above," Emmerson said, suppressing a shudder at the memory. "Cut right across Billy's cockpit. I saw the leather – his jacket, you know, and his cap – saw it jump and ... and sort of puff ... where the bullets hit. Then the blood. Splashing everywhere. Coating his wind-screen. Splattering my face, my goggles."

"If you'd rather not..."

"No sir, I do. I owe it to Billy. He'd want someone to ... to recount it. Especially what with there, not being ... well ... much left of him to send home, you see."

Pearce patted his arm. "Go on, then."

"He fell forward, against the controls. It was obvious he was dead. Obvious, slumped like that, his brains leaking down the side of his head. Didn't stop me yelling for him, yelling his name. I wiped my lenses and only smeared his blood. The plane nosed down, went into a dive, a spiral. Those Krauts who couldn't hit a piss-pot, they let us have it again, half shearing off one of our wings. Something had caught fire, I'm not sure what. Smoke everywhere, black and gritty, oily. I couldn't see worth a damn. Couldn't hear anything but the engines, the guns. I knew I was buggered – pardon me, Lieutenant..."

"Under the circumstances, what's a little strong language?" A pitcher and glass were on the side table; Pearce poured him some water and didn't do him the chagrin of holding it for him while he drank. "So, you bailed out?"

"I was sure I was dead anyway, that even if I got out of the plane before it struck and exploded, I'd get shot by the German aces, or chopped to mincemeat by a propeller. Or the 'chute wouldn't deploy, or it'd get holed or catch fire, or I'd be too low, or it'd slam me into a tree ... and, hell, sir, even if I made it to the ground in one piece, we were behind enemy lines by then. But some part of me wasn't ready to give up. So I unbuckled and jumped."

"And then what?"

Emmerson took another sip of the water; his throat had gone dust-dry. "Soon as I thought I was clear – or hoped I was; I couldn't tell – I pulled the cord like they told us. Saw other planes, ours and theirs. Saw one cartwheel into a barn and burst into flames, and the whole damn barn went up like tinder. The air all around me seemed full of smoke and noise. I may have been screaming."

"Wouldn't blame you in the least."

"Then … I don't really know … they say I might've blacked out … but…"

"But, next you knew, you were safe and unscathed."

"Yeah. I mean, yes sir."

"Not behind enemy lines after all."

"No sir. All I can guess is that a good breeze must have caught the 'chute, carried me back over."

The lieutenant bent down, opened a duffel, and gathered out a bunch of cloth. Silk. Once white, now charred and sooty. "Know what this is, Private Whitte?"

"A parachute … not *my* parachute?"

"Your parachute. With more holes in it than a Swiss cheese, and more burnt than a camp cook's first try at toast."

"Sorry, sir, but that's impossible. It's got to be a mistake. There's no way I could have…"

"Survived? Made it down without a mark? Not even so much as a bump or a bruise?"

"Well … yeah. Yes sir."

"Let *me* tell *you* a little story, now, Private. Two years ago, on my very first balloon observer mission, we got shot down. My captain ordered me over the side with the charts. The guns shredded the basket, and him with it. The balloon exploded and dropped out of the sky. I was surrounded by falling, flaming debris. The wreckage was practically on top of me and I was headed straight for a barbed-wire entanglement that looked as wide as a cricket pitch. Yet, somehow, Whitte, I landed in a clear spot, the only clear spot for yards around. Without a scratch. Without even a turned ankle."

Emmerson whistled, low, in appreciation. "Our luck must have been in for both of us."

"Maybe," Pearce drew the cloth through his hands, studying it intently. "I've spoken to a lot of other jumpers since then. Those who've been hurt and those who haven't, and some whose luck seems as incredible as our own. When possible, I've examined whatever was left of their 'chutes."

He held a section of the parachute taut and extended it toward Emmerson. A double-seam ran along it, joining two panels together, reinforced by another seam like a hem along the edge.

"I found something strange," the lieutenant continued. "Of all those 'chutes I examined, the ones still partly intact, the ones involved in those incredible lucky jumps had something in common, that none of the other ones did. Do you see it?"

Stitched into the silk, in a fine white thread nearly invisible but for a faint silvery sheen, was a design no bigger than a shilling. The shape of it made Emmerson think of church, and Christmas ... the outline of a robed figure ... suggestion of tiny hands pressed together in an attitude of prayer ... head crowned by a halo ... and wings.

"It looks like an angel," Emmerson said.

"It looks like an angel," Pearce agreed. "And I want to know what it means."

*

Snow fell in New Fairchurch, softly blanketing the rooftops and fence-posts, the yards and lanes and gardens. Frost patterned the windowpanes. Icicles dripped from eaves and tree-branches.

The factory stood silent. Its work-floor was a hollow, echoing vacancy. The large industrial sewing machines were long since sold off and shipped out. A lone, stray thread-bobbin had rolled into a corner and been forgotten.

Sarah Ellory exhaled a sigh into the cold, damp air. Her breath plumed in a pale billow, not unlike a blossoming dome of silk.

Paul had been partly correct. During the last year of the Great War, the demand for parachutes had indeed increased dramatically. Their fortunes had done likewise.

But, even after Armistice, the world was forever changed. Inflation raged. The recession dug its own trenches.

The soldiers returned – those who did return – shaken by their ordeals, by their injuries and suffering. They returned scarred as much in mind as body, if not more. They returned unprepared for a nation of women who'd grown strong in their independence, many more interested in jobs and the vote than in husbands ... though, in its way that was just as well, since there were so few eligible men available ... and even fewer jobs left for those men.

Influenza swept across the country, carrying her Paul away on its plague-tide. She couldn't keep the failing business afloat on her own; she had to close the factory, and give up the house, and move into the rooms above a little dress shop she'd been able to open with the last of their savings.

She made do. What else was there for it? She made do.

After another long, nostalgic look around, she sighed again, adjusted her scarf, and stepped out into the snowy street. Head bent to keep the whirling white flakes from her face; she walked up the hill toward the church.

At the gate, the low and respectful murmur of voices made her pause. She raised her head and caught her breath.

"They came," Sarah Ellory said to herself, blinking tears from her lashes. "Oh, they all came."

The churchyard was filled with people. Townsfolk, yes, friends and neighbors, but more. So many more. Several had wives at their sides, some with small children with them, or babes in arms.

"Mrs. Ellory," Captain Augustus Pearce said, touching his hat-brim to Sarah. He held the gloved hand of a pretty redhead tucked into the crook of his elbow. "My fiancée, Miss Renard."

He had been the one, the one who'd visited Sarah after the war with his enquiries about the parachutes. He'd traced them by manufacture, traced them to her factory. The parachutes of which perhaps one in six had gone out with something extra than what had been ordered.

Marlene Montgomery's work.

Marlene's deft touch with the needle.

Marlene's way of passing the time, between inspecting the seams on the finished product. Tiny angels embroidered into the silk.

What was it the old woman had said? Silly, but she'd meant well, and it did her heart good to hope they might bring those dear boys at least some luck.

According to Captain Pearce, they most certainly had.

Some luck? Miraculous luck.

They filled the churchyard. Young men. Soldiers. Pilots and navigators, balloonists, gunners, airmen. Every one of these men had leaped to safety, against sometimes staggering or impossible odds, carried by parachutes marked with Marlene's needlework.

Once they found out what they each had in common – again, Captain Pearce's doing – they'd have nothing for it but to express their thanks.

They'd wanted to see her, meet her. The months following the war had seen a steady stream of them visiting. They'd brought gifts, sent letters and parcels, arranged to have regular groceries delivered. They'd fixed up her decrepit shack into a proper and cozy cottage.

The elderly, childless widow had become an honorary grandmother to more than three dozen of England's best and bravest young men. She'd been invited to their homes for holiday dinners. She'd been to their weddings.

And now they had come for her funeral, to say a final farewell to their guardian angel.

Dig

Daniel I. Russell

"You have got through the difficult business, now you *dig, dig, dig,* until you are safe."

General Sir Ian Hamilton
British commander-in-chief, Gallipoli.

*

Five walked under the unrelenting Turkish sun, brows slicked and uniforms clinging to soaked skin. Two, Thomas and his brother, hadn't anticipated the heat to be so overbearing, yet marching through scrub from Ari Burnu, the Australian summer lingered like a sweet dream.

The squad trudged on, aiming for a far ridge. With each step came the sickening anticipation of a silent bullet. The ridges to the west were full of snipers. Such folly to undertake this mission in the middle of the day.

Hot, tired, and worst of all exposed, Thomas hoped his luck, which had safely seen him and Henry through the fight at the Suez Canal and landing at Ari Burnu, would hold true.

"Do you remember," he asked, trying to lighten the mood, "that trip when we were young 'uns, up into the hills east of Adelaide?"

Henry, the taller and stockier of the two, yanked off his slouch hat and wiped the sweat from his forehead. "Yes, I do. A long morning hiking up those damn hills. Thought I was havin' a heart attack at twelve."

"We stole some bread and jam from Mum and some of her tea. We also took Dad's camera! Remember that? What a day. Swimming in the cool streams and boiling the billy to sip tea and eat sandwiches on the grass. We'll have to do that again ... you know ... when we get back."

Henry replaced his hat, adjusted his pack and scanned the horizon to their right flank.

"If we *do* get back," said Henry. "When we enlisted, it was to see the world, not the peasant villages of Egypt and some godforsaken Turkish beach! I want to see England and France and push on into Germany. Our nation needs to be on the map, little brother, there when we put a bullet through the Kaiser."

Thomas sighed and stared at his boots as they pounded the hard, dry soil. He hadn't intended to spark another passionate rant from Henry. He'd had enough of those since August when war had been declared.

It had been an adventure. The fighting would probably be over by the time the inexperienced Australian and New Zealand troops reached the front lines. The war would be the only way most of these enthusiastic young men could escape their quiet lives working farms or laying roads.

Training in the Egyptian deserts had been tough going, but enjoyable with the new friends and camaraderie. Thomas' first taste of combat had been at the camp on the banks of the Suez Canal, where Turkish troops had attacked from across the water. The sides exchanged fire until British navy ships shelled Johnny Turk into pieces.

Before then, and with his training taking over, Thomas had taken a shot at a Turkish soldier and watched the man tumble and lie still. He still thought of the fallen soldier every night before blissful sleep washed the image away. None of this compared to the landing at Ari Burnu: running past the dead, waiting for that final bullet or piece of shrapnel. They'd dug in for days in an awful stalemate; one that the men expected might last for weeks.

"Can't you shut up?" spat Briggs. The cockney was a recent addition to the Battalion, and while he man had the wiles of a fox, he was a scoundrel at the best of times. "Your lot got us into this mess in the first place! You want the Turks to hear you yapping about the god ol' days?"

The previous day a squad of Australian soldiers, exhausted and dehydrated, had wandered over the ridge, dazed and confused. Their safe return gave Major Loach confidence that the right front was sparse of enemy, and that a particular ridge the major had been eying for some time might be within the Allies' grasp.

Furthermore, an abandoned Turkish trench that the crazed Aussies had rambled about, would be of use to house a greater number of troops as a go between. Loach had mustered a small band of scouts to find the trench and dig until nightfall, allowing space for reinforcements that would arrive in due course.

Henry and Thomas, the home-grown Australians and so diggers by decree, were selected for the party in addition to the more seasoned Briggs and a Frenchman: Durand. Leadership was handed to First Class Private Cecil Roberts, a no nonsense fellow from New Zealand, and so another soldier who by national reputation knew how to use a spade.

Their leader slowed his pace and unhooked a pair of binoculars from his pack.

"There we are boys," he said. "Turkish trench, two hundred metres ahead. Hope the gibberish from those Aussies was right and that it's abandoned."

"Would have taken shots at us by now, sir," said Briggs. "Five idiots like us walking through open terrain in the middle of the bleedin' day."

"Right you are, Briggs, but still, I don't like the look of the ridge to the right. We've been fortunate thus far, but a soldier must rely on his instinct and not lady luck. I want rifles ready. Eyes open, gentlemen. Two hundred metres and we have cover for the rest of the day."

Durand wiped the sweat from his narrow face and looked down at the floor.

"Someone's been through here," he said and pointed to a shiny coin half buried in the ground. He bent to pick it up. "I used to have a lucky coin when I was a boy..."

A small plume of dust shot from the earth beside his hand, accompanied by the whine of a bullet. Durand jumped back. A second bullet ploughed through his skull, ripping out his left eye and cheek and shattering his jaw bone. Half of his face sprayed out in a red mist. The Frenchman fell back, his body thrown into spasms and boot heels scraping the hard ground.

The men bolted for the relative safety of the trench.

Thomas' throat burned after a morning marching across the rough terrain, and his thigh muscles quivered and tensed with each furious step. He wanted to ditch his pack, but training had taught him better. He concentrated on the back of his brother who ran in front.

Bullets whistled and pounded the scrub.

Ahead, Roberts reached the trench and jumped over the edge, vanishing into the ground. Briggs arrived, quickly followed by Henry.

Thomas pushed harder, feeling every sniper's sights on his back and head. He leapt. The edge of the trench passed beneath him and he fell the six or so feet to the unforgiving ground. The pain and jolt of his landing barely registered as his pack was unstrapped and he found a position within the dugout, rifle at the ready.

*

"Okay, chaps," said Roberts. "I think the danger's passed. Perhaps they're wondering if we're worth bothering about now. Johnny Turk would have to leave his good position and get down and dirty with us, a foolish manoeuvre, but one we must be ready for. In the meantime, let's see what we have here and get to widening this crack in the ground before Loach sends his reinforcements."

Henry and Briggs grumbled their agreement and set to work.

Thomas slumped against the wall of the trench and propped his rifle beside him.

"Bloody hell," he stated. "Durand."

"Forget Durand," said Briggs. "It could have been any one of us, so I for one am glad it was him. All for a coin..."

The trench was short, perhaps only twenty feet end to end with only a tent for deeper cover.

"All we know is what those Australians told us," said their leader. "What little sense it made. They found this abandoned enemy trench and took shelter here over night. Williams..."

Both brothers looked up.

"Williams senior," said Roberts, nodding to Henry. "Check in the tent."

"Sir," Henry ventured inside and after a moment stepped back out into the sun. "Not much. Some provisions left behind, more bully beef and biscuits I'm afraid, and a standard issue pistol."

"Then I'm glad all of you had the sense to keep hold of your packs. Going to be a hard day's yakka, boys. We need this trench big enough to hold at least another twenty men."

Briggs sniggered.

"Something funny, Private?" said Roberts.

The cockney unfastened his canteen from his pack and took a sip. "Just you Aussies, mate. Dig dig dig! All you bloody do."

"And those are our orders, Briggs, so when you're done relaxing, pick up a spade and get to it. We're a man down and we'll be losing daylight in around five hours. We don't have the time to complain. If Loach's men arrive and this trench isn't fit to hold them, you'll wish it was your head that took that bullet and not Durand's." Roberts unhooked his spade from his pack and tossed it to Briggs.

"You heard the man," said Henry, a grin splitting his wide face. "Dig."

*

The going became a little easier after their spades had punctured through the sun-baked earth to reveal the softer clay beneath. The Williams brothers attacked the job with gusto, lengthening the trench by several feet over a few hours. At the opposite end, Briggs was not so enthusiastic. Only the constant supervision of Roberts, who too set to work with the energy of a man many years his junior, maintained the Brit's commitment.

"Hello," said Henry. "What's this then?" He brought the latest shovel load of dirt closer to his face.

Thomas glanced at the small mound of soil and seeing the glint of gold within, reasoned his brother had simply unearthed a spent casing and returned to the dig.

"Look, Thomas. I think I've got something here." Henry lowered his shovel and shoved his fingers into the dirt, pulling out the gold object. Wiping the soil from its surface he held up the round disc between thumb and forefinger.

"Not another *lucky* coin, is it?" said Thomas.

"What do you know … it's a pocket watch."

"Give it here," said Thomas, happy to use the find for a quick break. His brother handed him the watch.

An ornate design was engraved on the surface of the cover, which looked relatively new. He held it up to his ear. "Bugger me! It's still ticking."

"Rubbish!" said Henry. "I just dug it out the bloody ground! Who knows how long it's been there."

Thomas handed it back. "I'm telling you, its wound and ticking."

"What's all this?" called Briggs, using any distraction to escape the dig. "You find summat?"

"A watch," said Henry. "Right here in the dirt! Take a look."

He tossed the piece down the trench. Briggs effortlessly caught it.

"Don't give it to him," Thomas whispered to his brother. "He's a tealeaf! You'll never see it again."

"Calm down. There's only the four of us here. Once he's had a look I'll put it in my pack. Handy thing to find, that. Handy for trading with the locals. We're going to eat like kings for the rest of the week. Hey Briggs, throw it back. You've had a look."

The cockney closed his fingers around the time piece, trapping it within his fist. He looked up, fixing Henry with a cold glare. His lips and thin moustache seemed to peel back from his teeth in a sneer. "No."

The bigger Australian placed his hands on his hips. "What do you mean *no*?"

"You're not having it back," said Briggs. "It's mine."

"How the hell can it be *yours*?" said Roberts.

"Did you *see* them dig it out?" said Briggs. "Should have known. Bloody Australians. All criminals."

Henry dashed forwards, but Thomas, wary of his brother's quick temper, grabbed his shoulder and held him back.

"Easy now, fellas," said Roberts. "Let's not get carried away."

Briggs pushed his fist against his commander's chest. "Take a look. You'll see."

Roberts took the watch and held it up to the sun, studying the engraving.

"I recognised it straight away," said Briggs. "Present from the missus when I was called up. Went and bloody lost it during the landin', didn't I ... weeks I've dwelled on that time piece. One of these two tealeaves must've found it."

Henry tried to break free, but Thomas held him fast.

"Settle down," he told his brother. "I saw you dig it out. Besides, how can he prove it's his?"

Briggs smirked. "Pvt. Briggs. My bravest. Countin' the seconds." He turned to Roberts. "Open it, sir. Tell these thievin' Aussies."

Roberts rolled his eyes. "We have more pressing matters. But if this will settle the argument and allow us to return to the dig..." He popped the clasp and the cover sprang open. The older soldier squinted and held the watch closer. He studied the inside of the case for a moment, swallowed and wiped his face in the crook of his arm.

"Well?" demanded Henry.

Roberts looked up. "Pvt. Briggs. My bravest." He closed the watch with a snap. "Counting the seconds."

*

As the sun started to dip towards the jagged horizon, Roberts called for a brief respite against the back breaking labour. Sitting on their packs, the men unloaded a small dinner from the provisions found within. After the same diet for months on end, the food proved nothing but sustenance, their taste buds long habituated to the plain cuisine.

The Williams brothers sat at one end of the trench with Briggs at the other. Roberts, trying to stay loyal to his fellow ANZACS despite the overwhelming evidence, went back and forth but spent most of his time keeping Briggs company.

"I mean, I know we're all in this together," said the Brit, "but how can you trust a man with your life if you can't trust him not to nick your prized possessions, eh?"

"He wouldn't have known it was yours, Briggs," said

Roberts.

"I didn't take it!" Henry yelled from the other end of the trench. "How many more times? It was buried in the bloody ground!"

The men looked up at the sound of distant gunfire. Roberts shook his head and they returned to their paltry meals.

"You know," said the Kiwi, breaking the silence. "This is an exotic land. Many of the Johnny Turks we take prisoner are quite the affable chap. I got talking to one once as I marched him back. They share a great deal with the Maori and your Aborigines, you two. Myths and legends but … not many monsters and demons. More fools and heroes, folks of legend. Friendly spirits. Very natural."

"What has this to do with the price of eggs?" said Briggs through a mouthful of bully beef.

"Just saying. Maybe your watch has been returned to you by a good earth spirit."

"Ha!" said Briggs, spraying flecks of dark-pink meat. "More likely a pair of thievin' Australians! What would your Johnny Turk say, eh? Why would your Johnny Turk friendly spirit bring me back me watch, eh?"

Roberts sipped from his canteen and gazed out of trench at the sun dipping into the ground.

Already the evening had lost the desert heat of the day. Thomas shivered, again hearing a distant burst of gunfire.

"In the stories," said Roberts, "they usually provide a warning."

Briggs swallowed his mouthful and once again pulled the watch from his pocket, running his fingers over the engraving.

*

"Come on, boys," said Roberts, his shirt off and back glistening with sweat in the last light of the day. "We have twenty minutes I'd say before the dark sets in."

Thomas and Henry were similarly stripped, helping the increasing cold of night chill their skin. They had continued to dig through the afternoon and had almost doubled the length of the trench. They dared not light any torch a mile or so into enemy territory having already witnessed firsthand the deadly accuracy of the Turkish sniper.

Briggs threw his spade to the ground. "To hell with this. Twenty minutes won't make much difference. I have a better idea."

"Better idea then Loach's orders?" said Thomas. "I'd like to hear it!"

"The way I see it," said Briggs, "we don't know what state these reinforcements might be in once they get here, right? Out there is a soldier's ammo, provisions and kit. It's not much, but we're in no man's land 'ere lads."

"So what?" said Henry. "You're going back to Durand? You know that's in sniper range."

"Yeah, dark enough now. Be there and back in two minutes."

"Fine by me," said Henry. "Just make sure you leave your ammo and provisions here, mate. I don't want to have to go and find them in the dark."

Brigg's smirk fell. "Up yours, you thievin' convict."

Henry shrugged and planted his spade firmly in the ground, continuing the job.

At least he isn't rising to it, thought Thomas. Henry had always followed orders and believed that the Australian soldier would prove himself to the more military nations with unyielding commitment. Despite not sharing the degree of his brother's passion, Thomas' sunburned shoulders, and muscles that felt like dead weights chained to his bone, disagreed.

"What the hell?" said Henry and pulled back the spade. He dropped to all fours and began to sweep the dirt away.

"More watches, eh?" said Briggs. "Wife bought me mine as she thinks I'm the bravest soldier in the British Army. You ladies keep diggin' your little hole while I prove her right." He climbed the sloped side of the trench and pulled himself up onto the ground. With the sky glowing red behind him, the Brit gave a half salute before jogging away.

"Fool!" spat Roberts.

Thomas shook his head and turned his attention to his brother.

Henry sat back on his haunches, out of breath.

"My God," he moaned. "What is this? It feels … ah God…"

Thomas dropped to his hands and knees and helped his brother scoop aside the moist earth. His finger pushed through the soft loam and touched upon something cold, hard and covered in fur. He snatched his hand back, head filled with Robert's talk of monsters and spirits. His mouth dropped open, realising what they'd discovered.

"Henry," he groaned. "It's … it's a dog."

"Jesus!" roared his brother, diving back.

In the rapidly fading light, Thomas could just make out the black of the fur against the dark brown of the soil, and despite the state of decay that the beast must surely have been in, he only smelled the richness of the earth. Digging in once again, he cleared around the head of the dog, revealing the mouth and teeth, eternally grinning even in death.

"Briggs, damn him," said Roberts. "It's not total dark yet. If I can see him, so can the Turkish snipers. You two. Grab your arms. Get over here."

Wiping their hands on the backs of their combats, the brothers joined him at the wall. Foot holes had been punched into the earth and been sunbaked hard. Roberts stood on one of these makeshift ladders, binoculars to his eyes.

"This is your fault, you know. If you hadn't swiped that damn watch he might have stayed put."

Thomas glared at Henry, who thankfully knew better than to argue with a superior officer, no matter how slight.

"He's almost at Durand," continued Roberts. "I'm sure the Turks will have kept an eye on us. We might be few, but you can't have the enemy penetrating so deep. I want some cover fire, gentlemen. Might put them off. Bit of rifle fire might make them think we're on the offensive."

The brothers found their own precarious footing on the wall and peered over the edge.

Some distance away, almost hidden by the murk of the dying day, Briggs was crouched by their fallen comrade, struggling to untie Durand's pack.

Thomas scanned the ridge for any movement, but found none within the dark recesses. Perhaps the Turks had moved on?

"Ready those rifles," said Roberts. "I want fire the moment he starts back."

"Sir," said Thomas. "If Briggs gets back safe and the Turks are gone … perhaps we should head back. Take the chance while we can."

"Nonsense, boy. We have our orders. After all our hard work digging, we must defend this trench until Loach sends his reinforcements."

Thomas swallowed. Something Roberts had said stuck with him, a thorn in his thoughts. All the talk of spirits had been a laugh in the daylight, but here, in the dark … the ground held a chill that penetrated to his very bones. The mysterious watch and now a dead dog. What did it all mean?

The Cockney had pulled Durand's pack free and strapped it onto his back. Head down, he sprinted back towards the trench.

The first bullet zipped through the air, sending up a gust of dirt to Briggs' left.

"Snipers!" Roberts yelled.

Henry and Thomas alternated between firing and reloading, sending a steady stream of warning shots up at the shadowy ridges along the left flank. Briggs ran hard, switching his path side to side. Bullets continued to punch the ground about him.

"Run, Briggs," Roberts screamed over the relentless gunfire. "You're halfway home!"

"He's going to make it," roared Henry. "The lucky son of a bitch is going to make it!"

Briggs fell, and the men gasped, thinking him hit, but a moment later and he was back on his feet, dashing through the scrub, nearing the trench. The pack bounced on his back.

The sniper fire lessened.

"Lucky son of a bitch," said Henry again, lowering his rifle.

An explosion knocked the men from their perches on the trench wall, sending them hurtling to the ground.

Deaf from the ringing in his ears, Thomas tried to stand on jellied legs, fearing the Turks had moved heavy artillery into range and had begun to shell the trench. He blinked dust from his eyes and stared up into the huge cloud of disturbed earth a moment before the fluid hit. The warm rain slapped onto his face, head and across his front. Thomas spat the coppery taste from his lips.

"Landmine," moaned Roberts. "Goddamn landmine."

*

The night fell without further incident. The demise of Briggs, despite the man's almost unbearable attitude, weighed heavily upon their thoughts. Roberts appeared to dwell in particular, and Thomas had no doubts why. He had been placed in charge of this small band of scouts and had lost half of his men.

Thomas and his brother, expecting Major Loach and his reinforcements to arrive at any moment, passed the time by continuing the dig. The dog had been left in the open, yet another mystery that the earth had birthed.

"We ignored the signs," said Roberts, seemingly deep in thought. Sitting on the floor of the trench, he had chanced a smoke. The thin, rationed woodbine poked from the corner of his lips. "We ignored the warnings. Those Australians ... they were confused. Delusional. They found this place. The Turks had abandoned it. The earth itself throws out messages. Look! A dead dog." He took a long drag, mulling over his thoughts. He spoke through the haze of smoke. "We should not have come to this place."

His eyes long adjusted to the dark, Thomas caught the look of concern on his brother's face. They had both seen their fair share of soldiers driven mad by the war, the conditions and the endless threat. The human brain wasn't designed for such prolonged torment. Bodies can be bandaged and wounds stitched up ... but what field medic could patch the mind on the front line?

"The land," Roberts continued. "The land is tired. The blood has poisoned the soil. The shelling and the explosions have awoken something that should be dormant ... spirits..."

"That's enough, sir," said Henry, jabbing his shovel into the soft ground and leaning on the handle. "What would Loach say if he heard you like this, eh? The mission was a success. We took the trench and after all this digging can shelter the reinforcements. Don't go losing it now."

"The mission was a success? Try telling that to Durand and Briggs." He took a drag. "Dead. So many dead. As dead as that dog. At least he looks happy in death. I just to have a dog like that, you know. This was back in New Zealand, of course. Lived my whole life south of Wellington until I enlisted..."

Henry opened his mouth to speak, but Thomas stopped him.

"Just let him talk," he said. "It's helping him. Reminiscing about the good old days is better than babbling about spirits in the ground."

"Lucky!" cried Roberts, startling both brothers. "That was his name. My dog. God, I loved that dog. They don't call them man's best friend for nothing you know, boys. You ever had a dog?"

Both Australians shook their heads.

Roberts clambered on all fours across the dirt to the corpse of the dog. "You should get one. All that open bushland ... a dog would love it. When we get home." He stopped beside the dog and sighed. "Home. If we ever get home, right lads?" He ran a hand over the dark fur of the dog.

Henry wrinkled his nose, pulled his shovel free and returned to the dig.

Thomas, having seen Roberts' successful smoke, rummaged in his pack for his own tobacco tin. Let the Kiwi stroke the dead dog, he thought. Without a wash we're all covered in Briggs anyway.

He noticed the slow and steady stroke of Roberts' hand across the dog had stopped.

"This isn't real," whispered the soldier.

"Excuse me, sir?"

Roberts snapped his head up and stared at the sky, his eyes wide and teeth pressed together in a sickening grimace that aged the soldier to a cruel old man.

"Are they warnings?" he croaked. "Or taunts?"

"Roberts?" said Thomas, stepping forwards and placing his hand on the older man's shoulder. "Sir, this wasn't your fault."

"It's all of our faults," Roberts hissed and crawled to the

tent, nursing something in his hands. "The Kaiser, the Turks, the Brits, us ... we're all to blame."

Still muttering to himself, Roberts slipped between the flaps and into the tent.

"Good," said Henry, the muscles on his back and shoulders bulging as he scooped out yet more earth. "Let him get some rest. Might do him some good. We can keep watch until Loach's men arrive."

Thomas didn't agree. The look in Roberts' eyes ... he'd seen men go stir crazy in the weeks since landing at Gallipoli, and their commander seemed to be showing the signs after a few short hours. Picking up his shovel, he stood by his brother's side and threw some dirt over the dog. Better it be hidden back in the earth.

"Ah shit," Henry muttered. "What now?"

He leant his shovel against the wall and crouched to pluck something from the disturbed pile of dirt.

"Hey," said Thomas. "Whatever it is ... perhaps you'd better leave it, eh?"

Ignoring his brother, Henry pulled a square object from the soil.

"Henry, please."

"Don't tell me he has you spooked. He lost two men, Thomas. He's bound to go a bit ... odd after that. You really believe some spirit in the earth is spitting these things out?" He wiped the muck from the green object. It appeared to be a cloth bound book. Without opening it, Henry looked at the plain cover, grunted and threw it back. "It's nothing. Come on. Keep digging."

A deep gunshot split the night, and the brothers fell to the ground, hands over their heads.

"Shit," said Thomas. "That sounded close. Thought they'd come over the top."

Henry nodded and grabbed his rifle.

A quick check along the edge of the trench revealed nothing. The Turks hadn't grown impatient and staged an attack, nor had the shot come from any sniper.

"What the hell?" said Henry. "That sounded right on top of

us!"

Thomas pointed to the tent. "Didn't you find a pistol in there?"

"Ah shit..." Henry readied his weapon and gingerly approached the tent, pulling back the flap. "Roberts? Sir? We heard a shot..."

They were met by the ghostly wail of the desert wind.

"Roberts?" called Thomas. "Come on, Roberts."

Henry peered into the darkness of the tent.

*

Thomas roared and tossed his rifle to the ground. "Goddamn it, Henry! What are we supposed to do now, eh? What the hell are we supposed to do now?" He paced the trench. Down to just two men. The hills crawling with snipers and mines between them and the bulk of the Australian forces. His brother had always looked after him, but what chance did they have now?

Defeated, he fell to the ground, pulling his legs up to his chest, not a soldier anymore. Sometimes you want your games to end and to return to real life. Sometimes the game *is* real life.

"What are we going to do?" he asked again and sniffed, wiping his nose on the sleeve of his combats.

Henry emerged from the tent stone-faced.

Thomas had no desire to see the carnage within the canvas. Enough death for one day.

Henry stopped in front of his brother, something dangling loose from his hand. He held before Thomas' face. "You were right. Roberts was right."

Thomas stared at the dog collar his brother had found. Roberts must have taken it from the dead mutt.

Engraved in the metal tag, one word that mocked with a devilish malice.

LUCKY

Henry threw it high into the night.

*

Both brothers had abandoned the dig, and their shovels stood neglected against the dirt wall. They sat on piles of earth, far as possible from the shallow grave of the dog and the mess within the tent. Henry held the book, his fingers tight against the green cloth cover. It had no title, no author. Neither of the men had the nerve to open the book and see what, if anything, lay inside.

"I think," said Henry and shivered. He shook his head. "I don't know what I think any more. It was so simple, you know? We come here, see the world, serve our country. Put us on the goddamn map. Now … this…" He held up the book.

"Bury it," said Thomas. "What does it want? To warn us that we shouldn't be here? I think we're a little past that. It showed Briggs and Roberts something dear to them, from home. Maybe Durand and his lucky coin too. Something they missed. Since mum and dad died…" Thomas shrugged. "What do we have to go back to? An empty farm? We have no wives, no family. Just … each other I guess. What could it want?"

Henry turned the book over and ran his hand over the back cover. "Or like Roberts said, this could all be a taunt. Whatever the hell is going here, it could know that we're doomed, Thomas. We're the only ones left. There's no sign of Loach's men, and we have miles of snipers and mines between us and base camp. Maybe…" He fingered the edge of the tightly packed pages. "Maybe this is it. One last thought of home before we go west, if you know what I mean."

Thomas nodded and wrapped his arms around his thin body.

Henry passed the book back and forth between his shaking hands. "I had always had this fear. We always thought the war would be such a great adventure but I had this nightmare that threw a dark curtain over all the excitement. I used to dream we'd hit the beaches during a landing and run up through the surf, dodging bullets and shells, leaping the barbed wire, big heroes, you know?" He chuckled. "You and me together. The fear … of turning and not finding you there. Mum and Dad … now you. Didn't do a good job, did I? Not a very good soldier."

Thomas didn't look away from the book. "That's war. You play soldiers … most of the time you lose."

Henry flipped the book and held it between his hands, thumbs on the edge, poised to spread the pages wide.

"What are you doing?" said Thomas, bolting up from his

mound.

"It might be nice," said Henry, his eyes glazed and body twitching. "To have one last moment. You and me. Home."

He opened the book, and a piece of paper fell out and drifted to the ground.

Before Thomas could snatch for it, Henry scooped it up from the ground. Dropping the book, he dug into one of his pockets for a set of matches.

"What is it?" said Thomas.

Henry struck a match and held the flickering flame close to the paper.

Thomas approached his brother and collapsed into the dirt. Side by side, they gazed at the page.

Bound to the paper was a photograph taken one hot summer's day in the mountains east of Adelaide. Two young boys in black trunks sat by a stream, billy hung up over a modest campfire. The boys, both sharing the same dark eyes and hair, smiled out of the picture, happy on one glorious afternoon.

The Secret of Blackwater Island

Rima Devereaux

John Campbell flexed his arms and gave a great yawn. The January night air was chill and damp on his bare skin. He could hear the slow lapping of the waves against the stern of the naval motorboat that was taking him to Blackwater Island. The night was buried in a thick, foggy silence that weighed on his spirits. As part of the Mobile Brigade, it was his duty to survey the island and keep a look out for anything unusual. It was a thankless job in this forgotten spot off the cold east coast of England between the Trench and Windward rivers.

He remembered the radio and the bleak news of the slaughter of the Battle of the Somme in the summer. Stories of endless young women combing the hospitals for their fiancés. He thought wryly of the high spirits of the beginning of the war and the popularity of the catchphrase 'doing your bit'. He had difficulty believing in what he was doing any more. But he had something to live for – a fiancée of his own back in Oxford, and they planned to marry once the war was over.

John stared as the navy captain and skipper of the small boat strode up to him and said, "This is it, this is where we drop you. We'll be here in two nights to pick you up."

John nodded his assent and began readying his small bundle of belongings. He shivered as he looked over at the mud flats near where the launch was now moored. The night was deathly silent – not even any seagulls. He saw the skipper pointing to a tall signpost at the end of the mudflat where the dank grass started. "Wait for me over there at midnight in two nights," he repeated.

John shouldered his canvas holdall and moved off into the night. He needed to find shelter for the remaining hours of darkness. He struck a tarmac road, and turned along it in a direction that looked likely. Some minutes later he was rewarded by the sight of an isolated farmhouse looming up in the chill January air. Relief washed over him like a warm shower. Hopefully, he approached the thatched farmhouse with its porch hung with last year's roses, and knocked.

A plump woman with an oddly fearful, staring expression opened the door. "'Oo are you?" she asked abruptly.

"I'm an officer from the Mobile Brigade, stationed here for a few days. I'm looking for shelter for the night. Can you help me?" he said pleasantly, pulling his khaki coat close to him to keep out a sudden icy blast of air.

"You'd best come in," said the woman in exactly the same tone as before. John paused on the threshold in surprise. Her words had been welcoming but her gaze was pure terror. He was puzzled. But he had nothing to lose, so he entered the cottage.

The woman inched over to her husband, who sat in a rocking chair by the fire. They whispered together for a while, darting furtive looks at John. He could see fear and even cunning in their eyes, and it stunned him. His superiors had told him the island was isolated, certainly, but that the people were simple and friendly on the whole. He had seen none of it so far.

He was hungry and tired and disappointed at the lack of welcome. At length, the woman showed him into a narrow guest room with a simple iron bedstead and a chest of drawers, and gave him bread and soup. He tried to talk to her – he needed to ask her husband if he could borrow a horse in the morning – but she backed away from him in such alarm that he gave it up.

As he was stretching himself out on the bed and preparing for sleep, John heard the front door slam. Surprised at this, as it was after one o'clock in the morning, he peeked out of the casement window. He was just in time to see the husband hurrying down to the gate and along the road as if wolves were after him. John shook his head in disbelief and dropped back onto the bed. Why were the couple behaving so oddly? And had the man hurried off to give news of John's arrival? He guessed he would find out in the morning.

*

In the grey dawn, John awoke to the sound of milk churns outside. He peeked through the window and saw the woman, garbed in a charlady's dress of blue serge, getting ready to milk the cows. He shut the window hurriedly as a cold blast hit him. He dressed quickly, shouldered his holdall and tried the door. It was locked. He pulled at it tentatively, then shook it hard. He shouted, "Let me out!" and ran back to the window. The woman had disappeared into the barn.

He opened the window. It was high and small, but if he moved the chest of drawers and climbed on it, he thought he could just squeeze through. He dragged the furniture under the window, pushed his bag through first, checked that the coast was clear and writhed through head first, landing on his hands in the yard with a bump. He got gingerly to his feet and looked around.

He wanted the stables. They were opposite the big barn from which signs of milking were emerging. He stepped inside, and breathed the heady, musty smell of horses and hay. To the left stood a great bay carthorse.

Quickly, John saddled and bridled it with the tack that stood by, pulled pencil and paper from his bag and wrote a short note to his captors explaining that he had borrowed the horse and would return it. He climbed carefully on its back, dug his heels into its flanks and trotted smartly out of the yard and down the lane into the road.

The sun was up by this time but it was still invisible and the air was heavy, cold and clammy. John turned to the right along the road in the direction he had seen the man run the previous night.

As he rode, he fingered a letter from Alice, his fiancée, in his pocket. She was worried sick about her brother, who was serving in Flanders and hadn't written for some weeks. He was worried himself on her behalf. She would make herself ill if she went on at the high pitch she'd been living at. He sighed and shook himself free of the anxiety. Luckily he was going on leave soon, after he had completed this strange turn of duty on this very odd island.

He passed a few more outlying farmhouses before coming to a village with a squat Saxon church, a schoolhouse and a small store. Two or three horses were tethered outside the shop. John thought it would be a good place to find out more about the island before he commenced his circuit. A thin, grey-haired man in waistcoat and breeches had just come out of the stores. He stopped in surprise when he saw John.

"Hey, that's 'owd Bob, that there horse is," he stated, pointing to John's horse. "It's from up at Lawson's farm. Have you stolen it?" He peered at John suspiciously.

"I've only borrowed it," and John explained who he was.

The man's eyes narrowed. "Well," he said eventually, "You'll find that people are less apt to believe that pack of lies here on Blackwater Island, you know. Happen you'd best tell the truth." And without any further explanation, the man mounted his black horse and trotted off.

John was puzzled. Did people think he was pretending to be something he wasn't? What did they think he really was – a German spy perhaps? He shook his head in wonderment.

He decided to buy some tobacco from the shop before going on his way. He would buy lunch too, and tonight he would find shelter in someone's hay barn, not wanting a repeat experience of being locked in. Here he stopped with a jolt, his hand on the shop door. Of course, the Lawsons had locked him in because they thought he was a spy! But why should they be so suspicious? Soldiers from the Mobile Brigade were a familiar enough sight, after all. Bewildered, he walked into the shop.

He immediately saw that the village store doubled as a pub, café and general meeting place. Although it was still quite early, a number of men sat at benches drawn up to solid oak tables, tankards in their hands, playing chess and dominoes and talking constantly in their gruff voices. Behind the counter was a pleasant-faced, slim girl of around twenty or so, wearing an apron. An older woman, who looked so like the girl it was clear she was her mother, was bustling about between the kitchen and the main room where the men were sitting. John was amused. She looked very much in charge, and it was obvious that she was trying to protect her daughter from the overtures of the over-friendly clients as they soaked themselves in drink.

When John entered, everyone turned to see who the newcomer was, and a dead silence fell. It was so oppressive that John felt the urge to shout aloud to break it. The older woman stopped and stared, her tray of mugs forgotten. The daughter gazed in frank amazement, her jaw dropping. As John watched the closed, hostile faces in their serried ranks on the benches, something cold and clammy – like the air outside – took hold of his heart and he shuddered in sudden dread. There was something very odd going on. Without thinking, he turned and blundered back outside.

Dazed, for a moment John hadn't realised that a wizened old man with white hair had followed him out. He walked with the aid of a stick, pulling his woollen coat close to him as he did so. He came right up to John and tapped him on the chin. "Come with me, stranger," he said. "I have something important to tell you."

"Can't it wait till tonight?" asked John. "I have work to do."

"No, it can't," replied the old man. "Let's go to my house. It isn't far."

John shook his head in bewilderment, untied Bob and followed the man along the village street to a small grey cottage with a slate roof.

As the old man busied himself about the small front room, getting John a hot drink and some very late breakfast, John thought to himself, "Am I finally going to learn what is so strange about this place?"

He waited with anticipation as the man shuffled in with the food and two steaming mugs of weak tea, and settled himself under a patchwork rug in a chair by the stove. He began to speak, in a slow, sonorous tone of voice, rather grating on the ears but with a warmth and a depth in it. John stared at him as he spoke, looking into those twinkling blue eyes in that lined face. And the old man unfolded a strange story...

*

It was a bright, moon-enshrouded night in the late summer of 1915. The Zeppelin attacks had been especially fierce all week, and the people of Blackwater Island were inside with locked doors. Nothing stirred in the bleak east of the island where the wind blew across the bitter sea. A lone farmhouse stood there, a crouching shape defying the wind. The farmer had a cow in calf, and it was slow in coming. He had been up all night. He looked up at the starry sky as he walked across the yard to fetch a bucket of hot water, soap and a towel so that he could explore inside the cow.

Then he heard it. The unmistakable sound of a crashed Zeppelin, some few hundred yards away, just out to sea. He dropped the bucket and ran along the road some way. The 650-foot-long airship was lying in shallow water off the mudflats, and its commander was floundering and splashing around. The farmer held out a hand to help the German climb onto the mud bank.

"My ship, destroyed," said the German in a guttural accent. "I surrender to you. Please take me to the nearest police station. I give myself up."

"Certainly," said the farmer, secretly rubbing his hands with glee. Here was his chance to make good! He had had enough to eking out a living from the land. If it became known that he had captured a German airship, he would be decorated with a medal of honour.

The farmer helped the German youth to stand and asked him politely if he was injured anywhere. He took him to the only town the island boasted – a small collection of houses and shops on the north coast. He proclaimed his capture loudly to the policeman on duty. The German didn't contradict his story, although he could easily have said that he had surrendered willingly. The policeman thought that the farmer had really captured a German Zeppelin and its commander, and he clapped him on the back with thanks. The farmer began to feel very pleased with himself. *There'll surely be a cash reward for this*, he thought to himself.

The policeman took his details and promised to get in touch. The German youth was led off seemingly happily to a cell. His pockets had been searched. They had found a faded photograph of a young blonde woman with a slim figure and a narrow, pointed face, smiling up out of the picture. His fiancée, no doubt.

Meanwhile, the farmer went back home, but he blabbed, and the policeman blabbed, and very soon the whole island believed that Farmer Doe had indeed caught a German Zeppelin single-handedly. Whenever he went out, he was asked how he had shot it down, and how he had tricked its commander into coming to the police station. The story became more and more elaborate, until at last the farmer began to believe it himself. He no longer had the ability to distinguish between truth and lies. He was losing this fundamental human trait.

One still, cloudless night, only a matter of days after the Zeppelin had come down, the farmer was sitting cosily by his stove when there was a knock at his door. Outside a tall man stood swathed from head to foot in a black cloak, carrying a sickle in his hand. Farmer Doe trembled in his shoes as he gazed at him. The tall man in black swept inside without waiting for an invitation, and spoke his piece.

"You have lied so much that you are beginning to live the lie," he stated, and his voice was cold and thin, with an edge to it that was like ice. "All the good inhabitants of this island believe your lie. Therefore I curse you all, and you most of all. Henceforth, until one of you really captures a German Zeppelin, none of you will be able to leave this island. Goods and people may come in, but once in, they will not be able to leave, until the day you redeem yourselves by really achieving the courage and bravery to which you have pretended."

With that, the tall black stranger got out his sickle. One sweep of it, and Farmer Doe lay dead on the floor in a pool of his own blood. But the Grim Reaper's curse living on in the minds of all the island dwellers because, that night, they all dreamed the true story of treacherous Farmer Doe and the Zeppelin, right up to the curse. And that is the end of the sad story. But since that fateful day, we have all been marooned here.

*

John had been staring at the flickering light of the gas in the stove next to the wizened old man's chair, and stretched out his hands to feel its warmth. He felt too stunned to speak. That explained the suspicion, and the cunning, and the behaviour of the couple who had locked him in. It explained the attitude of the men in the village store.

But the implications of it were the worst. He was here now, and he wouldn't be able to leave until the inhabitants really captured a German Zeppelin. When that would be, he had no idea. Perhaps never. In which case he would be stuck there too.

John looked up to find the friendly old man peering at him with those bright blue eyes. He saw understanding in them. "Will you help me escape?" he asked hopefully.

"Alas, no," said the old man. "I cannot do that. It is against the law that set the curse on this island. In any case, nothing I could do would have the slightest effect."

"What do you mean?" John was irritated now. "The boat is picking me up late tomorrow night. Surely I have only to walk out onto the mudflats where it's meeting me, and board the thing?" He looked at the old man pleadingly.

"You can certainly try," replied the old man, "but I think you will find you are unable to leave, all the same."

John wasn't going to stand for that. He stood up, exasperation rising in him. "I'm grateful to you for telling me that story and befriending me," he explained. "But we men of the Mobile Brigade are realists, not tossed every which way by some cock-and-bull story about the Grim Reaper. I am going to make my circuit of the island now, and I do not expect to be hindered when I leave this place tomorrow night."

He could see hurt in the old man's eyes at these words. The man simply sat back in his chair, looked at him appraisingly. "Try, by all means. No one will hinder you, except the island itself."

John wondered fleetingly what that meant.

"If you need a bed for tonight," the old man went on, "you are welcome to my spare room."

Conflicting emotions struggled within him: disbelief, sick

fear, and an underlying deep gratitude. He nodded his thanks, tried to smile, and went to the door. "Goodbye until later then," he said, and headed outside into the foggy day to where Bob was tethered to the gatepost.

All that day, as he made his lonely way around the wild perimeter of the island on 'owd Bob, John thought about what he had heard. The story had been fantastic – it sounded like a case of mass hallucination. Farmer Doe had obviously taken his own life, and the shock had led to this very odd story being fabricated. As to the islanders' suspicion, it was an isolated spot, where visitors didn't come very often, and it was wartime after all.

Feeling suddenly better, John trotted on. The land on the island's coast was a mixture of marshy flats, tussocky grass and sparse woodland of hawthorn and alder. He picked his way carefully across the ground. That night, he accepted the old man's kindly offer of a bed and a square meal, and the next day, he continued his lone vigil, making notes for his superiors as he did so. He had not been told much about the purpose of his tour of duty here, but he knew there were plans afoot to use the island for the war, and his notes on the lie of the land would prove useful.

Promptly at midnight that night, John, having surreptitiously returned 'owd Bob to his stable, was standing by the signpost at the edge of the mudflat in the west of the island where the naval boat had dropped him. He peered into the gloom and shivered. It was a clear night but the temperature had dropped still more. Presently, he heard the lapping of water against the boat's hull, and there was the launch. He waved and shouted and made his way across the flats happily.

He was brought up short. An invisible barrier like stretched elastic seemed to spring him back. He tried moving to one side or the other, but the barrier was still there. Panic rose in him. "I'm here, it's John Campbell. I'm here to meet you, but there's something in the way. Can you throw me a line?" he shouted, flailing his arms against the invisible obstacle.

The skipper of the boat was only a few yards from him, but

seemed not to see him. He was looking past him, gazing at the signpost with a puzzled air. Then he muttered to himself, "It's not like John to be late," and the sound carried in the clear, cold air. Then realisation dawned on John. The skipper couldn't see or hear him. Something in the barrier distorted what lay behind it. He looked out angrily, and then sank to the muddy ground, his head in his hands.

It was true.

He was stuck on the island.

*

Sometime later – he couldn't tell how long, but the boat had gone – John slowly rose to his feet, and looked back at the island. In the pit of his stomach a sick feeling battled with a new-found determination to conquer this situation somehow.

One way or another, he had to capture a German Zeppelin.

He would start now.

John Campbell strode into the night, a lone figure in the bleak darkness.

He had a long vigil ahead of him.

After the Harvest

Bryn Fortey

George Albert Reece had never heard of Franz Ferdinand before the Archduke and his wife were assassinated in somewhere called Sarajevo in the June of 1914.

Neither was he aware of all the political whirlpools that had for some time been heading the European continent towards armed conflict. The world was shrinking, unknown to George, with less opportunity for Empire building in new territories. Some countries looked at neighbours while fading powers sought alliances as a means of protection.

Manipulating the Archduke's shooting, Germany had backed Austria-Hungarian threats and demands against Serbia while Russia part mobilised in defence of the Serbs. Great Britain and France were told by Germany to curb their Russian allies' militarism. Within days war was being declared by some, neutrality by others, and armies were on the march.

George Albert Reece knew none of this, though he had heard something about the British fleet being manoeuvred to block German access to the world's oceans. His employer, the landowner Squire Thomas, a stoutly patriotic man, was more than willing to pass on news to his farm hands.

With various armies moving on mainland Europe, the British government entered the conflict on August 4th when Germany refused to withdraw from neutral Belgium. Unlike most of the other major powers, the British army consisted entirely of volunteers and there was no conscription.

Needing to boost numbers, Field Marshall Sir Herbert Kitchener called for 100,000 men to sign up. "Your Country Needs You" said the posters and 175,000 volunteered in the following week. Squire Thomas had encouraged the young men in his employ to be amongst them.

"We will cope, lads," he'd said. "Us older ones will keep the farms going until you return, which won't be long. A couple of months should be enough to kick the Kaiser's backside."

So twenty-eight year old George Albert Reece, full of the Squire's patriotic fervour, joined with the other farm hands offering to do their bit for King and Country. Rebecca, his flame haired wife of only four months, had not matched his enthusiasm, but had come to accept the inevitability of it all.

"Won't be long, Becky. Like Squire says, should be over by end of year at most. Got to do my duty."

"Well all right, George Reece, but you had better take care and come home in one piece. Do you hear me?"

"I hear you, my love."

And he'd taken her gently into his arms. However short the war was going to be, he would certainly miss her while he was away.

*

Rebecca Reece had, in spite of her misgivings, felt a surge of pride upon learning that her George was a Pioneer in the Royal Engineers. It all sounded grand and adventurous, but that was because she did not know the rank was that of an unskilled labour force being put together as part of an enlarged R.E. Regiment.

"Sounds as if he's making his mark already," said Squire Thomas, who also lacked any knowledge of new army requirements. "He'll come back with stripes on his arm, you see if he doesn't!"

Rebecca and other womenfolk helped swell the depleted farm workforce, joining with the men either too old or too young to fight. The Squire had dismissed the one employee of army age who had refused to enlist. He was a hard but fair man with his own set of standards and treated his workers a sight better than many in the area.

She missed her George though, her husband of only four months, and their love still as fresh as the crops in the fields. Even if the blasted war only lasted a week or so more, it would still be too long for them to be apart.

The key to a woman was a man. The right man, and Rebecca had chosen well. George had been attentive but not servile, ardent but not demanding, generous but not indulgent. Just a farm labourer maybe, but possessing a maturity not all men attain.

Her life would be on hold until his return.

*

The seasons passed and a new year was born, but 1915 only ushered in grim and unwanted news. According to a despondent Squire Thomas, hopes for a swift conclusion to hostilities had ended with large numbers of casualties, a general stalemate on the ground, and further widening of the conflict. One of his nephews and a second cousin had already been killed in action and word arrived that David Hopkins had also fallen.

Young Dave, barely nineteen, who had travelled with George and the others to accept the King's Shilling. It all brought home the realities of modern warfare. The days of chivalry were long gone and Rebecca was filled with fear at the possibility of her husband not coming home.

As the days multiplied and the war dragged on it affected everyone. Even Squire Thomas was more withdrawn and looking older than his years. It rested heavy on his shoulders that he had encouraged so many to join what he'd thought would be a quick and adventurous victory. At least he had no sons to go and fight, though both daughters were helping to nurse the wounded.

The year ended with the government having to introduce conscription to make up for the terrible losses all the nations were suffering. This meant that even if they hadn't volunteered when they did, George and the others would have gone eventually. Which did ease the burden a little on the Squire's shoulders, though young David Hopkins would not have died when and as he did.

The bells seemed muted as they rang in 1916.

*

Pioneer George Reece, across the Channel, was too busy coping with atrocious conditions to worry about it being a new year.

Getting through each day was effort enough and he used the thought of Becky waiting at home to spur his attempts at survival.

Life was a never ending round of digging trenches, planting barbed wire, loading and unloading equipment. Rudimentary military training had been given but a Pioneer had more use for a spade than a rifle. And then there was the most distasteful of his duties, the removal and burial of the dead.

Oh Becky, my Becky, he would think, struggling through the lice and rat infested muck, *I will get through this somehow. I will get back to you.*

Then, later, he became a Mole. A nickname given to members of Pioneer Tunnelling Units as underground warfare gained a foothold in the seemingly never ending conflict. Both sides tried to tunnel under each other's trenches, from where they could either plant bombs or have soldiers burst up through. At times opposing diggers would accidentally meet while tunnelling and hand to hand fighting would result. Subterranean fighting that could bring walls and ceiling caving in.

Also, as if there wasn't already enough to contend with, there was the increasing threat of death or incapacitation by gas inhalation. Gas bombs could be exploded into trenches or dropped into tunnels. How many more ways could they invent to kill and maim? George wondered as the death toll mounted on both sides.

It did seem though, at times, that he led an enchanted existence. George dodged death by inches and always seemed to make the right choice. Men around him died: friends and strangers, comrades and enemies. And as yet another year drew to a bitter end; he was at least alive if nothing else. He was still on course to somehow get back home to the wife he'd left behind.

*

It was early in 1916 that the farm workers had their only sighting of a Zeppelin. An airship that was probably way off course since they were not near any of the industrial centres being targeted. Squire Thomas was said to have shaken his fists at the sky, his face dark with anger, while Rebecca herself felt an icy hand grip her heart as she watched the flying monster pass overhead.

The year dragged on and the news that filtered through, probably long after the events themselves, did little to raise the spirits. Germany failed to smash the French at Verdun but had survived on the Somme, with all armies suffering catastrophic losses.

Battle fronts in Europe.

Fighting taking place in Africa and Mesopotamia. It seemed as if most of the world was involved. Places Rebecca had never heard of before.

Then came the news she had been dreading, but never really believed she would hear: "Pioneer George Albert Reece. Missing in action. Presumed dead."

The words impaled her, through skin and flesh and bone. And a darker fear than she had ever thought possible engulfed her.

Some local women had already received similar messages. Others were hoping against hope never to. All joined to offer Rebecca what comfort and support they could, as was done for everyone in her position. Squire Thomas offered gruff condolences and promised that her place on the farm was secure. But, once the initial shock faded, her dogged resilience took them by surprise.

Rebecca refused to mourn. She had no body to weep over and no graveyard plot to tend. The words 'Missing' and 'Presumed' burnt their way through her skull and into her brain, giving her a hope and belief most refused to acknowledge.

Not dead, not her George. He had been all things to her, still was in memory, and would be again when he returned. Others might fall and be buried in a foreign field, but her husband was not like other men. He was out there, somewhere, maybe lost for now, but he would return. And nothing would persuade her otherwise.

"You must accept," said friends and family when she had continued to stare at the stars with a hopeful conviction that all would end well. "You must accept first before you can move on."

Move on?

The concept puzzled her.

From where? To where?

Rebecca thanked them for their concern but remained convinced that George was still alive and would be found.

*

The news she had been waiting for.

The news Rebecca had known would one day come, arrived in a letter as 1916 prepared to give way to yet another new year of continuing hard times on the home front and conflict abroad. She understood but little of the medical terminology, but that didn't matter as the one important fact sent her delirious with joy.

Pioneer George Albert Reece, previously missing, had now been found.

Alive!

He had been gassed, underground, where it had been thought there were no survivors. Unconscious and desperately ill, he'd had no identification on him so was not named until much later. George had been taken to a Medical Receiving Station at Allonville in France and had only now been moved back to Britain. The references to the seriousness of his condition were of secondary importance as she read and reread the official notification. Yes, he was ill, but if George had made it this far he would make it the rest of the way.

Suddenly Rebecca could stand the shaded loneliness of her little cottage no longer. She needed to feel fresh air on her face, see the fields and feel the breeze. Hear the sounds of life. No longer a person apart, she burst into the open, eager to share her wonderful news.

*

George's tunnelling crew had burst through into an enemy excavation and weary men grappled in an unexpected and unwanted subterranean battle. In these situations you used your fists or whatever came to hand. George killed one German with his spade. Nearly decapitating the man as he swung the thing in blind panic, and during the scuffles that followed his identification discs were torn from the twine around his neck.

The gas bomb was dropped into the British tunnel, but since the wall had been breached it snaked through into the German one as well. As they had been fighting one another, nobody realised the danger until it was upon them and suddenly they were all gasping, burning, struggling for their very lives. Mostly, they lost.

By the time the horrific spectacle was discovered it was assumed there were no survivors. In such a confined space the gas had succeeded, killing British and Germans alike. So it was with disbelief that one of the would-be rescuers noticed a barely perceptible chest movement on one of the fallen Pioneers. Unconscious, barely alive, and without any identification, George was lifted free and stretchered away. Later they transported him to Allonville, where his tenacity in clinging to such a tiny thread of life astounded all the staff.

With the limited means at their disposal, those at the Medical Receiving Station could do little more than pump him full of morphine. At least that way he was spared the agony of his burning throat and lungs, but it also meant he continued to have no name.

Knowing there was nothing they could really do there, it was decided to risk the journey and send him back to England. To a Manor House in rural Somerset that had been converted to a hospital for returning servicemen. For the very worst cases. It was there, during periods of induced awakening, that his hoarsely whispered name and details were finally acquired, and a letter was sent to his wife.

*

It was with a joyful nervousness that Rebecca had set out for her first ever train journey. Squire Thomas himself had driven her to the station in his horse drawn carriage.

"You give George my best regards," he'd told her. "The man is a hero and he'll always have a place in my employ. You tell him that, Rebecca."

And then she had swopped the horse drawn carriage for one pulled by a large and steaming locomotive. A noisy contraption that would carry her all the way to Somerset. All the way to see her George.

The miles sped by, the chugging train noises lulling her into a dreamy contemplation of what was to come. This was indeed a day of wonder. First the ride with the Squire, then her first ever time in a train, and a car to meet her when she finally dismounted at the small Somerset station.

It was an army staff car and the driver, though courteous, was just that, so could tell her nothing about her husband. Impatient, now that seeing him was getting ever nearer, Rebecca could do no more than look at the passing countryside and count each fleeting second. And then, finally, they arrived.

Major Tomkins, who was waiting at the hospital, seemed young to Rebecca for such a rank. Though probably, she guessed, promotions were quicker during wartime. Yet his eyes were old, and there was a weariness about him.

"I must warn you, Mrs Reece," he told her after the formal greetings were over, "before you see your husband. He presents a wasted figure. A shadow of the man you remember…"

His voice tailed into silence and though his words held pity his expression was one no doctor should ever lay bare. A look of despair, and Rebecca felt her body grow chill. She sensed that something was terribly wrong. This was not how their reconciliation should be. This was not how she had imagined it.

"But he will recover, won't he?" she whispered as, for the first time, tears filled her eyes.

Tomkins offered her a handkerchief. A conventional gesture, but providing an opportunity to retrieve his bland professional mask.

"We are quite confident," he replied, "but you must realise just how fortunate he is to be alive at all. Pioneer Reece was the only survivor from that particular event, and I don't suppose we'll ever really know why he didn't die with the others."

"Maybe George wanted to live more than them."

The major's smile was lacking in humour. "Will-power alone would be a poor defence against gas in an enclosed space. If it had been a disabling chemical such as mustard or tear gas, then others might have made it too. But it was almost certainly a more lethal agent, phosgene or chlorine at a guess, and an absolute killer under those circumstances."

"But be that as it may, sir," pointed out Rebecca, "George did survive."

*

The walk between the major's office and the ward had been short and Tomkins paused before entering. "Your husband is unconscious at the moment. We keep him in that condition for much of the time and thought it would be best for your first visit. Try not to let his appearance distress you too much. I'm sure it will improve, given time."

Such a caution should have prepared her for the worst, and Rebecca thought it had. But no, nothing could have forewarned her for the unmoving corpse-like figure lying in the hospital bed. Shining silvered needles stapled his arms at wrist and elbow. Bubbles frothing pink at one incision, before spattering the skin with tiny droplets of blood.

His face was hideous. It had the look of a strangled man.

She wanted to run, to hide. Do anything but stand and stare any longer, and was at least grateful that he was unable to witness the horrifying dismay she could not conceal.

The major, sensing Rebecca's distress, stepped forward, gripping her elbow in case she should fall. "Facts have to be faced," he said. "Your husband's condition is such that he will never regain his physical wellbeing. We have managed to stabilise the damage done to him, but no more than that. There is no magic cure. No tablet or potion. No way to be the man he was."

Like a sleepwalker stepping into uncharted territory, she allowed Tomkins to guide her back to his office and sipped dutifully at a cup of tea he got a ward orderly to bring.

"I never imagined..." she started to say, but lapsed into silence.

"This has been a great shock for you. I understand that."

"But surely..." She had to have some sort of hope. "Surely time and care will bring about some improvements, however limited."

"There is something," admitted the army doctor, "but first I must make you aware of Pioneer Reece's situation. He is now an invalid, and will remain so. The severity of his condition means he will be bedridden for the rest of his days."

Seeing the growing panic in her face he continued quickly.

"But there is something that might help. Not a cure, but a form of assistance."

Rebecca started to speak but he held up a hand to stop her. "Let me finish, Mrs Reece, and listen carefully to what I am going to suggest. While most of this old manor has been converted into a hospital, it does also house an experimental department working in the area of artificial aids. This mostly involves lost limbs, and great strides have been made in providing much improved substitute arms and legs. But they are always up for a challenge and the captain in charge thinks they can offer some small promise of help regarding mobility in your husband's case."

Rebecca grabbed at his words. "Can they make him walk?"

"Well … sort of." Tomkins cleared his throat. "As I understand it, they are proposing to build him into a metal frame which would enclose his torso and legs, thus supporting him for limited movement. The frame would be screwed through the flesh and into bone, meaning it could never be removed.

"It would not, and I must stress this, it would not enable him to enjoy a full and everyday existence. But even only limited movement is to be preferred when the alternative is to be permanently bedridden."

And Rebecca had agreed, wholeheartedly. "In sickness and in health" she had promised. She would nurse and care for him and honour their love, but would also be grateful for any help that was offered.

It not being his area of expertise, Major Tomkins had his doubts, but kept them to himself. "I am sure you will both be able to…" he paused a moment, searching for the words to tell this tragic woman that her husband would be more than just a freak. There were none.

"…adjust," he said finally.

*

George himself had been hoarsely optimistic when she had finally spoken with him the next day. It was difficult for him to dredge up words from his damaged lungs and throat. Like her, he was pinning his hopes on whatever support a manufactured frame would offer his wasted body. For all the terribleness of his appearance, he was still her George, and Rebecca did her best to reassure him of that fact.

"We will cope, Becky," he'd whispered.

"Course we will, George. Of course we will."

She had left the hospital then. Left Somerset and returned to their little cottage to prepare for his homecoming. There were people to tell, and to warn, about his condition. And a bed had to be placed downstairs since they had warned her that steps would be beyond his range of movements.

George was never going to work again. That was certain. "No matter," Squire Thomas told her. "We know how to care for our heroes. You and George need have no worries about that."

*

For all her happiness at having him home, Rebecca couldn't suppress a shudder as she watched the orderlies stagger into the cottage, heaving sighs of relief as they relinquished their burden.

The captain accompanying them was an outstanding talent in his field and an unpleasant man. *And* not *but*, for that would suggest some measure of excuse where none existed, which not even his acknowledged ability could justify. He seemed to regard all lower ranks with contempt. This did not make him unique, just unpleasant.

"Pioneer Reece posed many technical problems," he said. "Problems which needed to be overcome."

"But he's so big," said Rebecca, almost to herself. "So heavy."

George had been sedated for the long ambulance journey from the hospital. Soon he would awake and after a final medical check she would be alone with him. For all the love she felt, the thought did scare her a little. It would almost be like looking after a child.

Sourly, the captain agreed. "But consider what we have achieved," he said. "Even when the body is weak, the brain continues its active life. We have harnessed his useless flesh into a powerful exoskeleton. It may be somewhat cumbersome, but it will allow him some movement again. It will restore a certain degree of mobility.

"Otherwise..." he shrugged. "He would have been bedridden and probably hospitalised for the rest of his life."

Yes, I know, thought Rebecca, and I am grateful. But at the back of her mind she could not suppress a tremor of disquiet.

"You must always treat him as a *normal* human being." The captain stressed the word, and she glanced surreptitiously at the silent figure bulked beneath the red blanket.

Treat him as a *normal* human being!

Later, when George was awake and the medical team had left, he spoke of his hopes. "I will learn, with your help. Soon this frame will become as much a part of me as my own flesh and blood. We will both have to adjust, my love, but there'll be nothing we won't be able to meet and overcome, together."

*

At first he said he loved her; that they were still man and wife, and all that meant would always hold true. But when she continued to refuse he became angry and bitter, accusing her of going with other men and even naming Squire Thomas.

In his imagination George saw her in the throes of sex, her eyes half-closed, head thrown back, spreading her legs wide as someone else's penis plunged deep into her.

The thought filled him with revulsion ... yet excited him.

Later, as his frustration grew, he began pleading with her. "Let me," he begged in a little-boy voice. "I need you. Please."

Rebecca shook her head. "No," she replied quietly, averting her eyes. "I can't."

"Please!"

"No."

There was a long silence, as if a thick velvet curtain had descended between them.

"Damn you!" he shouted, suddenly and without warning,

as loudly as his poor body would allow, startling Rebecca with his vehemence. "Damn you to Hell and back! I want you ... now!" George began to sob. "Please..."

It was the final supplication. If she refused him now then all that had existed before was gone forever.

*

"Yes," she whispered, hardly believing that the word had finally been said.

*

Rebecca's eyes opened wide, then shut tight as the crushing weight bore down upon her, and she cried out against the violence of his need. There was a searing agony which seemed to wrench her apart the harder he thrust, until she felt that she could endure the pain no longer.

Until she screamed for it to end.

Until, finally, it was ended.

*

She looked down at herself: at the angry yellow bruises where his armoured fingers clutched her breasts, at the red wheals covering her body where the metal ribcage crushed her, at her thighs streaked with dried blood.

I wish he had died in that tunnel, she thought while remembering Major Tomkins telling her how fortunate George was to be alive at all.

I wish he'd die now, added Rebecca silently, bringing to mind the captain's vigorous entreaty: "You must treat him like a *normal* human being."

And the words began to hammer back and forth inside her skull, echoing until her head seemed to reverberate with the sound. Until it seemed that it would burst.

A *normal* human being.

Normal?

NORMAL...!

*

Outside in the fields the crops had been harvested. All that was left were broken stalks to be either ploughed back into the earth or used to feed the animals.

Inside their cottage a cold fear gripped Rebecca as she

wondered: how soon would it be before George wanted her again?

A Very Strange Tunnelling Company

Paul Woodward

A very strange Tunnelling Company passed through the Menin gate at Ypres on foot, in single file.

Four of them.

The first was tall and lithe. Behind her a younger and much shorter woman who looked furtively left and right.

All wore balaclavas, their uniforms, overalls, gumboots puttees and upwards, caked in white chalk from the South West of Vimy.

They could have been walking for days.

"Oh God, where are we Silver?"

The first woman turned around, "Don't call me Silver – call me Sergeant." The road was empty, and no-one to overhear. "And remember we're not women – we're men."

"Okay, okay but where are we?"

"This is a war zone and we're going to have to go underground to find the Black Turtle."

"A war zone? But there's no-one about..."

"There will be – and just remember to act like a man. If necessary leave all the talking to me, keep quiet and Jen, we're going to have to call you James."

The third in the troupe, Clockwork, interrupted, and looked into his hand as he spoke, reading from a dial. "We will soon find catacombs where you can rest."

Jen waved her hand at some elephant shelters they passed. "What's wrong with these?" The buildings were spaced out and rickety, and had taken some bombing. They appeared mostly empty, with an occasional single occupant sitting morosely in the doorway.

Shell-shocked, muttering incoherently, a soldier staggered

forwards and started shouting, but not actually at them, at something that only he could see. "Get away from me! Get away!" He jumped from one foot to the other, brushed himself as though vermin were crawling up his legs no matter what he did, or however strong he was.

Jen's eyes widened as she stepped towards him.

She saw what he saw: metal caterpillars boiled out of the ground and raced up his limbs, taking tiny slivers out of him before running back down. They were automated and remorseless in a fast procession.

As Jen reached for him they splintered and fell collapsed. Carapaces bubbled and popped under her gaze.

"What are these?" Jen asked, but Clockwork held his hand over her eyes as the tall woman, Hermione, led her away.

"This is why we need you underground. You can't go seeing things like this. It's not what we're here for. You'll be seen and we won't get the Black Turtle back."

The fourth, Carluccio, strolled over to the soldier who was now much calmer, though still befuddled. "What ... what's goin' on eh?" He led him back to the elephant shelter, dusted his shoulders and quietly re-seated him on a three legged stool in the doorway. He gently laid his hands on his head and the soldier slept easily for the first time since the war had begun.

*

The ribbed and bony elephant huts diminished as they walked further towards the front.

Eerily, a church loomed into view between a skeletal avenue of withered trees, stripped bare from war. Stumped and thwarted in shock, thin branches and trunks twisted and ended abruptly where once had been green shoots and shaded arbours.

A dusty wind followed them, rising at their tail and flapping their overalls.

Clockwork led to the rear of the church where a small old cemetery lay. Many of the stones, the markers of past lives, had fallen. Made brittle or left only in part. Swiped at in ignorance by the war. But otherwise not deliberately disturbed. No fresh burials here despite thousands of dead in recent times.

He pushed the lid from a mausoleum at the side of the church and headed down. A plinth remained above scarred and jagged where it had broken: enough left to see the vestiges of an angel. Stone wings sheared back to the shoulders. Half of one arm missing. The legs riddled with holes as though bullets had passed through: a failed attempt to topple the statue altogether.

Carluccio accommodated himself in front of the stone angel. Unfurled his backpack and his wings flexed out to replace the missing stone. The reaches of his wings glowed a pale and hesitant red until they took on the appearance and texture of the statue. His arm filled in for the one missing and his legs covered any bullet holes. All night he remained standing on the plinth, head cast downwards.

*

"We know that's Polyhedron," Hermione held Jen's hand. "Maybe those insects on the shoulder were just echoes?"

Jen stammered, not wanting to remember the one-eyed monster and his cave, and didn't say anything so Hermione continued: "It's because you saw them first. The soldier didn't see them the way you saw them."

Eventually Jen replied, "Yes, but he must have *felt* them. He was jumping with it. You saw him as well. Don't say you didn't."

"I'm trying to tell you he would have just felt a pain. He wouldn't even have thought about metal insects."

"So it's me then? I'm imagining them. But what's in that cave – that thing used them didn't it?"

Legions of metal insects had swarmed in and out of Polyhedron's cave with debris, wood foliage, animals, some alive, some not.

Anything animate or inanimate would go like a never ending river into the fire.

A horrible method of heat and distillation; pieces burnt down and blackened into cinders. Other metal insects at the rear of the flames pulled out the charred pieces with long pincers and mandibles, transferring them to cooling glasses or smaller fires, where they would be cooled or burnt again!

A scurry of activity that eventually produced sheets and lumps that Polyhedron considered with his one eye before hammering and twisting them into suitable shape for his mouth to ingest, or a layer to add to his armour.

Similarly if a vein burst, a burnt down clinker from his workshop acted as a suture – which he would slap into place with a bellow of pain, or a groan of satisfaction.

Remembering all of this, Jen asked: "But am I bringing it all back just by thinking about it?"

Hermione pulled her closer. "No – not in that way."

Jen though heaved deeply, remembering more. "It's my fault isn't it? I shouldn't have shouted. If I hadn't shouted!"

She was thinking of the taunts she threw at Polyhedron as they escaped. Of the metal slabs he'd thrown in retaliation and which had sunk their ship the Black Turtle, cursing them into perpetual war. "And if I hadn't shouted he wouldn't have known where we were, would he?"

With encouragement Jen eventually rested. Clockwork displayed a map of the underground tunnelling in the vicinity, hologramatic, including geological characteristics of soil and clay.

Both agreed the Black Turtle, now miniaturised, would be in the blue Ypres clay, firm enough to support its density, having doubtless sunk through the slippery waters of the upper Kemmel Sands.

*

Hermione sat in the office with Lieutenant Philip Hartley, the senior officer in command. He was barely twenty, observed Hermione; his cheeks were dusted with acne and powdered to disguise them, which only made it more obvious.

Her friends were separated by a woollen army blanket hung across the entrance to serve as a door.

Clockwork and Carluccio sat patiently behind bulky proto-apparatus which covered their faces in masks, although Carluccio left the mouthpiece loose against his neck. His wings were concealed in what looked like a secondary air tank on his back. Unable to hear any conversation the other side of the blanket, Jen became anxious and paced backwards and forwards. Eventually she put her head through, and the young officer spoke. "Ah, we have company – no standing on ceremony for Empire Jack's men I see!"

"Oh, hi," Jen read this as an invitation to enter and sat opposite Hermione.

He took this as irony and chuckled. "Not much headroom I know – your sergeant couldn't stand straight. Awfully tall fellow. But you and I we're okay hey!"

He stood to show a couple of inches clearance between his head and the ceiling then sat back down, behind a desk at the end of a low narrow dugout.

The roof: overlapping metal sheets; holding up tonnes of soil above them. Timbers formed the walls. No furniture – just a desk and two stools the two women occupied. Hangings on the wall were duty rotas, plans, all old and torn.

The young officer addressed Jen again. "As I was saying to your leader: I know you're civvies, and we're quite informal around here. No standing on, erm ... ceremony, so to speak," he stubbed out his cigarette and blew the remaining smoke from his mouth upwards, circulating it with his hands before coughing briefly.

Hermione unfolded her arms. "We're here for mine disposal."

"Yes, you've said that. Got no orders though. That's a tricky bit you know. What?"

Surreptitiously Hermione kicked Jen before she could giggle. "My corporal will have them in his bag."

Jen went through the blanket screen. Clockwork had produced official stationery and was printing across one sheet with his finger.

"Here you are, sir," Jen returned with a casual left handed salute to the lieutenant, handing him the papers.

"If I may ask – have you just come in off a ship?" He saw the shock pass across Jen's face and laughed. "And did it just sink?"

Hermione quickly interrupted before Jen could reply, "No sir, we've been down in the chalk for too long. Vimy way, sir!"

"Vimy you say," he loosened his cravat, pushed the papers aside just given to him and winked at Jen. "Aye aye sailor!"

*

"How does he know?" Jen asked.

"He doesn't. He's just making fun."

They were in a dugout assigned to them near to an entrance to the underground network.

Tomorrow they would start mine clearance and look for the Black Turtle.

Clockwork was busy transforming a geophone into a metal detector. Instead of listening for the sound of enemy tunnellers, they would be scanning for any bulky objects under the ground.

Unfortunately they would be unable to isolate the Black Turtle, though Clockwork would be able to read the approximate size and density of anything they found.

The Turtle: sank after Polyhedron's attack, drifted out of their reach – shrunk into the proportions of a large thick leg.

"But why did he speak about the ship sinking?"

"He doesn't know."

"But..."

"You know he likes you."

"Likes me? I'm supposed to be a man."

*

Jen operated the windlass. Her three friends descended, one at a time, down the vertical shaft through the Kemmel sands, before reaching the galleries below.

All that time Jen thought of what to say to the lieutenant.

He was quite nice in a boyish sort of way. His talk was quaint but direct. Jen told herself to concentrate on not being a woman, focus on what needed to be asked for. She had the list written down to fall back on if required. *Don't act casual – don't give the game away.*

Not in his office.

A half-dressed squaddie, leisurely adjusted his belt, eyes glazed, probably drunk, tunic undone and shirt open, directed Jen further along the tunnel with a smile.

She put her head through the indicated blanketed doorway and stopped. The lieutenant stood with his back to the entrance before a full length mirror. He was wearing a multi-coloured feather boa and nothing else. A sly smile creased his lips and spread slowly into his face. "Hello sailor."

Jen bolted and ricocheted off the tunnel's timber, not stopping until she stumbled across a group of men shrouded in smoke playing dominoes.

"Wow ... slow down there soldier." A large bare-chested moustachioed man said. "No sir, indeed! That's no soldier – that there's a clay-kicker!" He waved to somebody behind Jen. "I see you're with the officer – snap to it son!"

The lieutenant was upon her. He now wore a dressing gown and untied trench boots. Laughter behind them died away as he linked arms and led her back to his quarters.

*

He rattled off a series of questions to her she found difficult to keep up with. Asked where she was from and replied "Shore-side" which he heard as Shoreditch and canted a tune about bells and roses and places she'd never heard of.

He skipped a short while which she found infectious, glanced downwards and skipped with him, their feet light across the duckboards. "When will you grow rich ... say the bells of Shoreditch?" Jen sang along with him. Their voices echoed along the empty tunnels.

Philip Hartley, the lieutenant, spoke for a long time. Jen listened, mostly without hearing. His voice had an ebb and flow, sentences ended louder than they started.

He took the list of requisitions typed by Clockwork's hand without a glance. Cocked his head from one side to the other. He was looking at her while he spoke and she hadn't noticed. Off guard Jen beamed a big smile.

"I say – I'll get the men to bring you anything you want."

Later, with Hermione Jen could remember nothing he said. But she couldn't stop talking about him. His hands, his voice, his song, his...

Hermione folded her arms, "You've grown. You're not the little girl you used to be when you were first my stowaway. And now you're a woman."

She paused to allow her observation to sink in and held back the experience and events of hundreds of years behind the black dams of her eyes.

To Jen she seemed implacable and made her feel even smaller and insignificant before the tall woman than usual. Jen blinked, and didn't want to be reminded of the past. "You should be prepared for disappointment."

"What?"

"He likes men. We're supposed to be men, remember. But you're not. I suspect he won't say anything when he finds out, but just be prepared that's all."

Underground in the galleries Jen had little to do as the days passed. Occasionally at the face extending a tunnel where it was too small for Hermione or Clockwork. Discovered clay-kicking, resting her back against a cross and jabbing a shovel with her feet. Mostly they used adapted geophones, extended tunnels themselves or used large boring tools, too heavy for Jen to screw into the clay.

She became familiar with the lieutenant, or Lord Phil, whatever lord meant. Jen was drawn to him. Underground his quarters were a beacon of light in the darkness. A multi-coloured light. Lanterns and lights he shrouded in gossamer silks of many shades.

Lord Phil taught her a dance that consisted of holding one hand in the air and stamping one foot down, moving around in a circle. Jen copied but moved in the opposite direction looking at him all the time and laughing. Laughing in what she hoped was a manly way.

"You like this light James? I can tell you've never been in the army. But my father knows Norton-Griffiths. They're quite chums you see." She thought to ask later about this Norton-Griffiths.

At least Lord Phil was never suddenly naked.

Jen found she didn't need to speak much. Lord Phil liked to read aloud. He read poetry to her. They sang songs together.

Once the large man with the curly moustache entered, drunk, hardly able to stand, "What do you think – little clay-kicker, of our lord here?" he fell, eyes closed on top of Phil who couldn't hold him.

Together they manoeuvred him to Phil's bunk. His eyes

sprang open with glee, wrapped a tyre arm around each and bellowed: "Threesome!" before finally falling asleep, this time unconscious. Phil smiled apologetically, and Jen wriggled free.

*

In the tunnels Jen saw insects again.

Returning from clay-kicking she took a wrong turn. Hoped to emerge on a broad communication tunnel but instead the crawlspace narrowed.

The timber supports of three by two foot seemed to get smaller.

The wood became tin sheets.

The tin sheets started to move and rained upon her.

Expected to choke with a mouthful of soil and crushed by the weight of earth. Slithers, metal tendrils, probed her mouth.

Instinctively she knew they were Polyhedron's creatures. Jen bit down and opened her eyes. They had been closed in fear and expectation. Again these creatures withered in her gaze. Their metal bubbled and popped and faded away.

Jen cautiously retraced her passage. But resolved to say nothing, thinking it her imagination and claustrophobia being underground so long.

The Tunnelling Company waited for the windlass to take them up. Goggled and laden with excess cans of ammonal they did not see Jen. She took alternative ladder steps having no load to carry.

She found Phil immediately.

He sat her down and poured tea as she blurted about nearly being smothered by the collapsing tunnel. She didn't mention the Black Turtle nor the insects, but said enough to release her tension.

"Calm down," he stood above her conciliatory and loosened her overalls and worked his hands inside until: "A sailor girl – I could have guessed!"

His smile was unexpected, Jen thought he would be horrified. But he pinched her cheek playfully. She moved her arms and legs co-operatively as he peeled off slowly her layers of clothing. Knelt to the gum boots and pulled them off expertly from the heel, as if he had been her servant all his life.

Treasured each boot as he kissed them. "You are beautiful James – will you ever forgive me?" Jen looked downwards at herself, left and right. Phil slipped off his dressing gown.

Suddenly a large explosion went off nearby. The walls shook. Timber supports split. The metal roof shifted. Phil and Jen tottered, holding each other for balance. The sound was deafening. Jen's ears rang, she couldn't hear a thing.

Clockwork, heavy with balaclava and breathing mask, tore aside the blanket doorway and lurched forwards, swung at Phil and knocked him against the wall.

The comfy network of soft lights went flying in demolition.

Silks caught fire. Went up with an oomph, as though made from rice paper or something else equally impermanent. Shreds and circling dust remained.

"No!" Jen screamed and leapt onto Clockwork but she could not get purchase and fell helplessly to the floor. She desperately scrabbled at him as he broke Phil's neck. Jen got no response from Clockwork. He turned his back and left.

"Why!" Jen sobbed and rubbed her eyes. She knelt over Phil, "Why did you do this?" Clockwork had never behaved this way before. He'd always acknowledged her. Always sought her approval. There was nothing, no glimmer behind the balaclava. And what would she forgive Phil for? In death his body took on the same white pallor as his face.

Dressed, Jen lifted Phil. He was light as a feather. He could have been a twig or one of his coloured feather boas.

This didn't feel right. Jen shouted for Silver. Or tried to, she couldn't hear herself. But she picked up the slight body and ran through the tunnels. Passed the group of drunken squaddies who always seemed to play dominoes in a smoky haze, as though they weren't there.

"Silver! Silver!" she shouted and just began to hear herself. Jen ran holding the body to her chest with both arms. Skittered around a corner, struggled to find her footing and staggered up an incline.

At the top of the windlass she found Hermione. Bare to the shoulders, washing her head and face, ladling water from a bucket. Her skin glistening with water shone grey and silver in the underground lights. She wiped her head and shook herself dry at Jen's arrival, "Oh good – you've found it!"

Jen now held the Black Turtle, a small black submarine in her arms. But dropped it to the floor. "No – where's Phil?"

Hermione was puzzled. Clockwork looked up from where he sat opposite her, his lights too blinked curiously. The Angel Carluccio was quietly stacking cans of ammonal.

"What ... you..." Jen couldn't speak, "You ... Phil ... I saw you..."

"We're here. We've been waiting for you. Hermione spoke but Jen found it still difficult to hear.

Clockwork had been ready to go back down and look for her.

Jen told about insects in the tunnels and Phil and Clockwork – or something that looked like..."and I should have known, I should..."

Hermione held the young woman close. Forced her hand into her mouth and brought out a wriggling caterpillar. A hundred joints along its back twisted in as many directions to be free. Hermione's grip tightened and a bulbous scaly head emerged as the little creature's scales peeled back. She lowered this to Jen's level so she could see, and poked its eye out, "Gone Jen. Gone now."

Clockwork knelt on the duckboards of the trench, with his ministrations the Black Turtle grew larger and larger and would eventually burst out of the trench altogether...

Casualties

Anthony Hanks

The Gallipoli Peninsula – 1915

Hargrave Albion Willis didn't mind injuries, trauma or the general carnage associated with war. Though he would never admit it, the sight of arterial blood, raw exposed bone and torn and mutilated flesh excited him in a way most could never understand. In times of peace these characteristics were not accepted as normal and Hargrave would be labeled a madman.

A psychopath.

But in times of war … well … some might label him a hero, and a genius.

Hargrave Albion Willis stared out across Suvla Bay as he pondered this dichotomous opinion of himself.

Oh how I do love a proper hecatomb, he thought. *How I adore the carnage. How I delight in the slaying. And to think, here in this evil place people think of me a good man. A GREAT man. But they do not understand that in order for there to be good in this world there must also be evil.*

Hargrave had shown *them* that once.

A long time ago.

He walked a little further down the path towards the cliff-face, removing his pipe from his coat pocket as he went. He clenched the pipe in his teeth, struck a match with his thumbnail and brought it up to light the bowl of finely tamped tobacco. There was a sudden stirring to his left and a harsh whisper cut through the dark stillness, the thick accent ruining Hargrave's little moment of tranquillity.

"Aye! What are you, some kind of madman then? You tryin' to get yourself shot?"

Hargrave walked over to where the two men sat crowded in

their observation post. He leaned down and took a deep drag on his pipe so that the glow would illuminate his face.

He smiled. "A madman? Me? I'm afraid I'm not quite sure about that."

The two men stared at Hargrave's face and when they finally realised who they had addressed they straightened up in their trench and swallowed hard. The bigger man on the left spoke up.

"Sorry sir," he said. "Didn't realise it was you, sir."

The man's accent was pure Essex and Hargrave detested it. For an instant he visualised cutting out the man's tongue.

But he didn't.

Instead he smiled again and spoke to the man in his much more formal dialect – the kind he picked up many years ago while at Oxford. "Not at all. You gentlemen are just carrying out your duty, and doing a damn fine job of it. Damn fine. But I understand if my smoking makes you uneasy." Hargrave stood upright again. "Carry on then."

"Thank you, sir," both men said in unison.

Hargrave left them in their foxhole and continued down the narrow path above Suvla Bay. He understood why the two men had protested his smoking in the open. In the last week the Turkish snipers had picked off four British troops who had been a little too careless while up and about the camp at night. Hargrave himself had personally tried to save two of the men but to no avail. He refused to call it a failure, because the truth was he didn't put forth much effort to save them in the first place. During the operations his mind was on the chess game he had waiting in the tent of a captain from another regiment. He hadn't cared about the men, so it was of no matter whether they lived or died.

Hargrave paused and took another long drag from his pipe. The blue smoke drifted up into the tree tops above him. Some men – including the two back there in the observation post – would have thought him foolhardy, careless or maybe pompous to be smoking out in the open like that. After all, the glow from his pipe made the perfect target for snipers. Hargrave wasn't afraid though, and while he didn't truly believe that his fate was to perish at the hand of a Turkish sharpshooter, he was prepared for it.

However, deep down he knew he was destined for greater things. He'd already done *so many* great things. *Surely God can't be done with me?*

He smiled at no one, and stared out over to the other side of the ravine opposite the bay. It was approximately six hundred metres. *That would be a quite impressive shot.*

Hargrave himself despised firearms and much preferred the personal connection established when one's foe was dispatched with an edged weapon in close quarters. His little unit had been on this dreadful peninsula for three months and Hargrave had thought many times about sneaking over to the Turkish trenches at night with his amputation knife. Some of the younger soldiers might chuckle at this idea. He was, after all, a little old for a man of combat. But at fifty three he was thought to be the right age for a proper field surgeon.

Hargrave shook his head. *Fools. I'm in better shape than most of the men half my age.*

His thoughts drifted back to the two young men at the observation post. He could have killed them both in seconds and made it look like a covert enemy assassination. But in the end they had shown him the proper amount of fear and respect, and that's what he thrived on. For that, they got to keep their tongues in their heads and blood in their bodies.

Good Lord Man! It's as if you've an obsession with tongues now!

The tongue was considered an external organ, and Hargrave Albion Willis was more partial to the internal variety.

He continued back down to the encampment and eventually stopped just outside of the hospital tent. He knocked his pipe against his boot heel to extinguish the embers and then stepped inside.

It was quiet this evening. There were only four patients lying on cots at the far end of the tent. They all appeared to be resting peacefully – a pleasant result of the morphine shipment Hargrave had received the week before.

Hargrave continued on through the tent towards his patients. He stopped occasionally to straighten a random medicine bottle or to smooth a wrinkle in a bed sheet. The thing that set his hospital apart from others was that it was impeccably – almost impossibly – clean. His superiors credited this to a proper military mindset, and Hargrave let them think that.

The truth was that Hargrave Albion Willis was a gentleman, and as such he abhorred sloppiness. His own appearance was pristine. He was always clean-shaven, his hair perfectly groomed and his uniform looking as if it had just that day been unpackaged at the Quartermaster.

Hargrave had no patience for the soldiers that used combat as an excuse for laziness. Many men had found themselves on Doctor Willis's operating table sporting week old beards. Hargrave would fight the urge to remove the flesh from their faces with a scalpel, solving their shaving problem forever.

When he was finally done tidying, Hargrave stood over the four sleeping men. They were all that was left of a twelve man squad that had been hit with a vicious artillery barrage four days earlier. Hargrave smiled because they were all cleanly shaved, except for Private Becker. Becker's face was covered in bandages meant to hide his surgically removed left eye and lower jaw. *You'll never eat solid food again, but at least you won't have to worry about that dreadful stubble.*

Hargrave began to check the wounds of the other three men as well. Private Smith's left leg had been blown clean off at the knee, so Hargrave's work had been fairly easy. He'd simply stitched up the severed arteries, stretched the skin around Smith's knee before sewing it up into a neat little package. He appeared to be recovering nicely.

Private Collins had been the most challenging. Massive abdominal trauma had necessitated Hargrave removing ten feet of the young soldier's small intestine – a relatively new and complicated surgical procedure, and virtually unheard of in military field hospitals.

Hargrave Albion Willis had become an expert on colonic and rectal surgeries long before the medical community had accepted them as life-saving procedures, although he was sure that his alumni back at Oxford would not have approved of his practical training.

At any rate, his work on Private Collins had quite impressed the higher ranking medical officials of the 10th Division, and rumours of his surgical prowess quickly spread across the Gallipoli peninsula. While Hargrave didn't mind the publicity, he hated the nicknames his skills often bore and his latest was absolutely ridiculous.

The Wizard.

How absolutely juvenile, he thought. *To think that my work is akin to sorcery. One does not need magic and alchemy to perform miracles!*

Hargrave shook his head as he continued his check-ups. Becker's pulse was strong and he was stable, despite the severe injuries to his face.

Satisfied that Becker wasn't going to die in the night, Hargrave moved on to his final patient, Lance Corporal Bailey.

Both of Bailey's legs had been shredded in the artillery strike, and there was barely anything left of them when he'd been dropped onto Doctor Willis's operating table. Hargrave had gone quickly to work at amputating both legs just below the knees. Now, as he stood over the lance corporal, his brow furrowed and a sinister scowl crept across his face.

There was blood seeping through the bandage covering Bailey's stump of a left leg. The veins beneath the skin of his upper thigh were bright red. Hargrave leaned down and sniffed the blood-soaked bandage. He recoiled at the foul, rotting stench.

Gangrene.

Hargrave hated infection. He felt it ruined his work. That's why he had enjoyed the second Boer War in 1900. The hot and dry climate of South Africa made it easy to stave off infection. But here, on this Godforsaken Turkish peninsula, the conditions were hot and damp – perfect for promoting decay. He reached down and felt the fever emanating from the upper portion of Bailey's leg.

Well, looks like we'll have to take a little more off than we'd originally planned.

There was a medical transport due to arrive in the morning

and they would be taking all four soldiers back to England for recovery. Hargrave removed his pocket watch and discovered that there was just seven hours before the team arrived. He replaced his watch and stared back down at Lance Corporal Bailey. *That doesn't leave us much time.*

Hargrave injected an additional eight milligrams of morphine into the lance corporal's I.V. drip. Eight might have been a little excessive – there was a chance he would stop breathing. But Hargrave didn't care about that. His only concern was removing the infection from his work.

When he was sure Bailey was thoroughly sedated, Hargrave Albion Willis returned to his tent, where he retrieved his knives.

*

The transport team was late, so the following morning Hargrave once again stood alone over his four injured soldiers. His focus was on Bailey and the work he'd done the night before.

Although seven additional inches of the lance corporal's leg had been removed, so too had the infection and the smell of rot that accompanied it. Bailey was able to take the higher dose of morphine and hadn't died during the operation after all. Hargrave was smiling to himself when he heard the sound of a horse-drawn wagon pull up outside the tent.

Moments later, the entrance flap was brushed aside and two medics entered followed by a young nurse. As the trio approached, Hargrave focused on the woman and his heart began to flutter. She was young and she was beautiful, and she reminded him of a woman he'd known a long time ago. When the medical team had reached his side, all three rendered a salute, which he returned.

"Captain Willis," said the tallest man, a lance corporal. "It's a pleasure to meet you, sir."

"Corporal," Hargrave replied as he grasped the young soldier's hand.

The next medic stepped up and shook Hargrave's hand as well. "Sir, it's an honour."

When the young nurse extended her hand Hargrave took it

gently and turned it in his own hand. The practice of shaking a woman's hand as you would a man's had been growing in popularity since the turn of the century, but Hargrave simply could not suppress the chivalry he'd been instilled with. He bent at the waist and kissed the woman's hand gently. The young nurse blushed. Hargrave had a sudden vision of washing his hands in her blood.

"It's a pleasure to meet you, Captain," she said.

"The pleasure is mine, Nurse…"

"Kelly."

"Kelly." Hargrave almost burst into laughter at the coincidence. Instead he smiled charmingly. "But of course."

Hargrave assisted the young medical personnel in preparing the four injured soldiers, and eventually they loaded the patients into the medical wagon. When the appropriate transfer documents were signed, Hargrave bid the medics – and the young Nurse Kelly – a farewell. As the horses trotted off down the trail to the bay, Hargrave removed his pipe. Just before the ambulance disappeared over a hill the back flap was pulled aside and Nurse Kelly looked at him and smiled.

A burning sensation rose in his chest as Hargrave waved at the young woman. When she was finally out of sight he went back to preparing his pipe. As he lit it he fantasised about running his hands over Nurse Kelly's naked body.

Then he thought about skinning her.

Hargrave's fantasies were interrupted by a deep thunder that he felt before he heard. He instantly recognised the noise as a Turkish 18 centimetre Krupp Howitzer

He could hear the large shell whistling through the air and instantly knew that the transport team was the intended target. His thoughts again returned to Nurse Kelly, and he wondered what she'd look like if any of those artillery shells found their mark.

A dozen or so soldiers had run past him towards the trail, hauling their rifles with them. Hargrave took three more puffs as two more enemy shells flew overhead and exploded somewhere down the trail. He showed no concern whatsoever, and was irritated when the situation report traveled down the defensive line and eventually made it to him.

The ambulance had been hit, and four of the seven passengers appeared to be dead.

The other three had massive trauma and needed medical attention immediately. Hargrave ordered the private that had delivered the news to find all the available men he could and bring the three wounded passengers to the hospital tent. The private ran off in a sprint to carry out his orders. Hargrave knocked out his pipe and went back inside his hospital to prepare his surgical suite.

*

He'd donned his gown and laid out all of his instruments when the private he'd talked with outside arrived with six other men carrying the three wounded passengers on stretchers.

They set the wounded on three beds and Hargrave quickly began to triage his patients. They were a mess of blood, bone and tattered clothing, so until he stood right next to each there was no identifying who his patients were.

A quick examination of the first casualty actually stirred up some disappointment in him. The two missing legs were not caused by the recent artillery barrage, but the massive amount of blood pouring from Lance Corporal Bailey's neck was. *Shame I wasted all that time last night*, Hargrave thought.

"He's expectant, nothing we can do," Hargrave declared before moving on to the next casualty.

The tall lance corporal that had, thirty minutes earlier, helped carry Bailey to the ambulance was now lying next to him, unconscious. His right leg was shredded from the middle of his thigh down, and his right arm was completely blown off below the elbow.

Hargrave turned to the team of medics that had joined him.

"Get a tourniquet on his arm and leg and we may be able to save him." Before moving to the last casualty Hargrave looked up and saw that a decent crowd of soldiers had gathered in the hospital tent.

When he looked back down he couldn't help but smile underneath his surgical mask.

She was in much worse shape than the tall Lance Corporal.

Nurse Kelly appeared to be conscious but was unresponsive. Hargrave wiped some blood from her face and saw that her pupils were fat and black. Her right eye was rapidly filling with blood. Her blouse and skirt had both been nearly blown off, and he could see that her right breast was a mangled pile of jagged tissue. Her abdomen had taken the most damage. Several feet of intestine was piled on top of the gaping fissure in her stomach. One of the medics had done the correct thing by piling some fabric on top and soaking it with water. Hargrave was pondering what he'd need to do to perform the resection when one of the medics that helped carry Nurse Kelly in leaned over and whispered, loudly.

"Do you think you can save her, sr?"

Hargrave didn't have a chance to answer before someone else yelled from the crowd. "'COURSE HE CAN! HE'S THE WIZARD!"

A few cheers and words of encouragement erupted from the crowd of soldiers. Hargrave just shook his head. *There's that damned nickname again.*

He'd had many nicknames in his lifetime, but "The Wizard" was the only one he'd ever been able to claim.

"Leather Apron" had been his favorite.

"Jack the Ripper" had been the most famous.

He was thinking all kinds of vile thoughts when the medic on his left leaned in and whispered once more, much softer this time.

"Sir," he said, "you *can* save her, can't you?"

Hargrave Albion Willis turned to the young man and smiled. "Oh, I'm sure I'll be able to do *something* with her."

Truce

Shaun A.J. Hamilton

Far beneath the heavy grey sky of Christmas morning, troops gathered on the battlefield. Climbing over the top of their frozen trenches mazing through Belgium's deepest countryside, German, Scottish and French soldiers came together and made their pact.

Deep inside the wasteland's heart, enemies stood as allies.

Promises, gifts and stories of loved ones were exchanged as those gathered struggled with their prejudices. Some sang and others cried. Laughter and hope filled the void.

Fresh snow fell like tears from the Holy Deity whose birth they had come together to celebrate.

All nationalities enshrined by virgin white.

*

The order had been given.

They were to assemble their dead. Move them to a clearing in nearby Ploegsteert Woods. Frenchman would help Frenchman; Scotsman help Scotsman.

German help German.

But where needed, races would cross and help their fellow humans to shift their heavy loads.

Sergeant Simon Williams refused the offer made by the small German. As the thin Hun in the heavy coat approached, Simon stopped dragging his load and looked up.

The man held something dark in his hand, pointing it towards Simon. "Schokolade?"

His voice was soft; childish. He took a small bite of his offering to prove there was no sleight of hand trickery involved in this attempt at friendship.

Fresh snow crumpled beneath his feet as he inched closer,

arm outstretched once more. "Sie mögen?"

You like?

Simon said nothing. Did nothing.

He stared at the man, the frail man whom he knew he could take out silently with the knife concealed in his sock hidden by his overhanging kilt.

He knew how easy it would be to bring an end to this stupid farce and make enemies of them all once again.

To kill the murdering bastards.

Bring sanity back into this madness.

The German stopped. Snow landed on his shoulders and outstretched arm. His forgiving eyes changed as he recognised the fire in the man opposite him.

Fear replaced mercy. He saw a pain in Simon he had seen in many others out here in the wasteland.

A pain too raw to know forgiveness.

He dropped his arm and turned, giving Simon one last nervous glance over his shoulder as merged with the crowd.

Only when the man had left did Simon notice the adrenalin coursing through his veins. He felt the perspiration on his forehead begin to chill and turn to frost.

He breathed out hot plumes of white air like some great sweating stag about to go into battle. The tension in his muscles felt like his flesh were frozen. Walking back to the pile he had left behind, he thought he heard wet snaps as tendons broke their icicles and gave him his body back.

The body was wrapped in a cumbersome canvas cocoon. Placing it on a discarded tent already perforated by a German machine gun, he used this as his sleigh.

Threading thin rope through the bullet holes until large knots caught in the fabric gave him reigns. Before the Kraut had stopped him he had been pulling the wet twine like it was a game of tug-o'-war. But now, tired of heaving the 'dead' weight over terrain macerated by falling bullets and exploding grenades, he switched tactic, lassoing the cord around his chest.

Hurting, but refusing to buckle, he struggled onwards. Others trickled past him like stream water over a pebble. Bodies stiff with rigor mortis and ice were shuffled along the hoarfrost; dragged into the clearing beyond the dead trees marking the boundary between Ploegsteert Woods and the battlefield.

Lines of maggots following them like slug trails.

With an effort he refused to acknowledge, Simon finally joined the others at the perimeter, standing beneath a canopy of blackened branches. Spitting great lumps of snot and phlegm into the colourless snow, he saw faces and uniforms he knew.

Scots. 2nd Battalion.

Sent to Belgium to kill Germans, not befriend them.

Forming one fractious mass, the crowd looked towards the men standing in the clearing's centre. Three men. Three lieutenants. They each gave a nod. An orchestra of shovels and pickaxes scythed through the falling snow, hitting the solid ground in a single metallic melody.

Nothing fled the scene. The wildlife was all dead.

*

Simon screamed.

Each time the pick struck the solid ground he cried out. No longer could the man be heard. The sergeant was more beast than human.

Drawing in his breath as he sliced through the frigid air, shrieking as the impact's shockwaves reverberated through his arms. The metal tip bounced off the frozen soil, sounding like a blacksmith's hammer smacking his anvil. Gravel-sized earth chippings flew like so many bullets.

Some of those close to him watched. Others chose to shuffle their gruesome loads away from the madman.

No-one stopped him.

Vibrations tore through his upper body. Lightning agonies zipped through him. His back seared as a fire spread from his coccyx upwards. Steaming sweat coated his face, melting ice where it landed. His teeth rattled as again and again he hit the earth before him, tearing into it with rabid intent.

In less than a minute he had stabbed the ground over a dozen times but not hit the same wound twice.

Dislodged dirt fell like brown and black hail. But still he worked like a speeding piston, bringing the pick up and down, up and down, up and down. Smashing it into the hardened mud, marking his territory.

Ignoring the lead taste in his flooded mouth, the stretched veins pulsating beneath his flushed skin and the throbbing in his muscles, bones and organs, he swung and he hit and he yelled and he cried until the crust started to splinter and finally the grave's opening revealed itself.

Only then did he slump to his knees, breathless, exhausted. Throwing his pick to his right, not caring if it hit anything or anyone, he draped his left arm over his brother's chest.

And vomited.

He gagged, spitting out strings of scorching bile.

His face turned away from his brother so as not to dishonour his memory, he brought up whatever his insides wanted rid of. But he refused to let go. Just touching his kid brother brought back memories.

As fast and brutal as the bullet with his name on, childhood recollections not thought of in years trespassed his mind.

He saw them both in the street: playing football with Simon's best friend, Kenny Kilburn – whose mum left him and his dad behind so she could become a singer but never quite made it.

The sounds of their laughter and the smell from the street's shared shithouse down near the end of the alleyway. Thoughts of Sunday School; church; the toy battles they played together, using sticks as weapon…

Sticks.

He glanced at the silky baton hanging off his kilt's belt. If only he'd known then what he knew now.

Squeezing the canvas, cold fingers caressing a frozen torso, the memory of two brothers joining up at the war's outbreak made itself known.

Yet again Simon witnessed Jimmy's excitement.

Yet again he saw Jimmy's head splitting in two.

Devastated, he looked skywards and yelled out at the deity whose birth was to meant to put an end to all war.

He called out for justice. For salvation. Raising his hands he beseeched the sky, pleaded for an answer.

But none came.

No answer, no sign.

Weeping, gagging on his grief, he reached over, snatching up the pick. Still on his knees, he held the handle by the neck and renewed his digging. His furious efforts intensified to the point of fever. Gritting his teeth to keep the rattles at bay, he thrashed at the ground, raising the pick only a few inches before smacking it back into the compacted dirt.

Dragging it back, scraping the planet's skin. Gouging. Rubbing. Scratching. And when that proved pointless, he threw the tool away and continued with his hands, ripping at the ground as if it were bread. Flinging clumps of sod behind him. His tormented eyes seemed to be searching out for the opening to Hell itself.

With the grave barely dug, he abandoned the chasm. Staying on his knees he reached over and dragged his brother across, sliding the head down into what little there was of the hole.

The decorum and respect he had envisioned now shattered by loving memories and blind hatred for those he fought alongside. Their treasonable faces surrounded him as he fervently pulled, grabbed and pushed his brother's cadaver into the shallow quarry.

Despair, anger and impotence became one.

He had been unable to care for his brother; failed to save him. And now he was burying him in an anonymous plot in a Belgian countryside surrounded by enemies of all nationalities. The anguish was sickening. Panting, grunting, whispering curses, he strived to force the cumbersome carcass into the pit but it was too shallow.

The pool barely dug but Simon couldn't stop himself from trying to perform the impossible. He grabbed heavy clumps of cold soil and slammed them into the corpse.

Spittle, tears and sweat showered his coat as he struggled to do just one decent thing for his younger brother.

His face, normally so white, so pure, was a blood vessel swollen to bursting point; only his stiff beard remained the same coal black it always had been.

With no success in his efforts, he held onto the shoulders again and pulled. But still the body would not move. So he scrambled back to the feet and pushed, his body ready to explode like a water-bomb.

But the carcass remained stuck; the flesh within mutated to stone. He punched Jimmy's torso, slapped at where he imagined his legs would be, scratched at his arms. But the battle – yet another battle – was lost.

With the head pushed in as deep as feasible and the legs perched on the grave's edge, pointing towards the sky at an obtuse angle, Sergeant Simon Williams finally gave up burying Corporal Jimmy Williams.

Collapsing onto his brother's chest as though listening out for an impossible heartbeat, Simon gave up and sobbed until he was dragged away by his own lieutenant.

*

He woke on his bed: hard wooden slats lining a shallow cave cut into the trench wall. With his knees bent upwards, barely a few inches between them and the alcove's muddy roof, a stiffness spread across his lower back like frost over a puddle. Despite the sweat dribbling from his sodden forehead, he was freezing. His shivers were as extreme as any he had ever suffered before – even more than those experienced when seeing his first murder out in No Man's Land. If it hadn't been for Jimmy dragging his brother upwards...

The dead man hadn't been a man at all: he had been a teenage private who'd known the trenches for only a few hours before falling beside Simon.

A German sniper's aim, good and true.

The bullet had entered the youth's right eye before dragging the inside of his skull out into the night.

Shamed by his recollection, Simon realised he had already forgotten the boy's name. He had been in the trenches less than four months and already his memories of the fallen were dying.

Wrapping his arms around his midriff, tucking his gloved hands deep into his armpits, he squeezed his eyes shut, pressing his back into the splintered wood; shuffling to try and scratch new scars into the tired skin beneath the rough clothing.

But thoughts of a different pain eradicating the existing one were quickly swiped aside.

Pain bred pain. It didn't deny it.

Accepting this, he quit his efforts, choosing to rest as best he could. The cold was brutal. His face's naked skin held no feeling. The hovels gave soldiers a place to lie, but they were useless at keeping the weather out. These were things he and his comrades knew. Death, love and the elements dominated the thoughts of every man who had been forced to make these muddy veins their homes.

Above him he heard languages being exchanged.

Opening his eyes he saw, hard, compacted clay and the roots of flattened grasses and felled trees. Standing atop of these were the soldiers. Dozens (hundreds?) of soldiers. Foreign sides. Mixing together. Talking. Laughing.

Fraternising.

Light and heavy footsteps above loosened muddy fragments from his makeshift roof, sending a host of speckles to drizzle over him. He tried to swallow the small amount of saliva gathering at the back of his throat but his thorax was raw where hot bile had seared it.

Thin rivulets of drool slowly slipped down past his glued tongue and cheeks, falling beyond his epiglottis. He coughed, jerked; slammed the back of his head against his timber mattress; giving birth to a ridiculously spiteful headache.

The throb behind his eyes seemed to turn bone to elastic: his skull shrank and expanded in time with his breathing. The urge to vomit again roared deep within his withered stomach. He quickly scrambled upwards into a sitting position, swinging his legs over the bay's threshold. Gripping the edge, he sucked in air far brisker than the rancid, mouldy pus he was forced to swallow in his cave. Each breath cooled the pain; soothed his head's fury as though dousing it in water.

"You okay now, Sarge?"

The slight voice came from Private Jonathan 'Johnny' Leigh. He sat across the fetid trench from his sergeant on an empty wooden ammunitions box.

Only eighteen – he claimed – the man's adolescence had

been ruined by too many bullets. The lad had survived four "over-the-tops" since his arrival four weeks before – "one a week, you unlucky bastard" had been the general consensus when Leigh was told his fourth instruction had arrived.

His eyes were red and swollen from a lack of sleep; chestnut hair and beard, both of which contained white spots where thousands of nits and lice gathered; skin like cowhide.

Bent forward, he leaned his elbows on his knees, his feet lost in the trench's stream. Polluted waters lined every dugout in Belgium; soaking through boots and socks to rot feet.

Leigh's sodden flesh was just as bad as everyone else's. It had been weeks since he'd seen the dead skin within his muddied boots and may well be weeks before he saw his feet again – that was if the Germans didn't get him first! The searing pain felt as gangrene set in was agonising, but usually offset by an itching fury caused by the birth of another hundred head-lice.

"I ... er," Simon rubbed at his throat. His thirst was rapacious. He pointed at the small metal water canteen Leigh had on his belt.

"You don't look so good," Leigh stated, handing it over.

The first mouthful he swilled about, detaching flesh from calcium before spitting it out. The geyser of brown liquid splashed into the tributary. After a couple of gulps, giving his stomach something to savour, Simon handed the bottle back to Leigh. Taking it, the private then offered a lavish rectangular tin in its place.

"Chocolate? Courtesy of the King?"

Simon's stomach went into spasm. "No ... no thank you ... Leigh".

As Leigh secreted the tin about himself, Simon took in more fresh air, savouring a taste clean of gunpowder for the first time in so long.

"They're full o' shit!" the voice came from Simon's right. Staff Sergeant Wayne Bruce leaned his back into the mud wall next to Simon's bed space, his arms folded but his right hand hovering over the revolver hitched into his heavy cloth belt over his left hip.

Usually massive in both height and girth, months in a series of Belgian trenches had shrunken Bruce's waistline and forced the six-foot-eight-inch Glaswegian to improvise when it came to keeping his kilt in place. The gun now acted as a belt buckle. "Standin' up there and chattin' away like they're all at some school fuckin' reunion."

"We managed to bury our dead, didn't we?" Leigh said.

"Aye, dead all those bastards out there murdered. Dead who were all either frozen stiff or full o' maggots because they'd been left too far out in the open for us to get at without those bastards killin' us too!" Pointing at Leigh, Bruce added, "so don't make out they're doin' us any favours."

Finished, he opened his mud encrusted sporran and retrieved a pewter hip flask as big as Leigh's head. After taking a swig he offered it around his companions. Leigh took the smallest of sips but Simon fed on the cheap whiskey as if it were the first tasting of his mother's milk.

"Hold on there, Sarge. You're not supposed to take the whole fuckin' thing. I knows it's Christmas and all tha' and you're in a bad way like, but you're not the only one sufferin' here. My ma gave me that special."

"Sor ... sorry," Simon managed to say over the intense heat mushrooming up from his belly.

Hot. Fiery.

But cleansing. He returned the flask, his eyes focused on his boots dangling three feet above the ground.

"Nay issue, Sarge. Just that bullshit out there is makin' me feel like getting pissed." To confirm his intentions he drank deeply from the returned flask. When finished, he added, "There's no way I'm breakin' bread with them murderin' bastards."

Simon looked at the tall Scotsman who smiled back, his teeth broken and brown like shot branch stubs. He tried to find his own smile but it was too well hidden.

Looking beyond Bruce, Simon saw others who had refused to join in with the party. A small number of tired, worn, frustrated soldiers who shared space and ignored rank on this most unusual of Christmas days.

Like Simon and his comrades, these men shared presents and resentment. Tears of anger were spilt. Words of hatred shouted over the uneven ridge into the grey sky above.

Simon heard their cries of: "Judas bastards!" and "how could you?" and felt like joining in. They were right. Bruce was right. But then so was Leigh. Without this ceasefire, when would he have been given the chance to bury Jimmy?

A man approached. His head hidden by the lowered brim of his tin helmet. He was one of a few still wearing their head protection; refusing to trust the Germans even when the white flag had been raised.

Simon recognised the man; one who had fought alongside him in many battles. He watched the gaited walk through the roughshod catwalk and remembered when he had last seen the soldier.

"Jimmy!"

"Wha'?" Bruce said, turning. "Wha' ya on abou'?" Leigh looked at Simon before following his stare. All three men watched the approaching soldier: Simon felt something cold and wet in his stomach as the putrid water and cheap whiskey threatened to loosen his bowels.

He scrunched himself inward: his belly tight; his back taut; his scrotum shrunk and his rectum sucked in somewhere near his navel. Sweat broke out as though his pores were taps. He leaned his hands against the cavity's edge and scrunched the hard mud until it melted in his palms. The man – boy – was less than ten metres from him.

His dead brother approached him.

"It's not me," said Jimmy.

The soldier lifted his head. "Can you believe those wankers up there? Fraternising with the Kaiser's quim dribbles like they're virgins in-front of a whore raffle. What's up with you three?"

"Told you."

It wasn't Jimmy.

He had the same build, but it was clear to all that Jimmy was dead and this youngster was just another in their ranks.

"There's nothin' up with us," Bruce told the boy, standing

straight and putting his arms around the new arrival.

"You sure? I mean, Sarge, you don't look so good."

"Too much whiskey on an empty stomach, isn't that right, sir?" Leigh said, stepping over the trench to help his superior.

Simon's face was as grey as the morning clouds. He tried to shuffle back into his cavern. He didn't want to look at the boy. Simon knew his name but couldn't remember it and didn't want to. He wanted the boy to go away. He had tricked Simon. Tricked him into thinking the impossible. That Jimmy was...

Jimmy was...

"Dead, Simon. I'm dead."

Bruce shared more of his hip flask with his new comrade as Leigh tried to help Simon hide from the world. "Too ... too much whisk ... whiskey," Simon managed to confirm just as he lumbered his backside over a ridge in his lumber bed and hit his head on the underside of his muddy ceiling. Clumps of soil rained down. The voices above seemed clearer. Lying back, he looked up to see what he thought was a tree root coming towards him: a thick, luminous stem from some long forgotten shrub falling through the earthen sky.

But they all knew exactly what it was when the maggots showered down and the dead man's head followed.

The weight of those congregating above was too much. The depth between the open ground and the trench bunks too shallow – and yet they had buried their dead where they fell.

At nightfall. With no lamps.

Unable to risk taking them into the woods; comrades buried above the beds of the living.

As the Christmas socialising between enemies continued, the original burial ground had been disturbed; its occupants were falling through the layers.

Simon and Leigh fumbled out of the recess, falling into the freezing stream as they fought to get as far away as possible from the macerated corpse that now rested in the ligneous cot. The small wet snap of Simon's right wrist breaking was lost in the yells.

*

There was no point in being coy about it: his wrist hurt like a bastard!

The break's clamping ache refused to leave him. According to the spiteful doctor who fixed him up, he was lucky to still have a hand. Somehow he had managed to pull it so far back his fingers were facing his elbow. It had taken a lot of manipulation with very little pain relief to reset it. Now he had a series of wooden splits tied around his forearm, all of which pinched his flesh.

Tucked tight into the bottom bunk, Simon lay on his back, resting his damaged arm in its sling across his chest, fingers scratching at the infuriating itch tracing the void between sweaty skin and grey bandage.

In some respects he was grateful for the distraction. He had never been good on water – the journey to Belgium, across the English Channel, had been laden with episodes of violent vomiting and painful stomach cramps.

Jimmy had helped his elder brother with a wet rag to the forehead and a barrage of abuse at those others who thought the sight of a grown man puking was hilarious. Simon had yet to bring anything up on this return journey but his insides rocked in time with the sea's call.

They had given him his own space. The room had four beds built into the boat's wooden hull, two each side, but he remained alone. Portholes cut into the lathe timbers between the bunks offered a blanket of icy light across the lower beds and floor. Watching white foam and brown waters wash the glass beside him, Simon thought of the ales he and Jimmy shared in the club back home.

Before the war.

When they were with the ones they loved.

The thought of seeing his mum and knowing what he had to tell her sent a lurch through him far stronger than any seasickness gag.

Envisioning his mother and the grief and agony he was about to bestow on her ensured the need to vomit bypassed the pain and itching in his wrist and wrapped itself around his heart – that most useless of organs. He turned on his right side, his head hanging over the bucket the boat owner had kindly placed there when leading Simon to his bed.

The stench of fish guts emanating from the tin pail brought forth the first bellow of hot puke.

"There, there, Brother, just bring it up."

The voice did nothing to sooth his hurt. His eyes remained squeezed shut as his ribs were pummelled by the retching. The image of his mother's pain crucified him. Seeing her bent double when he told her about Jimmy...

He heaved.

"It's okay, Si. Bring it up. Get it all out." The hand on his back was warm. Slowly it ran across his shoulders; thick fingers kneading the muscles. He wanted to smile at their touch.

Collapsing back on the mattress, hot sweat stinging his eyes, he stared up at the bunk's underside, the room brightened by the lights sparkling around his skull. He clasped the fingers of his damaged wrist tight to his ribs, calming the internal cramps.

"Jimmy!" he cried, sitting up sharply.

No-one answered. The room was empty. He knew it would be but that didn't stop him from searching the remaining bunks.

*

He saw her from the top of the hill. She couldn't see him. Her back was turned as she chatted with a neighbour.

The bus from Dover had carried him and his fellow travellers over anonymous roads and through forgettable towns and villages, randomly distributing passengers across the country.

By the time they had reached his village, the majority of Simon's fellow commuters were in their homes, soaking up the celebratory love afforded to families whose brave men had returned from a landscape too foreign for them to imagine. The journey had been a quiet one as they all dealt with the memories of a world too horrific to leave behind.

Simon walked slowly down the bank towards his street, passing homes that still smiled with Christmas decorations. It was unusual for them to still be on show so many days after Christmas – it was already the second day of 1915. This time last year the street was empty of such celebration with its occupants living their normal lives.

The war had changed more than just those in the trenches.

Familiar faces materialised at windows as he marched past. On each side of the cobbled roadway doors opened before and behind him as people realised one of their own had returned: survivor of the horrors they'd been reading about in the newspapers.

Joy ran down the street like spilt water; rising high above the undulating line of slate roofs to merge with the grey clouds hanging high above the terraces. They called out to him with warm words and hopeful cries, telling him to "come have a drink" with them or "come over and share an Oatcake" whenever he had the chance. A young boy asked him about his arm before his mother gave him a whack behind the ear-hole for being so "bloody nosey".

Simon tried being polite. Their words meant something – they were another link to Jimmy – but at the same time he just wanted to scream at these people; wanted them to just shut up and leave him alone.

They couldn't understand what he had gone through or what he was about to do so why assume it was a time for celebration?

Couldn't they see what was written on his face; had taken residence in his eyes? Did they not recognise grief? Guilt?

The woman his mum had been talking to pointed at him. Following her finger, his mother turned round to look at her son.

His world faded into the background.

Now there was just the two of them.

He standing less than thirty feet from her. His legs stopped working. He tried to move but he couldn't. Fear and shame rested like lead in his bones. He should be running. He hadn't seen her for so long. When last they shared time together he had been a boy eager to do his duty by his King.

He had been an elder brother.

"She knows. You can see it in her face. She knows what you've done."

"Shut up!"

The kids running towards him hit the brakes when they saw his face twist in fury. "So ... sorry," he said realising how he must look to them: the bogeyman made real.

Accepting his apology and acting as if nothing had happened, the three boys and one girl, all still months away from their seventh birthday, reached out and shook the sergeant's hand. Their silent smiles enveloped his cold heart in clouds of childish warmth. For the briefest moment he understood what his going and fighting the Germans on their behalf meant to these people.

Turning away from the retreating children who found the warmth of their homes just as quickly as they had found the soldier, Simon looked towards his mother but she was no longer there.

The lead drained from his limbs.

"She knows," Jimmy said again.

With friends and strangers alike watching him, Simon walked home.

*

He stood in the open doorway; at the entrance-hall that over the years had known so many happy faces. A hall that had remained sober and solemn as the coffin of his and Jimmy's father, husband to their mother, had been carried from his home for the last time.

A luxury not afforded for Jimmy.

Entering, he closed the door behind him, shutting away the outside world. The only natural light allowed into the compact room and stairwell came from the half-circle fanlight above the door: stained glass shaped by lead lines casting ruby and green ghosts across the orange floor tiles. Dropping his heavy rucksack at the foot of the stairs, he softly rubbed his splintered wrist, easing the sticks out of his skin.

"She knows" said the familiar voice.

"Are you comin' in or just gonna stan' there?" his mother called out from the room to his left.

"Just taking off my bag," answered Simon with a quick and easy lie.

The room was just as he remembered it: dominated by a loud coal fire that burned brighter than the sun. A quiet square dining table with four lattice-backed chairs were all tucked in tight in the alcove opposite the door. In the alcove to the fire's left, his father's brown leather chair still sat as though waiting for its owner to return.

Opposite the fireplace, her bent frame almost consumed by the small sofa's garish flowers, sat his mother: her head bent forward as though she were studying a bunion.

"Mum?"

She said nothing. Did not move.

"Mum. I ... I tried to ... tried to save him, Mum, but I ... but I ... I failed him mum. I failed our Jimmy."

He stumbled towards her, tears falling with his footsteps. Collapsing at her feet he shuffled his head onto her lap as though he were a persistent dog. At first she did nothing. Her arms remained still as though allergic to his touch. But when he wrapped his arms around her waist her reluctance shattered. She took him in. Pressing his head against her breast, she squeezed her only son.

"I'm sorry, mum. I'm so, so sorry." Again despair clamped his insides and forced his agonies to spill. "I tried to save him but, but the bullet ... the Germans ... I couldn't mum. I couldn't."

"Shush," she said, twisting her waist so that she rocked his head. "I know. I know."

"Out there. In a muddy field. They made me leave him, mum. They made me leave him there."

"It's okay. Get it out. Tell me everything."

"They killed him, mum. They killed him. And our supposed betters broke bread with them! They shared drinks and laughed! I wanted to kill them, mum. Wanted to kill them all. I buried him and wanted to take my gun to each and every one of them: Scottish, French, German. Bastards!" He spat the word into his mother's lap.

"Don't use language like that in this house, please Simon."

The mechanics of her voice surprised him.

There was no emotion. No upset. Like she was reading a

script. This went against every vision and dream he'd ever had since Jimmy's death. She should be bawling.

Slapping him in anger for failing to protect her youngest. Reaching for him for protection and solace but being repulsed by his weaknesses. Even the way she held him felt wrong. She'd pulled him close as though it was what she thought was the right thing to do rather than wanting to do it. Letting his hands drop from her, he tried to push back but her arms refused to budge. They gripped his head tight against her.

"Mum. Mum, what's wrong."

"You know what's wrong, Simon."

"I don't. You're acting strange." His voice broke as tears and snot gathered at the back of his throat. Leaning his hands into the sofa he pushed back, breaking her hold. She was staring into the fireplace; her face rigid and as cold as the sky beyond the netted window. He had come here seeking solace and retribution for the horrors he had already faced but seeing his mother's tearless eyes ... he knew there was something more to come.

"I told you to tell me everything," she said in that harsh voice he hardly recognised.

"I have."

"Really?" Breaking her stare she looked at him. "Don't lie to me, Simon. You know how I hate lying. I and the Good Lord both despise liars, Simon. So tell me the truth. Tell us both."

"I don't know what you're talking about, mum. Mum, what's wrong with you?" He stood, backing away towards the fireplace. His words continued to dismantle themselves. He knew what he thought he said but couldn't be sure his mother had heard him correctly. When she looked up at him, rather than seeking out her son, her eyes passed right through him as though there were something staring down at her from behind him.

"I told you she knew. Didn't I tell you?" Jimmy said.

Simon said nothing.

"Answer your brother," his mother insisted.

"What?" Simon managed to gurgle.

"I see him. He's there. Behind you. In the fire. He came to

me through the flames on Christmas morning. Told me everything. Now I want to hear it from you. Tell me, Simon. Tell me the truth!" Her words barely registered, coming to him as if she were speaking from a pothole and he were buried beneath the rocks.

"Tell her, Simon. Tell her the truth. She deserves to hear it. From you." The voice did indeed come from behind him but when he spun round all he saw was the wallpapered wall over the roaring fire.

He didn't even feel its heat. "I... I..." The words were scorching his vocal chords. He had to get them out just to stop his throat from burning. "I buried him, mum. Out there. In the field."

"Yes, I know that."

"She knows that, Simon. Tell her the rest."

"And ... and I ... I killed him." There it was. The thing that had been resting deep inside his memories. The thing that had made him collapse at his brother's burial site. He saw him and Jimmy and all of the others, out in the middle of No Man's Land. Dodging hundreds – thousands – of German bullets; firing back their own in retaliation.

Jimmy stepping across Simon's firing line; Jimmy's head exploding as the bullet entered the *back* of his head and exited through the *front*.

"Oh my God," Simon said as he collapsed to his knees, hugging himself tight. This time the real tears fell.

"That's better, Simon," his mother said, her arms enclosing him. This time he felt their warmth. "That's better. Isn't it always better to tell your mother the truth? Now then, let's have a cup of tea and the three of us will talk about things. Together."

Morningstar

Emile-Louis Tomas Jouvet

The Abbé rested his foot on the half-buried stone and stared out at the wilderness. The land was as it had always been and that gave him some comfort, some satisfaction. He coughed, a dry and raspy cough, and thought about when this 'always' was exactly.

He guessed he meant the seventeenth century, when the foundations of the abbey were first laid by that saint ... what was ... oh yes, Vindicianus, the disciple of the great and revered Eloi.

It was all coming back to him – the abbey's grandiose history: by the time of the Middle Ages it had become a place of great learning but following the Revolution it was but a ghost of its former self.

He coughed again, scratched his forehead. Christ, did that actually make sense? One moment he had said that it was as it had always been, the next he was calling it a ghost. Was he talking about the land, the abbey or the country? What was the matter with him? It was all so confusing ... or was it contradictory? Things didn't always make sense nowadays.

The Abbé was full of contradictions.

Well, he actually prided himself of that if he was honest. Some called him rude (some called him worse!) but he would say that it was more of a case of social awkwardness – ironic then that he believed he was born to fulfil the role that was now his vocation.

Abbé.

Abbé to the Mont-Saint-Eloi Abbey.

Abbé.

Ridiculous. A word which was a contradiction in itself.

232 in real life it's low

His chest hurt as he heaved.

He stared onwards – that barren wasteland. Those bastards knew full well what they were doing when they built their abbey here: the middle of the valley. The middle of fucking nowhere. Nothing but a small stream nearby, two day's walk to the nearest town.

They weren't the only bastards of course – what about those so-called enlightened *citizens*? He spat out a globule of phlegm – *they* came during the Revolution and began dismantling (no damn it, he wasn't going to let them off that easily – they raped, they pillaged) the stone that gave the building its very soul.

What was left now wasn't much, but it was worth fighting for.

For good measure and to accentuate his point, he whacked the stone with his stick, undid his breeches and urinated, groaned as he did so. Why did everything hurt nowadays? Had he spent too long out in the open air? Was it time to go ... home? Where was home anyway?

He finished, put himself away, and wiped his hand on his tunic.

"Come Milou," he called to his Petite Gascon Saintongeois, his faithful companion who frolicked nearby. "Time to get back."

He sighed, turned and began the slow descent back to the abbey; Milou, by his side.

The Abbé inhaled, frowned. "Can you smell that?"

Milou barked as if confirming his master's enquiry.

"Then it's not just me old friend..."

He bent down (Sweet Jesus! His back was killing him) and picked up the dog – who licked his master's face.

"Something foul is headed our way Milou, mark my words, something foul."

*

"Who goes there?" the private raised his rifle.

The Abbé tutted. "Stand down Claude, it's only me."

"Indeed," the soldier stated. "But who are you exactly?"

"Do we have to go through this every time?"

The private stared on.

"Fine," the Abbé raised his hand. "I am Abbé Guérisseur. We have known each other for what? Sixty-two, sixty-three years? When we were runts playing in the orchards of the Duc de Ganbry."

"Loic?" the soldier appeared momentarily confused.

Guérisseur laid a hand on his friend's shoulder. "Yes Claude, it's me."

The private motioned with his weapon. "What is that?"

"That's not a 'that' Claude, that's Milou, you remember Milou don't you?"

"Abbé," a much sterner voice said. Guérisseur looked past his friend who was now standing to attention, as erect as his old age allowed.

"Capitane," the Abbé nodded in recognition.

"Let him pass, Private, all is well."

"Sir!" Claude knocked his booted heels together, stepped to one side. Guérisseur and his faithful companion entered the ruins of the once prosperous abbey.

"Something on your mind, Capitane? It's not often I'm met at the gate," the Abbé asked as Milou scampered past them both; off to search for scraps near the cook's billet.

"I would like to talk to you about something. In private if you don't mind." The capitane held out his arm, motioning for the Abbé to go with him. Guérisseur took a deep breath as they strolled in between the rows of dirty white tents, located where the cloisters once would have sat.

As they walked, the Abbé tried his best to disguise his utter contempt for the capitane and his men. Of course he knew there was a war on, and yes, they were just doing their duty – he understood that. But why in Hell did they have to bring all that nonsense here, to his abbey? It was supposed to be a place of sanctuary ... the Government Minister who had informed him of their plans said something about its location being 'territorially significant' due to what had been happening at the Lorette Spur and Vimy Ridge.

Yes, yes, yes, he understood all that but if it was that important, then whey use only old men to defend the abbey? A Battalion of men in their sixties, most actually past that and in their seventies – some even older! The Government man had just smiled and said that everyone had their part to play.

The capitane was different. He wasn't even thirty. Guérisseur wondered what he had done to deserve such a posting, probably got caught with the major's daughter or something ... the Abbé had never asked, had always thought it better not too.

They entered the capitane's tent. Guérisseur pulled up a chair. He rubbed his thighs, his knees were killing him. The capitane sat down on the edge of his cot, took off his cap, ran a hand through his hair, twiddled absentmindedly with the end of his moustache. Neither man spoke for a moment or two and their silence hung heavy.

Eventually the capitane leant forward. "I'm worried about the men Abbé, I'm worried damnit!" He stood, paced backwards and forwards. A strange expression on his face.

Guérisseur had always viewed the capitane as a man in total control but now he was shaking, sweating. His uniform was crumpled, slept in almost. He looked like a man coming apart at the seams. Literally.

The capitane picked up his shaving mirror, stared at the reflection. Frowned as if he had never seen his own face before. He put the mirror down, and then turned it over.

"I believe there is something out there Abbé. Something dark and evil. The men talk about it all the time. They don't think I know, but I do. Rumours. Stories around the camp fire ... don't tell me you haven't heard them ... I know that you have."

Guérisseur smiled thinly. "There will always be rumours. Especially at times of extreme duress."

The capitane looked on, at nothing in particular. "I understand that man, but I'm talking about something else entirely." He paused. "The men, they are worried about something ... no that's not ... they're scared. Terrified."

"The enemy do seem to know our every move."

The capitane appeared lost in his own thoughts. "They're so close; they watch us every second of every day. They pick us off one by one ... yet you ... you walk out there every morning," he gesticulated with his hands. "Yet you are never harmed, never shot at..."

"I hope you're not suggesting that..." Guérisseur snapped.

"No, no ... what I'm trying to say is this: where you walk, God walks with you."

The Abbé clasped his hands together. "The Lord will protect us all, Capitane, we only have to ask for his Grace."

The solider looked as if he wanted to say something but stopped himself short, just nodded his affirmation. His eyes narrowed as he stared at the flecks of dust on his boots. When he looked up, there were tears in his eyes.

"Strictly between us Abbé, I have been having some peculiar dreams recently, peculiar dreams indeed."

Guérisseur drew a circle in the dust with his stick. "That's not uncommon is it ... you ... we ... are under acute strain, stress, pressure. The human brain can..."

"No, no, that's not it at all. If only ... no this is something else entirely." He stood at the tent's opening, pulled back the flap. "Come here a moment."

Slowly the Abbé stood. "What is it?"

"Look past the tents, past the gates, what do you see?"

Guérisseur shrugged, not entirely sure where the capitane was going with this.

"Humour me please; tell me what you see *exactly*."

The Abbé sighed. "I don't ... fine, fine ... well I see the hills, I see the valley, I see..."

"And? You see what?"

"Well I don't..."

"Use your eyes man!" the capitane pointed.

It took Guérisseur several seconds. "You mean the clouds?"

"Damn right the clouds! Don't you think they look odd? That yellow hue, that's not usual, is it? And what about that whiff?"

The Abbé continued to stare. Perhaps the capitane was right, but then again maybe it was just a trick of the light.

"And I'll tell you something for nothing, it's ever since those damn clouds appeared that my dreams began. I've also taken the liberty of speaking to the doctor and he agrees with me.

There's something uncanny out there Abbé, something uncanny indeed..."

*

Sleep evaded Guérisseur. He'd tossed and turned for hours and eventually admitted defeat. In the valley he could hear a splattering of gunfire but it seemed too far away to be of any major concern. Though it was times like this, the middle of the night in particular that he wished everyone would just lay down their weapons and talk. He was adamant that was all that was needed to stop the bloodshed.

He swung his legs over the cot, rubbed his eyes. Several almost burnt out candles glowed in the nave and chancel. They created very little light and even less warmth but they were a necessity – it was just so damn dark. Milou fidgeted in his basket. "You restless too boy?"

The Abbé stood up. That fetid aroma in the air again but he was becoming used to it. He tip-toed across the stone floor, went to one of the small windows and looked out.

"Another heavy fog," was about all he could make out. He knew the moon should have been full but he couldn't see it in the sky. He'd spent his formative years on a farm and most of his adulthood in the countryside, he knew much about lunar and solar cycles.

Someone moved behind him, he turned; it was one of the old priests that the Ministry had also put under the abbey's protection. Thomas Le Farge. The blind Curé from Rennes.

"You couldn't sleep either?" Guérisseur asked.

"I heard something. Something above us."

"There's nothing out there, nothing that I can see anyway."

"I was dreaming of the seven trumpets. The gates of hell were blown wide open and thousands of unclean spirits were spewed forth. Can't you hear them howl?"

The Abbé looked about him. What was the old fool on about? Perhaps it wasn't just his sight that he'd lost ... one thing was true though, his hearing was second to none, could even give Milou a run for his money.

But before Guérisseur could repeat that he'd been wrong, that there was nothing to worry about that he should go back to sleep, the sky became illuminated – a bright white then yellow then red flash that lasted several seconds.

"What was that?" Thomas asked.

Milou barked loudly.

"I don't..." was about all the Abbé managed to say before there was an almighty BOOM! The sky rumbled with a massive crash of thunder, shaking the very foundations of the abbey. Guérisseur was thrown to the floor, glass smashed, bricks and stone, wooden beams from the roof, came crashing down.

Dust. So much dust.

Coughing.

Another flash and night became day.

BBBBOOOOOOOOMMMMMM.

Chaos reigned.

The Abbé tried to get to his feet but something pressed down on him. His chest and right arm hurt. A rib or two possibly broken. He couldn't breathe, could only manage shallow breaths. Milou too sounded in pain, was making a queer sound. Moans and groans, crying, screaming ("...he's dead, he's dead ... Lord why...") came from the other priests but there was nothing he could do about it.

A third almighty bang. A mammoth smashing of glass. Voices. Shouting. Orders being barked. Artillery shells. Something must have hit the stained glass window that depicted Lucifer being cast out of Heaven.

Thinking was difficult. A cold darkness crept up his body. He was sleeping into unconsciousness...

*

"Abbé? Guérisseur? Can you hear me?"

Slowly, he opened his eyes. "Christ, tell me I'm dead." His throat was certainly killing him. He tried to move but screamed in agony. A wet towel dabbed at his forehead.

"Rest now, Abbé."

"Capitane," he whispered. "I... I..."

"Rest. I don't want to lose anyone else. There has been so much ... death ... as it is."

"What happened?" he croaked.

"Some kind of attack. There was an explosion, it was pretty

close. We're not sure exactly, but it certainly knocked us for seven." He sounded exhausted. "There's been much destruction ... not many of us left..." He coughed, obviously in an attempt to hide his emotion, but he failed miserably. "The radio is out ... everything is damn well out!"

"I feel cold ... so cold..."

"You've lost some blood, broken a rib and your arm. Now that you're awake you'll probably have one helluva headache. But, you were lucky that we found you when we did ... some of the others ... well they're not so fortunate."

The capitane leant down, picked up a bundle of dirty fur, some of it scorched.

Guérisseur smiled. "Milou! Thank God you're safe."

The little dog barked, happy to see his master alive, it not entirely well.

"His leg is broken," the capitane explained. "But we've given it a splint, bandaged it as good as we could. He should be okay in time."

"Thank you, thank you..."

The Abbé's chest rose and fell. He'd never felt so weary. It was a struggle to keep his eyes open.

"Sleep Guérisseur, sleep. But when you wake, I have something unbelievable to show you. I did tell you something uncanny was going on and now I have my proof."

The Abbé drifted away, losing sense of the capitane's words ... odd indeed because he was positive he heard mention of the Devil but he knew then that it was just his mind playing tricks on him...

                                    *

"How's the head ... hope you're feeling a little better?"

It had been several days since the attack. It had been fairly quiet; only one minor skirmish from the enemy. However, the yellow fog was an eerie constant in both the day and night skies.

Guérisseur was now able to sit up. His arm was in a sling, the minor cuts and bruises to his face were healing nicely and shouldn't have left any permanent scarring – his cracked ribs were also well on the road to recovery. It was safe to say he was now low on the doctor's list of priorities.

It was mid afternoon. "I was wondering," the capitane continued. "Do you think you can walk?"

Milou, who had been resting in his makeshift basket darted (well, limped) under the bed, a ball fashioned from old socks in his mouth. The Abbé was worried about his friend, since the explosion he was off his food and appeared terrified of the slightest noise, but he guessed it would take some time for both their wounds to heal completely.

Guérisseur smiled. "I'd actually do anything to get out of this bed for an hour or two ... what do you have in mind?"

The capitane, with a deeply furrowed brow, held out his arm. "If I wasn't a believer in the Good Book before, then I certainly am now. Come, I've got someone ... no, some*thing* to show you."

*

They stood outside the large wooden doors that led to the nave. The Abbé was soaked in sweat, perhaps it hadn't been the best of ideas to get out of bed but he knew he had to get some circulation in his ancient legs.

He had felt an uneasy atmosphere in the camp. He'd felt it with the capitane, the doctor and now the two soldiers who stood guard. What was the matter with everyone?

From around his neck, the capitane removed a thin leather thong, a key hung from it.

"We couldn't risk anyone ... unauthorised entering here. They might not understand," he said by way of explanation. "Are you ready for this?"

"Ready for what? You're not exactly making any..."

The capitane held up his hand. "What you're about to witness, well, you need to see with your own eyes."

He put the key in the lock, turned it clockwise, a click ... he hesitated however, before pushing the door open. Both soldiers crossed themselves.

"God forgive us," one of them uttered.

*

What was that stench?

"Sulphur," the capitane stated as he closed, and then locked, the door behind them. He reached inside his trouser pocket, handed the Abbé a small surgical mask. "This may help."

"Where's yours?" Guérisseur asked from behind the gauze.

The capitane shrugged. "There's no need. I've been spending a great deal of time here ... contemplating. You grow used to it after a while," he sat down on a pew.

The Abbé frowned. "You're making quite a mystery of all this. Why have you brought me here?" He was out of breath.

The soldier pointed to the far end of the chancel, towards the altar. "Take a look; I'm sure you won't be disappointed."

"Yes, but I..."

"Please. Loic. Just do as I say. I'll wait here ... I can't ... I can't..."

Guérisseur stared, but couldn't see what was getting the capitane so worked up ... there was so much damage caused to the nave and chancel that he wondered whether the building was still structurally safe.

His interest piqued, the Abbé headed deeper in, mindful of the rubble which lay strewn all over the floor, he made sure his steps were unhurried and true. He couldn't risk any further injury. His heart was beating fast.

There were large holes in the ceiling. Roof tiles were missing – allowing more of that damned yellow fog to flood in, mixed with whatever sunlight was able to penetrate through, the dust motes swum.

Several of the wooden pews were upended, some even broken and destroyed altogether. The Abbé also did his best to ignore the dried puddles of blood that stained the stonework. The old priests' cots had been cleared away, thank God.

"Who's there?" an elderly voice called.

"Thomas?! Thank God you're alive." Guérisseur slowly removed his mask.

"Abbé ... I thought..."

"Likewise Thomas, likewise, seems the Good Lord was watching out for the both of us."

The blind Curé stepped forward from the darkness, his arms outstretched. He had a nasty looking gash on his forehead but other than that he seemed as right as rain.

"Have you come to see the wonder?" he asked, grabbing the Abbé and hugging him tightly.

"Wonder?" Guérisseur groaned in pain as he struggled himself free. "What is all this about? The capitane said something about the..."

"Ssshhhhhh," Thomas put a finger on the Abbé's lips. "He will hear you."

"Who will hear me?"

"Praise the Lord. When you see him, tell me what he looks like, is he as beautiful as they say? We truly are blessed."

The Abbé sighed. The yellow air was certainly musty and foul, but here there was a certain sweetness to it that he hadn't quite appreciated before. There was something ... yes, that was the word: addictive, about its potency. Somewhat lightheaded, he breathed in.

"Who...?" he began but the Curé motioned with his hand. "What you seek is beyond the yellow veil." He stepped backwards, letting the darkness swallow him.

Guérisseur wiped the sweat from his face. He tried to focus. He felt bizarre, out of kilter, intoxicated.

He stared into the mist, but all he could really make out where several beams of light attempting to break through the damaged roof.

"Go, go..." the Curé's voice echoed around him and the Abbé felt he had no choice but to obey.

*

The fog became thicker, denser, seemed to stick to his clothes. Felt damp. He searched for the mask but damn, he must have dropped it when the Curé hugged him. As best he could he used his shirt sleeve to cover his nose and mouth but he wondered if already it was too late, wondered how much of the stuff had entered his system, working its dark magic.

His eyes were streaming, red raw. It was agony if they were open, it was agony if they were closed. He walked forward, once or twice he stumbled, almost lost his footing ... but after what seemed an eternity, the mist began to dissipate.

In the cleaner air (well as clean as he guessed it would be) he paused, took several short shallow breaths – he was getting far too old for all this *excitement* – very, very slowly the tears stopped falling.

He took a moment to get his bearings, he had become disorientated. Yes, there was the altar, the purple drape ripped and torn. The large wooden crucifix which usually hung on the way lay broken in several pieces on the floor. There was glass everywhere, damn it, the revered window must have been damaged and perhaps Lucifer had had his day...

Breathing.

He could hear breathing.

He wasn't alone.

Guérisseur looked up.

"Jesus wept!" he crossed himself. In total shock, he took several steps backwards, reached out for something to support him.

Some*thing* was there, hanging upside down from the roof. It was staring at him. It made a guttural noise in the back of its throat. Reached for the Abbé with its talons, wanting to squeeze him tight.

Quickly – because he knew his life, no, *his very soul* depended upon it – Guérisseur tried to take stock of what he saw.

First: yes, the window had been totally obliterated, all that craftsmanship, that work ... destroyed beyond all repair now.

There, in the wreckage, dangling from a criss-cross network of ropes, cords, metallic bars was, no doubt about it, the Devil itself – all red-skinned, naked and violent.

To Guérisseur it appeared that it hadn't had time to form properly as it was cast from Heaven, stuck between this world and the next. Covered in blood, its flesh was torn, raw, its skin burnt, hair sizzled, limbs fused together, one foot now only a frazzled stump.

The Abbé crossed himself. "Jesus ... Jesus Christ..." The adrenalin was flowing, his heart threatened to beat right out of his chest.

The creature moved, the web of restraints creaked. "Aggghhhh bbbbiiitttttt."

It spoke! The Devil was speaking to him! *Christinheaven.*

"What do you want? What do you want of us?"

The thing's taloned fist opened, several of its fingers were missing. It made that sound again.

To say that Guérisseur was frightened wouldn't have been missing the point, but as the seconds passed he realised that as powerful as this Devil certainly was, it was bound up so tightly with no means of escape, that the Abbé had the upper hand – unless of course that a choir of Fallen Angels followed closely behind their leader (he put that idea out of his mind as he didn't want to think this was the first of an invading army).

"Impressive don't you think?" Thomas said as he bowed before the thing.

"Are you so sure that..."

The Curé rested a hand on Guérisseur's shoulder. "Can't you smell the corruption? The stench is palpable." He crossed himself. "Sent to us for a reason," he clasped his hands together.

The Abbé frowned though still couldn't take his eyes from the hanging monstrosity. Perhaps Thomas was right but even so. "Why here? Why us?"

"It had to be someone, somewhere, eventually didn't it?" the Curé shrugged "So why not here, why not us?"

Guérisseur nodded, agreed with that certain line of logic, though perhaps it was too big a question ... his head hurt just thinking about it.

The creature moved again, trying to break free from its captivity but the more it struggled, the tighter its bondage.

It opened its mouth and screamed.

The Abbé covered his ears but the sound was piercing, penetrated his soul, shook his very bones. "Make it stop, make it stop!" Guérisseur shouted and eventually it did cease though not because of any human intervention.

"He's so beautiful, isn't he? I don't need my eyes to tell me that. Imagine all that pain, all that agony, all that evil in one flesh and blood form ... God turned His back on him but should we do the same? Should we not show him sanctuary – here of all places?"

Guérisseur felt he was losing his grip on both his reality and his sanity. He couldn't look any more, he had to turn away, it was just too ... horrible. He pulled Thomas out of the way, hopefully out of earshot. "What are we going to do?"

The older man appeared confused. "Do? What do you mean do? We're not going to do anything."

"Surely we must, we can't just leave it here, hanging..."

Thomas smiled. "We can and we will. If it is here then it is under our jurisdiction, under our control. It can't cause havoc, it can't unleash Hell. Then we wait."

"Wait? For what?"

The Curé paused. "Not for what ... for whom. It will only be a matter of time, the Resurrection will now soon be upon us and we will be right at the centre of it. The war outside those doors, that will pale into insignificance. This building, your revered abbey will become a place of pilgrimage ... I, you, we will become Saints. They will build statues ... they will write stories."

Something snapped in the rafters and a broken piece of timber came crashing to the ground, missing Thomas by only a few feet. Not that he noticed, he was in his element, his arms were open wide, his head back, he was chanting Hallelujahs.

Guérisseur was beginning to see a different kind of light. His head was clearing; something wasn't right about all this.

He looked skywards, the Devil watching them.

"No Thomas, you have this all wrong. We have to cut him down."

"Cut him down?!" the Curé snapped. "What in God's name are you talking about? Will you be responsible for letting the Lord of Flies loose upon the Earth? "

Perhaps sensing this was its last chance; the creature screeched, writhed, kicked and fought. Dust clouds were thrown up. The Abbé covered his face, but sneezed once or twice as he breathed some of it in.

Thomas was in his element, he had the bit between his teeth now. A beam of light illuminated him. "The Lord wills this Guérisseur. God wills this! They said this was the End of Days that this *war* was just the beginning ... and they were right ... the Rapture will unfold..."

The creature looked down upon them both. One eyeball hung useless from a socket, but the other: it stared right at the Abbé, an impassioned expression upon its bloody face. Its mouth opened, teeth like gravestones, a large chunk of its lower jaw missing.

Imagine that pain, imagine that agony. Like a wounded animal...

"Thomas, you've got this wrong, so wrong." Guérisseur searched about for something suitable...

"What do you think you're doing?" Anger rising in his voice.

"We've got to get him down and quickly, before it's too late."

He groaned as he picked up a piece of thin timber. He wasn't entirely sure what he was going to do with it, or was possible of doing, considering his broken arm and cracked ribs – but he had to give it a try.

"Don't move. Guérisseur, I said don't move." Thomas held a small gun.

"Come now, there's no need for this. You know what I'm going to do makes sense."

"There is every need. I can't risk you ... I can't risk you destroying our last and remaining chance."

The Abbé was confused. "Thomas, you're not making any sense."

"The world is changing," the Curé took a step forward. "And just because I'm without my eyes don't think I can't see it."

"Yes, but..."

"...but nothing. And stop moving, I can hear your footsteps. Stay exactly where are you. I have no qualms about pulling this trigger. What is one more death in this bloody war? You won't be missed."

Guérisseur stood still though he wasn't going to just give up as easily as that...

...he coughed, the yellow mist was thickening. The creature groaned.

"He's singing to us Loic, a song I have heard my whole life. Don't tell me you haven't heard it too. What I am doing is just.

What I am doing is holy."

"Then just put it out of its misery, please Thomas."

The Curé leant back and laughed. "Kill him? I'm but a humble man – it isn't for me to kill the Great Beast ... I TOLD YOU STOP MOVING! I will sacrifice you Abbé if it is for the greater good, do not doubt me again."

Guérisseur had tried to sneak a couple of paces forward but had then stubbed his foot on a piece of fallen masonry – that had obviously given the game away. Discovered, he stood like a statue, took several short breaths, he had to come up with something and quickly. Realistically there was only one clear way out of this and that was rush Thomas and hope against hope that if he moved quickly enough then the older man wouldn't be able to get a true shot off ... he needed a distraction.

The creature screamed as it tried to get some purchase on a rope or cable that was wrapped around its leg. Several shards of glass fell to the ground, smashing upon impact.

"Thomas, the building ... it's coming apart around our ears!" Guérisseur called.

"You may believe that, but not I," the Curé countered, though his voice did appear to have lost some of its previous steel. "God, God will save us."

Stone, brick, wood, began to fall, the walls crumbled.

"We have to go now Thomas!" the Abbé coughed, a lung full of dust.

"We won't be going anywhere," the Curé replied.

*

What followed, happened so quickly.

There was a massive crash of what Guérisseur thought was thunder. Then lightning. One of the walls exploded, masonry was sent flying in all directions – a brick hit the Abbé square in the head. He collapsed to the ground.

A gunshot rang out.

*

He lay still for several moments, but was fully aware he wasn't dead. The pain and agony (that thumping in his skull) reminded him of the fact.

Outside, a battle raged. Gunfire. Explosions. Screams.

The chancel was full of dust, the heat was stifling. He coughed. He choked. Grit in his eyes. There was nothing he could do about that, he had to force himself to his feet and get out swiftly, they only had a matter of minutes probably before the remains of the abbey fell down around them.

"Thomas? Thomas are you there?"

He could hear someone fighting for breath but wasn't entirely sure whether it was the creature or the Curé.

After several failed attempts he did manage to get up. He screamed in anguish.

His eyes were barely adjusting to the poor light; he ducked (out of instinct more than anything else) as another bombardment shook the building.

"Thomas?" he called again, stumbled his way to where he thought he'd last seen the Curé standing.

"Damn it," he crossed himself.

Thomas was dead. Decapitated. Guérisseur prayed that it had happened quickly and that the Curé hadn't felt a thing.

"Go in peace brother," he whispered, reaching down and removing the pistol from the old man's hand.

A gurgling sound from above his head, something wet hit the ground.

"Are you not dead?" the Abbé called. He looked up. The creature had been dislodged (breaking its leg and hip in the process) but it was still trapped there in the criss-cross lattice of ropes and cables.

Guérisseur's mind was made up. It was clear to him now. He knew what he had to do, even if it meant the loss of his own life.

It felt natural to be holding the weapon. He had used a gun once or twice before and of course he was a pacifist (that went without saying) but when push came to shove...

...the pulpit still stood and by the looks of it, still accessible. It would be the best vantage point. He could climb to the top, take a closer aim and finish this once and for all.

Slowly, surely, he took each step of the wooden stairs in his stride.

Something dropped onto his face. He put a hand to his cheek. Red. Blood.

"What kind of creature are you?" he asked, more to himself than anything else, just concentrated on his own journey. He faltered, reached out for the rail to support him. It did. Just.

A flash of light. Something landed on the ground. A flare, no: a canister. Spewing more of the yellow mist. A gas of some kind? Yes, that made sense now.

Pounding from within the nave. Was that the capitane shouting, barking orders? Another gunshot.

He thought of Milou. Prayed that he was fine and that one of the soldiers were looking after him.

There was a ringing in his ears. His throat dry. His nose and were streaming.

Guérisseur reached the top of the pulpit, he stopped and stared.

"Ugly looking bastard aren't you?" he stared looked the creature right in the eye.

"Biitt ... biiitttt..." it cried, then coughed, blood dripped from his lips.

The Abbé laughed. "It's too late to beg for your life now."

Tears fell from its one good eye. That close to it, he could make out in greater detail its burnt flesh, its charred bone. He now wasn't sure it was a devil at all but a wounded man, hanging there, entwined in a web of rope.

"Zzzzeeepppiiillllllinnn," the thing gurgled as well as some other words which sounded vaguely foreign ... vaguely *German*?

Guérisseur ignored them; put the pistol to its head.

"Drop that weapon," a voice ordered.

The Abbé looked down as soldiers filed into the chancel. Their rifles aimed at him.

Ah they were trying to trick him obviously. A legion of demons dressed as German soldiers. Masks covering their faces, protecting themselves from the yellow fog. Clever, very clever.

He turned back to the Devil before him and smiled. "May God have mercy upon your soul," he lamented.

And pulled the trigger.

One shot was all that was needed.

At that range, the creature's head exploded, covering the Abbé with brain and bone. Sickened, he dropped the pistol, it clattered to the ground.

Someone shouted something and as Guérisseur turned, the demons let loose their cannons. The Abbé was catapulted over the top of the pulpit.

He hit the dusty stone floor.

Bullet wounds peppered his body. Blood poured from him. But he had a smile upon his face. He knew he had done right, he knew he had done God's work.

He looked up; already they were cutting their fallen comrade down. Did it matter now? It ... he, was dead anyway. No bringing him back from whatever Hell he had been dispatched to.

Something nuzzled at Guérisseur's neck. "Milou!" he whispered. "You made it..." He was happy; even though his whole body was suffering he was now reunited with his best friend.

The Abbé's attention was diverted momentarily. One of the demons stared down at him, rifle lowered.

It removed its mask, eyes fiery red, teeth barred. "French bastard!" it spat then stabbed Milou with its bayonet. The poor little mutt yelped as it died.

"MILOU! NO!" Guérisseur screamed as the demon placed the rifle between his eyes and pulled the trigger...

Somme-Nambula

Allen Ashley

My father first took me to the theatre when I was eight. It was a respectable end of the pier venue with only the occasional bawdy song up from town to suggest there might be a repertoire beyond the hymn book. *Double entendres*, however, went right over my callow head.

What really interested me was the headline act - Casper Fallow, a white-haired, silk-suited hypnotist and magician. Commencing with card tricks and coin manipulation, he swiftly moved onto false-bottomed wardrobes, a sawn in half female assistant and a claim that he could put anyone into a deep trance and control their mind for as long as he chose.

At this particular performance a raucous young fisherman suggested Casper "put a spell on all me creditors so's I never 'ave to pay me bills again." When the amused hubbub died down, the fisherman - Henry, I think he was called - was invited onto the stage and with hardly twenty words and only the subtlest change of tone, Casper had him sleep-walking and impersonating all the creatures of the deep for everyone's amusement during the succeeding five minutes.

I was both impressed and annoyed. Impressed for the obvious reasons; annoyed because even at a tender, barely schooled age I'd wanted to be the one chosen to go under and experience that slightly distanced state. I thought I was the obvious choice for it because I was already a noted somnambulist.

Not that I said anything of the sort to the recruiting officer as he placed light pencil ticks on my enlistment papers.

I could imagine his likely reaction. At best: "I'll have to speak to my superiors."

More probably: "I'm afraid we can't have you wandering

out of your trench at night, sonny. Not under orders, you see."

So I waffled on about King and country and how I was School Dash champion two years running and did a bit of boxing in my time there, as well.

They let me in, of course. Too desperate for saps to do otherwise. With my father's business acumen and my well-read pretensions propping me up like the fingers of a ventriloquist, I even managed to scrape my way onto an officer training course. I'd landed in clover, I thought.

Clover in the path of a scythe.

*

"A show," the captain called it.

But it wasn't the sort of show I used to frequent back home far, far from Ypres. It's how we deal with things, how we've always dealt with things - by using silly little euphemisms:

"Poor old Charlie bought one last night."

"Chap who lent me a fag is pushing up the poppies now."

"We'll be safe from the bloody Boche in this trench, old son."

I used to go to the music halls whenever I had the cash about me. The reek of cheap gin and stale cigarette smoke was all part of the experience and just occasionally there was a petticoated lovely of dubious reputation to help while away the after hours with my half crowns or shillings.

Indeed, I harboured thoughts of a stage career in either mesmerism or sleight of hand until maybe a year ago when I finally had to admit I was neither dextrous nor fast enough to make a go of stage magic. Now I was crouched, freezing and hungry, in a French foxhole worrying that I might not be swift enough to dodge the enemy bullets.

But I might try again when - if - this lousy war is over and we serving soldiers are taken with the urge to live more hedonistically than ever.

*

Snapper caught me sleep-walking last night. He's a good chap and will keep it from the other fellows. I don't want to lose my authority over them, for what it's worth. And what is authority worth, anyway? *Trust* is the all-important commodity.

Snapper, Ginger and Haddock talk about 'calculated risks' when shuffling the francs and the playing cards in the mess tent of an evening. We have lost any residual faith we might have had in the blind orders issued by Headquarters, which leaves all their lives in my probably incapable hands.

I dreamed that I was a boy again, but a boy in a uniform like my own and not the popular sailor suit of yesteryear. I was watching Casper Fallow on stage again, all white hair, neatly trimmed beard and piercing blue eyes.

This time he had responded to my wishes and hypnotised *me*. The distance from stage to stalls must have been over twenty yards but my dream state accepted his long-distance ability without question.

He held an oddly shaped bell and when he rang it the first time I was to rise to my feet. I did so. The attention of the audience was upon me but I could not respond to them in any way as Fallow almost immediately rang the bell a second time to usher me forward into his presence.

It was a theatre of the common sort because I could smell and almost taste the rancid odours of cigarettes, spilled tea, old vomit and booze-assisted urine.

But it was dark, too, dark like the trenches on a quiet night, lit for brief snatches by the bright flare from a Swan Vestas. I stumbled once or twice and even in my mesmerised state remembered to mutter apologies.

There was now a short flight of steps ahead of me and I could clearly see that in his left hand the magician held not a gong or a bell but the square-topped grey helmet of the Rhine Army. He raised a thin stick in his right hand, ready to strike again with a resounding clang. And on the third stroke I would —

I felt Snapper's strong arms around my somnambulant shoulders preventing me from raising my bare head above the parapet. His onion and tobacco breath was pungent in my nostrils as he pleaded with me to return to the land of the conscious.

We shared a tot of rum later and I pressed a half crown into his sweaty palm but he returned it with a shake of the head as if taking it upon himself to clear away the last remnants of my troubled dreams. A flare went up to the east and the silence of the night was temporarily punctuated by the stuttering of a German machine gun. I returned to my bunk, wondering when my night wanderings would eventually lead me into its murderous path.

*

To the Boche, with their guns ever trained on us, we were all identical, just a bunch of Tommy targets. Worse still, our own top brass perceived each of us as merely another expendable pawn in the sacrificial chorus line of the latest bungled show.

"Several gaps in the front row, old chap? Never mind, there's a bunch of willing young recruits on the next boat from Dover. Soon have them marching like ants again, what ho!"

Whereas, of course, a couple of cold trench nights spent talking and gambling with the chaps proved to any doubters that we were all finely honed individuals and certainly not the round pegs the army and the government required us to be.

Perhaps it was this right to selfhood that we were ultimately fighting to uphold. When the war was over - if it was *ever* over - the survivors must return and build a society broad enough to encompass our valuable differences.

It was at one and the same time both an indispensable and a dangerous commodity, this comradeship of battle. Snapper, Invisible, Rapunzel, Chalky, Haddock and the others - they were all my mates and I would gladly risk my life to protect them which is the very essence of soldiership.

And yet these friendships were so fragile and tenuous, liable to be irreparably broken at any moment by a sniper's bullet or a stray piece of shrapnel. What was the point of all this fellow feeling when at the next pointless charge across No Man's Land or even simply patrolling this six foot deep, sandbagged ditch of death our best friend in the muddy universe could be snuffed out quicker than a candle on the altar?

Forgive me for rambling on and raising so many questions, rhetorical or insoluble. I had an onerous duty to perform tonight.

One of our number - Private Mark Jones, better known as

Sniffer - had volunteered to venture out beyond the barbed wire in order to retrieve some of the guns and ammunition from yesterday's fallen.

In a war of attrition it might come down to who had the last magazine or mortar bomb left up their sleeve, or so we were reliably informed by HQ.

Jones was a wiry but immensely strong chap, an ex-farmhand; technically too young to enlist but that hadn't held him or thousands of others back from the front line. He'd ploughed fields, milked cows, shorn sheep and sustained a slight rash from visiting a brothel in Bethune, the one time he'd known the pleasures of a woman. We called him Sniffer because he was desperately trying to grow a moustache even though the black hairs on his top lip were a constant irritant to his nostrils. We'd arm-wrestled for a wager that very afternoon, best of three, and he'd beaten me two-nil.

Crossing the mud and the debris in a low crouch he'd accidentally stepped on an unexploded shell. And yet even as his boot came down he must have withdrawn it slightly because instead of being blown to pieces he'd lost a leg and suffered serious chest and facial injuries; but was alive enough to spend the next two hours emitting tortured screams for merciful relief. Even with our hands over our ears or the gramophone turned up to full volume we could not blot out his agonised cries.

After about an hour of this aural torture, the local CO called a party of us together and demanded something be done.

"Come on, you chaps," he chided, "it's a mercy mission. I need a volunteer."

Silence as we studied the mud on our boots or scratched surreptitiously at the lice lining the seams of our trousers.

"Are we not English?" he demanded. "Where's your mile-wide brave streak? Where's your fellow feeling for a comrade in trouble?"

Eventually, we tired of his ranting and raving. Snapper scanned the horizon with the captain's field glasses. The blokes had a whip-round for cigarettes and chocolate rations but, really, I was more interested in shutting up the CO as I clambered over the parapet in the semi-darkness armed only with a revolver and a grubby handkerchief which would show up as white in the beam of a searchlight. I hoped. If the German sentries decided I was leading an advance party I could have no real complaints at their obvious response.

Oh God, let me die instantaneously when my time comes!

I found Sniffer sprawled amid an array of helmets, spent bullets, half-buried skulls and glutinous mud.

"Come on, son," I said cheerily, "let's drag you back over our side of the fence and let the medical boys sort you out."

We both knew this for a kindly meant falsehood. The stretcher parties had been drafted over to the fighting on our left flank and news reached us regularly that those with more than a simple case of trench foot were left groaning in a crowded corner of the clearing station for days on end without attention.

"I'm done for, sir," he whispered.

"Nonsense," I countered. "You might not play football for England but in the country of the lame the one-legged man will be king."

He smiled, holding back a grimace with courage beyond his years. "My leg's not the worst of it, sir. I can't breathe much longer. It's like I got a whole Hun battalion on me chest, sir. Make it easy on me, sir, I can't fight any longer."

I bent down to put my hands under his shoulders. Blood erupted from the side of his ribs and he began coughing and choking without the physical capacity to make his position any more comfortable.

One eye was already hollow and he'd lost half the caterpillar moustache along with the skin covering jaw and cheekbone. Put a mirror down his middle and he might have passed as presentable in the moonlight.

He screamed suddenly like a soul in torment and I laid him back down on the squelchy ground. Momentarily fearful for my own safety, I glanced across at the dim shadows of the German entrenchment. Maybe they were busy cooking and consoling and would not jump up at every squeal unless the sounds became too proximate.

"Make it easy, sir," he gasped again. "Please."

I unholstered my pistol. A bullet to the brain would be quickest, I judged. I held my gloved hands steady as I rested the barrel against Sniffer's skull but I averted my eyes. It was just another pointless death among so many but was no easier to bear for all that.

The sound of the shot echoed off the barbed wire entanglements and the low-lying clouds which promised further rain within the hour. I did not hang around to witness my handiwork but scuttled back to our position like a rat to its lair.

Chalky broke the outmoded rules of etiquette by clapping me on the shoulder and stating, "You did the right thing, sir. You had no choice."

I spent the rest of the night awake in my cold, damp dugout wondering how one could ever know what was 'the right thing' and when exactly any of us had last had a real choice.

*

I was given a few days recuperation back at HQ. The chance to sip fine liqueurs, scoff palatable three course meals and spend all day perusing jingoistic newspapers was a welcome relief to my shattered nerves. There was even talk of me being shipped home with an honourable discharge. Mother would have been thrilled and the chance to track down my beloved Mary - the lost Eurydice of my youthful fumblings - was a prospect I savoured.

Perhaps too obviously, for it was snatched away from me just as I'd dared to believe in its probability. My hands had ceased shaking and in all other respects I was as normal and average a citizen as any chap within the uniformed ranks. Perfect cannon fodder, in fact.

This was the moment to mention the re-occurrence of my somnambulating and thus at least achieve a stay of sacrifice. But I kept a typical British stiff upper lip, accepted my lot and was back at the front line before you could say General Kitchener.

Dimwit. Dunderhead.

Patriotic simpleton.

*

When I saw Casper Fallow's magic act again he had added a new trick to his repertoire: he claimed to be able to catch a live bullet fired through a pane of glass.

It had to be enormous sleight of hand, I assumed, and yet I went again to see his demonstration on the following evening and was lucky enough to be the Johnny Public invited up into the spotlights to check his hands and various pockets for hidden props and replacements.

His assistant squeezed the trigger and there was the cone headed cylinder caught perfectly between thumb and forefinger like a metallic cigarette butt. Still warm to the touch and grooved from its rapid expulsion. The man's reactions, I had to believe, were faster than the eye could see and no doubt faster than the photographic processes of Mr Eastman or Mr Kodak would be able to capture.

He would have made a great comrade in arms. He had the necessary trait of trench humour, also. With a thin-lipped smile, he turned to his applauding audience and said, "Promise me that you won't try this trick at home."

*

For King and Country
            Against Kaiser Bill

A gentle breeze across the downs,
The thwack of willow upon leather,
Cucumber sandwiches and evensong.

                    Another broken night.
                    Wet feet and mud-stained clothes,
                    Blood seeps through the gaps
                    in the sandbags.

The pealing church bells.
Victory will be ours with God on our side.
Men of Britain - Enlist!
Save our schools and our Empire.
Save our stately homes.

The stench of gas and urine.
Rations not fit for a pig - when there are any.
Give us a light, boy, but quench the
match before the Boche sees us.
Dead horses and gun carriages sinking
in mud like quicksand.
Reminds me of when I —

Buckets and spades and bathing machines,
End of the pier shows and
"What The Butler Saw".
Throw another shilling in the pot:
we'll have a right good old knees-up.

Endless, senseless killing.
Face down in Flanders.
Certain death on the Somme.
Lights out and don't listen
to the wounded wailing.
Hush, here comes a whizz-bang.

*

Rumours sweep along the front line like the early morning mist off the stinky Somme.

The casualties from the last show are put well into the hundreds. By afternoon the figure will have been exaggerated into thousands. Still, we reputedly gained twenty square yards, so that's all right then, isn't it?

Twenty stinking yards of stinking, cloying, grey French mud that might once have nurtured a vineyard but is now ruined for agriculture and building alike for at least the next decade.

I'm no mathematician but it seems to me that if we lose men and gain ground at this stupendous rate we'll need the population of China and Mongolia on our side as well as the current allies in order to make headway into the Fatherland. That's if we did actually move our barbed wire emplacements forward at all yesterday.

No doubt the top brass are ensconced safely back at

Divisional HQ - General Haig and all his bloody cronies getting saddle sore in their comfy armchairs - and *our* positions and *their* positions are carefully plotted and pinned upon a large-scale map and it maybe makes some kind of sense but to me out here it's just the usual mess and confusion of all infantry based wars through the ages.

My battalion has gained no ground. My nerves are shot to pieces and I can hardly hold this pen or grip my tin mug of lukewarm tea. My colleagues have suffered serious injuries and are even now being carted back through the communications trenches to the Field Hospital where their chances of surviving are slight at best. For the honour of England? Fighting to save our green and pleasant land? Showing a firm hand to a hated aggressor? I don't think so.

General Haig, don't be vague,
How many yards did you gain today?
Douglas Haig, king of slaves,
How many men need a fresh-dug grave?

I've been here less than six weeks but already I am completely disillusioned with my life, my lot and the team I'm ballistically representing. So why do I not simply throw down my arms and surrender? Or desert?

Like any soldier at almost any other stage of such a protracted engagement, I fight because I fight. Nothing more. I'm a soldier; it's what soldiers do.

*

Another grey dawn somewhere in the Autumn of 1916. The sun rose behind the enemy lines, shining onto the barbed wire enclosing their fortifications as if illuminating the thorny hedgerows of the mechanical age.

I was partway through my first cold water shave of the week when I was summoned to Captain Featherstone's dugout. I hastily wiped off what little lather remained, checked the straightness of my shirt and issue tie and made my way through the two closest communications trenches - Harrow Road and Rayners Lane - to his palatial abode.

The sound horn of the gramophone was showing signs of damp-induced rust; the wooden supports by the rear wall looked ready to give way at any moment. Still, the metal pot was gurgling on the hob and I gratefully accepted his offer of a hot drink.

"Is there something bothering you, sir?" I inquired. "Over and above the usual," I added.

"Yes, Lieutenant Dove, there is something more than the usual. I'm concerned about Private Fairclough and Corporal Boatman. Rapunzel and Haddock, I believe the chaps call them."

"That's correct, sir. Fairclough has unruly ginger curls somewhat longer than regulation length, hence the fairy tale reference. Boatman is from a fishing family, sir."

"Yes, thank you, a very fine lesson in etymology, I'm sure. What concerns me is that I discovered these two in intimate contact last night and I'd like your advice on what action I should take."

"Uh, how intimate, sir?"

"Let's just say their contact was of the Oscar Wilde variety. Bloody nancy boys! My school was full of them, you know. They ought to be rounded up and shot at dawn as a moral example."

I smiled. "Well, Captain, it sounds like you've already made your mind up."

He banged the folding table, spilling the remnants of both our teas. "That's my heart speaking, Lieutenant!" he roared. "My *gut* feeling, if you will. I remain, however, a professional soldier and will be guided by the head in matters such as these."

"Well," I began, "one or two snide comments were passed along the line about Rapunzel simply because of his physical appearance. Haddock, however, has never once given us cause to question his masculinity. The point is, sir, that these are men under fire and we all require a comforting arm from time to time in the face of such stress. With no wives and girlfriends on the front line, some blokes can't help seeking, uh, physical solace with each other. I believe similar instances have occurred in His Majesty's prisons and on board ships long out at sea."

"Hmm, Dove, very eloquently expressed, I'm sure, and,

frankly, the sort of justification I half-expected from you. So, what disciplinary measures do you suggest I take?"

"Uh, none, sir."

"None!"

"Who has been harmed by it and who even knows about it?"

"It's illegal and immoral and downright depraved! And you suggest I do nothing!"

"Let it go, sir, as a temporary aberration. They're both good fighting men and, in any case, we might all be mown down in another over the top charge in a few days time."

He wrinkled his nose as if I'd emitted an unpleasant eructation. Not that the trenches could have smelt any worse than they already did.

Eventually, he answered, "Have it your way, Dove. Typical *laissez faire* attitude. The sort of outlook that got us in this mess in the first place, if you ask me, but an expedient one in this instance."

"Think of their families, sir," I suggested.

He required a moment to glean my meaning, then nodded silently.

"Get back to your duties, soldier," he ordered.

"Yes sir."

                                    *

Notions of home comforts and hearth fires burning took my thoughts scurrying back to Mary, my lovely Donegal lass with the shiny chestnut hair and rounded hips.

My father had worked his way up the slippery Adam Smith ladder and by my teen years we were quite a well-to-do family with a respectably addressed property in central London. Ours was new money, so polite society was less than welcoming. It was money, nonetheless.

Mary's mother, Mrs O'Keane, had prospered in service after arriving penniless and with a babe in arms almost two decades previously. She worked for one of my father's business associates and when we were able to afford a housekeeper her daughter came with the highest recommendation.

She was a couple of years older than I, her face already a

little care-worn by burdensome domestic duties but bright and smiling during our shared moments. Yes, I know, I know, the old master and servant set-up but I really felt passionately about my warm Irish miss, even to the extent of professing love and a desire to legally cement our union.

Besides, I was not so much a master as a penny-pinching student struggling to compete with the lush lifestyles of my college peers. I told none of them that Mary was of the servant class; nor did I speak of the affair to my parents.

When we met for chaste woodland walks we were as any other two love-struck young people. Our intimate contact occurred mostly in her own chilly quarters. Such fecund treasures lurked beneath her starched linen uniform, such Grecian alabaster thighs were uncovered by her ridden-up lacy petticoats!

She left our employ suddenly.

I neglected my classes for a full two weeks as I attempted to track her down. Eventually I received a tip-off that she was hiding in a sorry and penniless state in the back room of a laundry near Whitechapel.

She'd had "some business I had to take care of, John, sir." That she was no longer with child left me with sorely mixed feelings. At that time I was not in a sound enough financial position to adequately care for her and any offspring. I emptied my pockets, implored her to stay in touch, swore fidelity that I held onto for more than a year. Inexorably, it seemed, she slipped out of my life.

If I'm fighting for anything, it's perhaps for the chance to re-create my life with Mary within a juster, fairer, less class-restricted society where I would not be frowned upon or disowned and she would not be viewed as an opportunist or gold-digger.

She was my comfort. Socially right or wrong. An earthly paradise ... lost.

*

Then suddenly I was up and over the barbed wire again. Usually, it was never anywhere *near* quiet at night, what with the stray shells, the creaking wheels of the corpse collecting wagons and the anguished cries of wounded men in muddy trenches. And yet a certain calm seemed to descend over me and my surroundings also as I stepped light-footedly through the patchily lit quagmire of No Man's Land. Half-awake or half -asleep, I wasn't sure which mental state was dominant. In theory, I was in more danger at this moment than at any other during this so-called Great War and yet I felt almost divinely protected as if surrounded by an invisible shell rather like the Martians in Mr Wells' fine novel.

Nothing could touch me. I could undertake the glorious one -man death or glory mission so beloved of our top brass, our sat at the rear "we sustained a few hundred casualties today but gained two and a quarter yards of Somme River border bog land so that's all right to print in the papers" blundering generals and majors.

I moved beyond bitterness. Light as Ariel, errant as Puck. The incessant rain was back to its mere drizzle stage and a hint of moonlight teased and tantalised way on high like a whore to a sailor. Or an angel like the one so many claimed to have seen at Mons.

I must have walked a good mile and a half along the disputed hinterland. It was as if I was outside time. I watched a horsefly cross my path about ten feet in front of my nose, its progress slow and laboured as if swimming in glue.

I walked to *their* barbed wire unseen and unhindered and was about to vault across and wreak bloody havoc when something - Caution? Fear? Morality? - got the better of me and I opted instead for a casual stroll back to my starting point. The ditches and the foxholes were uncannily quiet, as if everyone had suddenly seen the pointlessness of this attrition and gone back to grooming horses or driving trains. Only the irritable lice in the lining of my trousers kept up their busy night's work.

"Are you all right, sir?"

It was Snapper, a good old East End boy on sentry duty, breaking my reverie as I stumbled back into the firing trench.

"Just stretching my legs, Private. Too much weak tea - made me restless, what?"

"Yes sir. I thought for a moment you'd - no, that's ridiculous. Well, good night, sir. Hope you settle to sleep soon."

"Thank you, Private. Good night."

*

For a time I harboured youthful ambitions of becoming a stage magician. I nagged at my father to take me to as many performances as he could. The nature of the theatre was changing, however, and some of the shows we ended up frequenting were of the less salubrious variety, to say the least. Bawdy songs with sing-along choruses delivered by over-painted ladies in frilly French petticoats seemed to be the order of the day. On closer inspection, some of these songstresses proved to have dark stubble to match their husky voices.

I returned to my books but found I could not properly manage the swift sleight of hand necessary to pull off even the simplest card tricks, let alone produce rabbits from hats or apparently saw some buxom lovely into two pieces.

I managed to see Casper Fallow again, however. Some ten years on from that first occasion, he seemed to have aged at an alarming rate, rather like Dorian Gray's hidden portrait. From my seat at the edge of a side aisle, I espied a stagehand up in the rafters responding to the performer's nods and winks by pulling levers and ropes to keep the illusions coming fast and fleeting.

Casper caught the bullet again and I was struck by the way a silver-haired, somewhat shabby old man could still command dominance over our state of the art killing technology. It was a matinee performance and afterwards a couple of shillings placed in the caretaker's grubby mitts enabled me to nose around the empty theatre for half an hour or so on the pretext of having lost a sentimental fob watch.

A cursory examination of discarded props and partition boards yielded nothing of the mesmerist's secrets. I began my search anew and just before the doors opened for the later audience I found what I was looking for: a pointy-nosed, still slightly warm, brass shell along with two, unused live bullets. The trick was surely in their composition. I broke both open with a pocket-knife. They seemed to be of the regular sort and contained a substance which looked and smelled like gunpowder, so I was none the wiser. Maybe Casper Fallow really could stop the bullets in their flight. Maybe it was genuinely *speed* rather than *sleight* of hand.

Short of confronting him in a dark alley with the advantage of a sharp dagger in my hand, I might never know the truth. I wasn't sure the knowledge would in any way justify such ungentlemanly unpleasantness.

*

Enlist now!	Die later
Your country needs you	Your country considers you expendable
We must stop the advance of the Kaiser's war machine	We must continue with the advance of our own
Are you a man or a mouse?	Only rats have a realistic survival rate in the bogs around the Somme
With your education and background we could get you a commission as an officer	You can watch your subordinates die five minutes before the bullet comes for you
All the nice girls love a serviceman	Catch a dose of the clap from some French whore old enough to be your grandmother
Daddy, what did you do in the Great War?	You'll never be a daddy with your bollocks shot off

*

I think I have been sleepwalking again, although it's so hard to differentiate dreams from reality.

The blood in my body, perennially frozen by the ceaseless

rain and deprivations of trench life, must have risen to the surface because the sensation I was most aware of was warmth. Not the so-called heat of battle but the blazing of a summer sun bringing rivulets of sweat coursing down my forehead like tiny tributaries of the stinking Somme.

Yes, it was daylight. Yes, therefore, I was almost certainly dreaming. That doesn't negate my experience any.

The tanks had arrived to save the day for the brave English. I saw huge, futuristic machines and gigantic guns out of the imaginings of Jules Verne.

Instead of the inconsistently issued - and often ineffective - regulation gas masks, many of the combatants around me wore whole suits to protect themselves against the chlorine and mustard potions from our Mephistophelian enemy.

Manoeuvres were underway, if not an actual conflict, and occasionally the air was rent by the banshee scream of aeroplanes unrecognisable from the buzzing hornets barely able to stay up more than five minutes I'd seen demonstrated down at Farnborough in 1914.

Either our government has followed the conjuror's example and kept a huge arsenal of technological marvels concealed up its collective sleeve awaiting the opportune moment to smash the Kaiser's minions or else ... or else, I had, like a shell-shocked Nostradamus, fallen into prophetic mode and been transported like the traveller in H. G. Wells' *Time Machine* to a yet more violent future. This latter improbability was given possible credence by the way in which I seemed to be both present and absent at one and the same time.

Careless of my own personal wellbeing, I reached out to grab several of the uniformed personnel as they scurried busily past me. Most would not meet my eye or simply shrugged away my gossamer touch. When one finally did acknowledge my existence he proved to be one of our Yankee cousins. I was not aware that they had yet sided with us *militarily* in this current conflict. He had remarkably good teeth for a front line soldier. He gave a crisp salute at my stripes and said, "Have a nice day, sir." Who said Americans can't understand irony?

The sky to my right was hellish red and I became aware of

the pungent and almost overwhelming smell of burning oil. This olfactory impression must have jogged some safety mechanism in my brain as the next thing I recall is jerking awake to the sight and smell of Snapper greasing his gun and dragging hard on a weedy little hand-rolled cigarette.

"The first one of a new day and the most important, eh, sir?" he grinned.

I muttered something haughtily incomprehensible in reply.

My recollections are *so* mixed up. I may have wandered or I may merely have writhed in my slumber. Only time will tell.

*

I was shaking and crying but Mother's loving arms were around me.

"Poor Johnny," she whispered like a religious ritual, "there, there, it's all right."

"Was I dreaming again, Mummy?"

"Yes, darling. And walking about the house. We were worried you might have an accident."

"I saw Billy again, Mummy. He was calling me towards him. I... I was so happy to see him again."

"I'm sure you were, darling, but ... your brother's with the angels now. He's peaceful and happy there. He wouldn't want you to join him just yet. Not till you've lived a long life just like Grandpa did."

"I'm not going to die yet, Mummy, am I? Not like Billy did?"

"No, darling, you're going to be with us for ... ooh, ages and ages! Just as long as you keep taking your tonic."

She pulled me in to the warmth of her bosom. Although I was five I was still reminded of milk and sugar by her tender proximity.

"Mummy," I mumbled, "I don't mean to walk in the night. I was just thinking about Billy, that was all."

"I know, darling. I never suggested there was any mischief about it. I'm sure you'll grow out of it but I'll speak to Doctor Cranleigh again in the morning."

*

"Who was that strange looking guy I saw you talking with?"

"Dunno, didn't get his name. Some Brit. Cuckoos in the nest, if you ask me."

"Waddya mean?"

"Kept going on about fighting the Germans and digging trenches and stuff. Weird shit from, like, donkey's years ago, you know what I mean?"

"Jesus. Reckon Saddam's gases have really got to that one?"

"Yeah, I guess. Unless he's that famous unknown soldier the sarge told us about back at base camp."

"Aw, come on, that's kids' stuff! You're having me on!"

"Yeah, course I am. Just some poor saddo lost his gas mask. What're you drinking?"

"Pepsi. I'll pretend it's got some Bacardi in it."

"Yeah, fucking A-rabs and their alcohol ban. Should let 'em fight their own war, if you ask me."

"Can't. All wars are American wars from now on. And don't forget you heard it here first."

"Meathead!"

"Cornball!"

*

Looking for a nice little two up two down or a country manor with a bit of an estate, sir? Maybe I can interest you in *Five Trench Chateau*, an extensive property on the banks of the picturesque River Somme that's been on our books for several months now without anyone taking firm possession? Ah, the delicious smells of the countryside! The stench of mud and urine. Somebody crapped themselves by the mobile canteen but nobody really noticed. Wonderful indigenous wildlife! Rats the size of cats that nip at your exposed features and run off with the bulk of your meagre rations. Lice in whole colonies down the lining of your trousers. That comforting, itchy feeling day and night; who would be without it?

The place comes with a whole coterie of youthful and manly domestic servants. Admittedly, some have been crippled during the course of their duties. That there's Mister Haddock, the world's first arm-less butler. Young Master Snapper would be pleased to look after your dogs and horses once he's picked up his spilled guts and sewn them back into his bullet-riddled torso.

We believe in the class system, of course, sir. It's the natural order, ain't it? It's what made this country great. So do your new neighbours, in their own way. Yes, I admit they're a little lively but that's to be applauded, surely? They're German and they do like their beer gardens and patriotic songs. But we exchanged presents with them at Christmas and reputedly some of the lower orders engaged them in an association football match. I'm a rugby man, myself. And they have such heavenly voices when you can hear them above the mortars and whizz-bangs. *Stille Nacht...*

The area has many claims to be an important historical site. The major landmarks are indicated on this rather quaint hand-drawn map: that's where Ginger lost his left leg; over there Jenkins stepped on a live shell; and a yard to the east a dozen men lost their lives on a forgotten charge over the top. Some suggest the plot is haunted - like the Angel of Mons and all that rot. Not a superstitious man myself, as it goes.

It's a property that comes highly recommended, sir. As the Great War poets would surely say, "There is some shit hole in a foreign bog that is forever England."

*

I grew up essentially as an only child. My brother Billy was two years older than I but died of pneumonia when I was only three. I, too, was afflicted and temporarily weakened by the disease. *Why* I should have recovered whilst my seemingly stronger sibling succumbed remains a painful mystery to this day. Though I knew him for just a few formative years he left a huge impression on me and his loss is something I've struggled to come to terms with every day of my life.

My mother did give birth again much later in life, a girl and a boy twelve and ten years my junior. They are more like a niece and a nephew to me. I've had little contact with either of them what with boarding school, college and work commitments.

I know Billy would see through the iniquities and blunders of our commanders and yet he'd still be proud of me for signing up to fight the Hun. I said nothing at my interview or medical about my childhood somnambulation. Why should I? Until I set foot in the trenches I'd been cured of it for over a decade.

Maybe we're never really cured of anything; perhaps all we can ever hope for is an extended period of remission.

*

It had rained all day. We had fired the occasional useless volley through the barbed wire at our invisible foe but mostly we had spent the time crouching in whatever makeshift shelter we could find with our scrofulous socks and wet cigarettes.

Even Jerry seemed to have called a temporary halt to the ceaseless chatter of his machine guns so that today's danger was falling props and sudden mudslides caused by the deluge. One such avalanche revealed a stray right arm from some hapless Tommy who'd have difficulty performing juggling tricks or shaking hands with Saint Peter.

Tonight, however, the clouds had moved away to allow a sliver of moon to illuminate the ghostly desolation that had been home to us survivors for the past few months. The last home we all might ever know.

And there I was, *again*, upright in No Man's Land, a stupefied, somnambulant target careless of my personal safety and hardly in control of my actions.

"Come and get me, you bastards!" I wanted to call out but in truth my voice was little more than a phantasmal whisper in the semi-darkness. "Do your worst, see if I care."

No volley of metal-death was forthcoming. Not a peep. It was as if the German platoons were all fast asleep with not a single sentry minding the shop. Maybe they weren't even there at all any more, if they ever had been. The enemy we fought was some sort of grotesque supernatural projection of ourselves: the devils within us, made substantial.

"All right, Fritz and Hans," I offered in a stage whisper, "ready or not, I'm coming to get you."

I maintained a lightness of step despite the quagmire beneath my booted feet. *This time*, I promised myself, this time I would exact sweet ice cream cold revenge for all my late or maimed comrades. If it meant laying down my own life as a glorious sacrifice, so be it. What are we here for, anyway?

Oh Mary, I want to come home a hero and sweep you up into my arms and say, "Hang the class system, we were destined to be together!"

But she's probably found a companion of her own station in life by now. And after all I put her through, who would blame her? If only ... if only I can survive this endless battle of attrition and return to London, I *will* seek her out and we will be married. Oh, to rest my hands on those warm, firm thighs again!

As I crossed over into enemy lines, I amended my earlier dancing acrobatics to the more considered progress of the tightrope walker. At the very edge of their barbed wire I became aware of a slight buzzing in my ears. I paused. Midnight was usually a quiet time for flies and mosquitoes, or so I had always assumed.

To my left, at the periphery of my vision, I spotted something *burrowing* through the air like a whisk churning through a vat of butter. I reached out with a curious, rapid, grabbing motion worthy of a creature in the London Zoological Gardens and grasped the airborne object.

It was a bullet.

But travelling *so* slowly? Had that been how Casper Fallow performed his act? And yet, in that case, most of the audience would have perceived the deception. Besides which, this was a combat zone in the war to end wars - what use would a *slow bullet* be here?

With a nut-cracking pincer movement, I broke open its casing. Like birds and rabbits from a conjuror's hat or an endless string of flags from an illusionist's sleeve, the contents seemed to be too bulky and too *many* to be contained within such a small vessel.

To my astonished eyes, I withdrew: a twist of silk, its heady perfume still detectable above the mephitic odour of mud and carnage; a gold wedding ring, inscribed microscopically with four initials; a valentine's card quoting a Shakespearean sonnet; and a miniature baby's crib which fell out of my tired hands and seemed to inflate into full size as I watched open-mouthed!

I ran my fingers over its wicker-work, feeling a little like the Egyptian maid who discovered the infant Moses in the River Nile. What strange sorcery was this - a bullet containing all these icons from a man's life?

Then I did something you should never do on a battlefield at *any* time unless you have an over-riding desire to join your ancestors: I closed my eyes.

I held the bullet like a precious jewel. My vision cleared to reveal a spring day in leafy England and two young people absenting themselves somewhat from a mixed age group exploring the edge of a coniferous forest.

She lifted the train of her white skirts as she set a dainty foot on the forest floor and his gentlemanly hand supported her and stayed clasped even when conditions underfoot improved. I guessed them to both be on the cusp of twenty. The woman giggled as the man's pencil moustache tickled her lips when they kissed for the first time. But she invited him back for a second and third helping. Then they both became a tad embarrassed as if scared of detection.

They made their way back to the main party and the vision faded.

The crib, I noticed, had almost sunk into the welcoming mire. I continued walking.

I could see the German soldiers now, sleeping and immobile like the lions in Trafalgar Square. All except for one private who moved in a painfully snail-like manner as he attempted to turn his machine gun and spray a further barrage of bullets into the chill November air. *Slow bullets...*

Was he crippled in some way? Were they *that* desperate for fighting men?

Or was it that, in some inexplicable manner, I was able to move with greater speed and grace than those around me and thus possessed an insuperable advantage? *This* was my chance to achieve the glorious retribution that not only would avenge my dead companions but might even gain me deserved promotion *away* from the Eastern Front.

Oh Mother, look at your little studious boy now with his guns and his uniform ... and his heart full of hatred!

I moved slightly to the side of the Jerry's firing line - it was an easy task, believe me. I casually picked more of the flying cylinders out of the air. I broke a couple open. More mementoes and memories: a fading photograph, a school certificate, a gold cross and chain and entwined locks of blonde and brown hair. Their purpose seemed clear to me now; their easy avoidance, too.

The square head finally managed to get his weapon trained upon me. I let the lead bullet crawl towards me and caught it more casually than Casper Fallow could ever have dreamed of doing. This one I didn't open. Instead, I placed it safely within my jacket pocket and stepped towards the sluggish aggressor.

I thought of using my pistol but decided that an unsheathed bayonet was probably a better bet. The fear on the man's face was brighter than a hundred Pole Stars. I thrust, wounded him in the side of his chest. The blood trickled out red and torpid. He required one more blow to finish him off, what our French allies call the *coup de grace*. But I didn't want to deliver it.

The bullets I was collecting all had their set targets, identified by the significant contents they contained. I was beyond their range; no bullet had my name on it or my identifying icons within. I was the soldier who could not be killed. I had my time, so why not extend his for a little longer? Oh, nowhere near as long as mine will last, but measurable in minutes, maybe hours. Let him try to slither away.

And let me wander. There was no rush. There *is* no rush.

No rush at all.

The Treasure

Rupert Brooke

When colour goes home into the eyes,
    And lights that shine are shut again
With dancing girls and sweet birds' cries
    Behind the gateways of the brain;
And that no-place which gave them birth, shall close
The rainbow and the rose: —

Still may Time hold some golden space
    Where I'll unpack that scented store
Of song and flower and sky and face,
    And count, and touch, and turn them o'er,
Musing upon them; as a mother, who
Has watched her children all the rich day through
Sits, quiet-handed, in the fading light,
When children sleep, ere night.

Contributors' Notes

Allen Ashley is a British Fantasy Society Award winning editor, writer, poet, columnist and writing tutor. He runs five writing groups across north London, including the prestigious Clockhouse London Writers. His most recent book was *Astrologica: Stories of the Zodiac* which he edited for The Alchemy Press. His next books include *Sensorama* (as editor) due soon from Eibonvale Press and *Dreaming Spheres – Poems of the Solar System* co-written with Sarah Doyle and due soon from PS Publishing's Stanza imprint.

allenashley.com

Mike Chinn has published over 40 short stories, from westerns to Lovecraftian fiction; with all shades of fantasy, horror, science fiction and pulp adventure in between. He's scripted comic strips for DC Thompson's *Beano* and late-lamented *Starblazer* digest; along with two books on how to write comics/graphic novels – which saw translation into several languages. The Alchemy Press published a collection of his Damian Paladin fiction in 1998, whilst he has edited *Swords Against the Millennium* and *The Alchemy Press Book of Pulp Heroes* and *The Alchemy Press Book of Pulp Heroes 2* for the same imprint. He is presently working on a third volume in the *Pulp Heroes* series, along with a Sherlock Holmes Steampunk mash-up for Fringeworks – in which he gets to send the famous detective to the Moon.

saladoth.blogspot.co.uk

Rima Devereaux studied Modern Languages at Oxford and holds a doctorate in medieval French from Cambridge. She is an editor, writer and translator. She is working on her first novel, a quest fantasy inspired partly by her knowledge of medieval literature, and has written a number of fantasy-themed short stories. She is the author of two works of non-fiction. In her spare time, she enjoys playing the flute, medieval seminars and medieval re-enactment, European cinema, learning languages and country walks

Stephanie Ellis Stephanie writes horror and genre stories which have found success in *Massacre Magazine* and *Sanitarium Magazine* as well as in anthologies by a number of publishers including: Angelic Knight Press' *Demon Rum and Other Evil Spirits*; Death Throes Publishing's *Peripheral Distortions*; KnightWatch Press' upcoming anthologies *Cadavers, The Last Diner, Pun Book of Horror, Dead Man's Tales, Raus! Untoten!*; Visionary Press' *Horror in Bloom*; Sky Warrior Books' upcoming *Vampires Don't Sparkle.*
 stephellis.weebly.com

Bryn Fortey appeared in various short story anthologies during the 1970s, including Fontana titles edited by Mary Danby, as well as enjoying an active participation in the British small press poetry scene. Since reigniting his interest in writing fiction in 2011 he has appeared in anthologies from Shadow Publishing, Gray Friar Press and The Alchemy Press, with the latter bringing out his collection *Merry-Go-Round and Other Words* in 2014.

Christopher Fowler is the award-winning author of over 30 novels and twelve short story collections, including the Bryant & May mystery novels, recording the adventures of two Golden Age detectives solving impossible London crimes. His latest books are the haunted house thriller *Nyctophobia*, the Bryant & May novel *The Bleeding Heart* and the memoir *Film Freak*. Other work includes the *War of the Worlds* videogame with Sir Patrick Stewart, a graphic novel, and a *Hammer Horror* radio play. He has a weekly column in *The Independent on Sunday*. He spends his time between King's Cross, London and Barcelona.

christopherfowler.co.uk.

David Jón Fuller was born and raised in Winnipeg, MB, with a one-year stint in Edmonton, AB, and also lived for two years in Iceland studying Icelandic language and literature. He holds a B.A. (Hon) in Theatre and his short fiction has been published in *Long Hidden: Speculative Fiction From the Margins of History*; *Tesseracts 17*; *In Places Between 2013*; and *The Harrow*. He also has fiction appearing in the upcoming *Tesseracts 18: Wrestling With Gods* and *Guns and Romances* anthologies.

davidjonfuller.com.

Writing on a part time basis for the last ten years, **Shaun Hamilton**'s work has been published in a number of magazines and anthologies, both print and digital. His long-suffering collection *Witterings of an Unshackled Dogsbody* will be published eventually, as will his small medical compendium *Under the Skin*. He lives and works in North Wales with his amazing wife, and intends to "sort out" his novel.

shaunhamilton.wordpress.com

Anthony "Tyson" Hanks is a fan of horror—both literature and film. He wrote quite a bit when he was younger but was struck with a tragic case of adulthood. He has recently taken up the craft again and is thrilled that some folks have deemed his work worthy enough to show the public. His work has previously been published in *Sanitarium Magazine*. He lives in Florida with his beautiful wife and daughter, and when he isn't writing fiction, fishing or working the dreaded "day job" he writes film, book and haunted attraction reviews and articles.

nerdcronomicon.com

Nancy Hayden is a writer, artist and organic farmer living in Vermont, USA. She has an MFA in creative writing from the Stonecoast Writers Program in Maine; a BA in English and studio art; a PhD and MS in environmental engineering; and a BS in forest biology. In 2014, she published (or soon to be published) several short stories. She has been researching and writing about WWI for the past few years and is currently working on a WWI novel.

Amberle L. Husbands is a writer, sheet-metal mechanic, and a native-daughter of the Okefenokee Swamp. Her short stories have appeared in such publications as *Shock Totem*, *The Alchemy Press Book of Pulp Heroes*, *Underground Voices*, and elsewhere. Her short story 'Only Whistle Stops' took third prize in the reader-voted 2014 summer issue of *Sixfold*. Amberle's novel, *See Eads City*, is currently available through Amazon and Barnes & Noble. Additionally, a book of her poetry is available from Maverick Duck Press. When she isn't writing, Amberle spends her time throwing knives and teaching the English language to houseplants.

Born in Evry, France in 1993, **Emile-Louis Tomas Jouvet** has won many scholastic prizes for his minimalist short fiction. Now completing his Literature degree at the Sorbonne he is working on a collection of horror stories, *The Condemned*, which will see publication in the very near future. His stories in English have appeared in *Phobophobia*, *Cities of Death*, *The Demonologia Biblica* and *Demonology*.

Peter Mark May was born in Walton on Thames, Surrey, England, way back in 1968 and still lives nearby in a place you may now have heard of called Hersham. He is the author of *Demon*, *Kumiho*, *Inheritance*, *Dark Waters*, *Hedge End* and *AZ: Anno Zombie*. He's had short stories published in genre Canadian and US magazines and the UK and US anthologies of horror such as *Creature Feature, Watch,* the British Fantasy Society's 40th Anniversary anthology *Full Fathom Forty, Alt-Zombie, Fogbound From 5, Nightfalls, Demons & Devilry, Miseria's Chorale and* Western Legends' *The Bestiarum Vocabulum*.

petermarkmay.weebly.com.

Christine Morgan works the overnight shift in a psychiatric facility and divides her writing time among many genres. A lifelong reader, she also writes, reviews, beta-reads, occasionally edits and dabbles in self-publishing. She has several novels in print, with more due out soon. Her stories have appeared in more than three dozen anthologies, 'zines and e-chapbooks. She's been nominated for the Origins Award and made Honourable Mentions in two volumes of *Year's Best Fantasy and Horror*. She's also a wife, mum, and possible future crazy-cat-lady whose other interests include gaming, history, superheroes, crafts, and cheesy disaster movies.

Mary Pletsch is a glider pilot, toy collector and graduate of the Royal Military College of Canada. She is the author of short stories in a variety of genres, including science fiction, steampunk and horror. She lives in New Brunswick with Dylan Blacquiere and their four cats.

fictorians.com

Chris Rawlins has a passion for history and art, and to bring history to life through his artworks is a dream come true. His puts the viewer there in order to bring a true-to-life realism that the books of his childhood lacked. He is passionate about strong composition, realism, detail, accuracy and dramatic lighting. Chris has lent his brush to a huge diversity of subject matter and styles. The portrayal of humans, horses, animals, and landscapes, using contemporary and modern techniques, has earned much admiration and acclaim. Chris' artwork has been used for numerous book covers, albums and magazines, as well as for entire books, gaining a large audience of appreciative scholars and enthusiasts.

christopherrawlins.co.uk

Australian Shadows Award finalist **Daniel I. Russell** has featured in publications such as *The Zombie Feed* from Apex, *Pseudopod* and *Andromeda Spaceways Inflight Magazine* #43. Author of *Samhane, Come into Darkness, Critique, Mother's Boys, The Collector* and *Tricks, Mischief and Mayhem*. Daniel is also the former vice-president of the Australian Horror Writers' Association and was a special guest editor of *Midnight Echo.*

Thomas Strømsholt is a Danish author of short stories. His first collection of fiction in English, *O Altitudo,* was published by Ex-Occidente Press. His fiction has appeared in various anthologies and magazines, including *Urban Cthulhu: Nightmare Cities, Sorcery and Sanctity: A Homage to Arthur Machen, Bête Noire Magazine, Sacrum Regnum,* and *Supernatural Tales* (forthcoming).

thomasstromsholt.wordpress.com

David Thomas is the author of a novella, dozens of short stories and a screenplay. His work has been published in the UK and America – even as far as Japan! He also draws and writes comic-strips and poetry. He lives and works in Cardiff, Wales.

Paul Woodward has always been a writer and has had some success as a performance poet in the past. Recently he has concentrated on writing prose of a fantastical nature and is currently working on a novel which re-imagines Homer's Odyssey in a futuristic science fictional setting. The story included in this anthology is set in the same milieu.

The Editor

Dean M. Drinkel is an author, editor, poet, award-winning script-writer, theatre & film director. Read more about Dean at deanmdrinkelauthor.blogspot.co.uk, ellupofilms.com and in issue 331 of *Fangoria*.